INVITATION

TO

A

HANGING

A NOVEL

Bonnie – All the best to you,

INVITATION TO A HANGING

A NOVEL

KARIN RATHERT

atmosphere press

Published by Atmosphere Press

Cover design by Matthew Fielder

atmospherepress.com

for Theo

ADVANCE

The children were embarrassed by the circus. They sat silently on the corner benches, pulling on the too-tight collars of their mission school uniforms while the mostly white audience pelted them with hostile glances. Even the teachers occasionally looked their way with what felt like disdain. But then the band of Indians charged into the arena whooping and hollering, and the children felt a gush of pride. The warriors, with their long headdresses and flying hair, were their people. They rode tight on the backs of their horses, like man and beast were one. And they shot their arrows on the fly so straight and true. A few of the children reached up and touched their own hair, which had been chopped upon their arrival at the school the same day the reverend had confiscated their moccasins and forced their feet into stiff shoes.

The warriors chased down the stagecoach, and several leapt on top of it to wrestle with the whip and conductor. But then, the cavalry broke into the arena blasting their rifles and defeated the Indians with ease. When they took the chief hostage, the audience applauded wildly—except for the children. They sat motionless, stiff from dissonance and shame, and they remained that way through the rest of the performance. Even the cowgirl shooting apples from the mouth of a dog failed to bend their lips into anything resembling a smile. Afterward, the general and chief circled the arena, and the chief smiled and waved and cursed the crowd in Siouan. Only then did the children laugh. They understood the subversion.

Later, they marched through the menagerie tent single file, the old teacher slapping his thigh and chewing his lip. When the children started whispering in the language of the chief, the teacher snapped his stick against the thigh of the nearest offender.

“English!” he commanded, and the children fell silent.

They drifted by the cages, horrified by the imprisoned animals, most of which were mangy and listless, barely alive. John, a thin boy no older than twelve, stopped in front of the tiger. He was amazed by the geometry of stripes, all fire and ash, a conflict of color. The tip of the tiger’s tail hung through the bars like a fat lazy snake. Of course the boy knew better, but he had to touch that tail. And then, the beast opened the cool flames of its eyes and stared. The cat, the boy understood, was Iktomi’s brother, a sleeping demon, and he understood that the white men caged their gods.

CHAPTER 1

ADAM

He took it as a sign—not from God; this place had been abandoned by God. It was a sign from his mother. She was dead, but that didn't stop her from making an appearance from time to time and speaking to him. He tossed the empty bottle and watched it shatter against the side of the hotel, then stepped from the boardwalk to crunch his heel down on a large piece of glass, just because. The space between the hotel and newspaper offices was littered with trash and smelled putrid, so Adam stepped back onto the boardwalk and surveyed Main Street. Several wagons and cars were clustered in front of the hardware store farther down, but otherwise the town was quiet for this time of day. Adam spun slowly, swiping at mosquitos buzzing around his face. The sun was burning, and he could taste the dust in the air. He glanced at Bert's Saloon. There were a couple of stray bottles still standing on the railing, and he thought about walking across and nabbing one, but then a cowboy stepped from the bar and leaned against the railing, and Adam thought better of it. He turned back to the posters plastered on the facade of the *Yellowstone News,* then dug his hand into his pocket and pulled out the tiger. It was worn a bit by now; the ears had grown increasingly rounded, and the stripes carved into the bone had faded, but there was no doubting its nature.

He held it up to the poster. Other than size, color, substance, form, and dimension, the two were indistinguishable. The tiger jumping through the ring of fire on the storefront was a stunning beast—a blaze of color with claws like knives. It was surrounded by exotic animals and acrobats and whiteface clowns twirling or lounging or jumping from a kaleidoscope of planks or ropes or rings. And because one wasn't enough, the same tiger repeated the leap, one on top of another, so that a streak of cats covered the facade, and each one was exactly the same as the others. They were all part of the Most Wondrous and Spectacular Show on Earth! And according to the script, they were all arriving in less than two weeks.

This was, Adam knew, his escape.

"Hey, son. I've been looking for you."

Adam spun. The man coming toward him was more bear than man, huge and lumbering like he was all set for hibernation, with the same pent-up rage. A line of sweat dripped down either side of his face, which he dabbed from time to time with a folded handkerchief.

"Yeah?"

"It's sure a hot one," Jake said, still dabbing. Adam didn't respond so Jake continued. "I've got a job for you."

Jake was always coming up with jobs for Adam. For as long as he could remember, the big man had been insinuating himself into Adam's life, looking out for him, checking on his schooling; and on occasion, he'd even taken him fishing, though he had no knack for the sport. There was a tethering of sorts—Adam could never wander too far before Jake would pull him back into his fold.

"Yeah. What is it?"

"Get that friend of yours. The tall one. With the runny mouth. What's his name?" Jake's tie bulged above his shirt, and Adam had the urge to yank it and tighten it.

"Cecil." Adam kicked a stone into the dusty road.

"Yeah. Cecil. Get him and bring him down by the livery."

Adam said he would and watched Jake lumber off, then he retrieved Cecil from the river where he was fishing, and the two of them waited at the livery for Jake to give them directions. By midafternoon, the boys were hitching a couple of old horses to the wagon. It was a short distance from there to the sporting house where they rattled to a stop. The horses stretched their necks to reach the grass as best they could within the confines of their harnesses and shafts while the boys gazed upon the rotting corpse of the house with reverence. It leaned to the southeast, submitting to the perpetual winds blowing off the Rocky Mountains from Canada. Weeds grew from the sideboards, and the broken windows had been boarded up and then the boards had been ripped away and tossed into the yard, which was littered with scraps of wood and broken bottles, rusted cans, and strips of filthy, faded fabric. But the boys knew from the stories it had been a grand place in its heyday, that the clients had drunk their brandy from snifters and music had played on the gramophone six nights a week and the girls had been youthful and pretty and had voices like bells that chimed when they laughed.

"It must have been something," Adam said.

"Well, it was a sporting house," Cecil snickered. Adam didn't notice his patronizing tone—he was thinking about all the amorous adventures that had happened within the walls of the old house.

They took their time getting down from the wagon bench and then approached like monks to a temple. They had to pick their way through broken boards to the front door, which hung on its hinges so that the door was jammed at an angle. Adam ran his hands across the gray slivered planks, avoiding the protruding nails. They ducked inside and stood while their eyes adjusted to the dim lighting. The velvet walls were peeling, and the heavy velvet curtains dangled from a falling rod or lay crumpled like drunks in piles on the floor in front of the broken windows. A chandelier, sharp-toothed and rusted as a bear trap, swung from the ceiling. Cecil crunched across the room and Adam followed, stopping before a heavy wooden bureau. He ran his hand along the top, then clapped off the dust. The drawers had been removed, and the contents were scattered across the floor. The bits of clothing were muddied and soiled from exposure to seeping rain and snow. Along the wall, a stained and sunken settee sat in a nest of broken bottles, the springs partially exposed. Some of the bottles, Adam noticed, had faded labels, and some of the bottles looked new—even still, visitors took it upon themselves to make themselves at home for the night. Adam imagined how gentlemen of old had waited patiently on that couch for their lovers or how an outlaw had paced the room wearing a six-shooter and a charming smile.

"I bet the ladies were fancy," Adam said.

"They sure were," Cecil replied. "I saw pictures." He held his palms in front of his chest to indicate big breasts, and they both laughed. Cecil was a year older and spoke with an authority Adam admired.

Adam imagined a tangle of bodies and shoes on the floor behind the closed doors, thoughts that set his heart to racing. He stepped into a current of cold and he could feel them, a gathering of ghosts. And maybe he imagined, or maybe he could see, the bent cigarettes and hats—a broken-down farmer, a newsman with his too-tight vest, a young woman in a flouncy dress—all leering. He could smell their sour sweat and wafting perfume.

"Whatcha waiting for?" Cecil gave him a shove and the phantoms scattered.

Adam crunched across shards of glass and slipped through

a door into a hallway withseveral rooms attached and a narrow door that led to a staircase. He went up the stairs to the ladies' rooms. They were small, with barely enough room for a bed. Several were carpeted indiscarded clothing, the material like cardboard when he gave it a kick. In one room, a mattress lay like carrion on the floor, wounds covered in black mold. The mattresses in the other rooms were ripped or missing or thick with the dirt that had swept through the cracked windows.

Adam returned downstairs to find Cecil in the kitchen pulling open cupboards. They would need help, he saw, loading up the big iron stove.

"Thought there would be something more interesting," Cecil said, slamming a cupboard. "What's he going to do with this place?"

"Beats me."

Adam didn't say it, but he thought the house was plenty interesting. He stepped into what must have been an office. There was the same peeling velvet as well as painted black shelves built into the wall. Adam sat on a small stool in the corner of the room facing the door. After Josephine's departure, business had fallen away, was how he'd heard it told. The house had taken a shabby turn. The ladies and clientele had become increasingly wretched until it served only the lowest class of men. Business drifted away to better houses until Jake kicked out the few whores that remained. The house had been standing empty ever since.

Cecil came into the office and spun in a circle.

"What a shithole," he said. He kicked a broken board and it cracked in half, and a slice of sunlight spilled onto the floor.

"He should just burn it to the ground."

"At least he's paying us. It's better than cowboying or planting wheat."

Cecil grunted, which was the same as agreeing.

"Maybe he's going to plug up the holes, put in some new carpet, and open a hotel."

"That's the stupidest thing I've heard."

Adam rubbed his hands along the shelves and scraped up bits of paper and years of dust, which he rubbed off on his pants.

"He's a hell of a cheapskate, if you ask me." Cecil stabbed his finger into the corner of a small cupboard built into the wall.

"Has people filing false claims, is what I heard. Heard he had a guy file a claim on a dollhouse 'cause the homesteading law doesn't specify the house has to be measured in feet! . . . What's this?" He pulled out a thin chain and dangled it in the air. He fingered the pendant, then pried it open, and there were two tiny pictures too inky black to make out.

"Bet it's worth something," he laughed, and stuck it in his pocket.

"Jake will have your head." Adam shivered as a wave of cold air rushed over him. He forced himself to remain calm.

Cecil shrugged. "Let's go upstairs."

It wasn't until he and Cecil lifted the mattress from the bed to haul it down the stairs that Adam found the book lodged under a floorboard that had curled up along the edges.

"Hold on," Adam said, setting his end of the mattress down.

"What is it?" Cecil balanced the mattress and watched Adam peel the book out from the floor.

The book was made of black leather, severely damaged, and the pages were yellowed. Adam flipped through the pages—the first few were a ledger of some sort, a list of random items with numbers: perfume 80, stockings 100, cigarettes 100, rouge 20, rum 250, ribbons 80, linen 55; and then the writings took on the appearance of a diary—short notes and long scrawls—the often bold ink cutting into the paper.

September 13

Hazel's been frequenting the laudanum. It's curtains for her, sure as eggs. Stupid girl will end up in some filthy crib or hog ranch working renegades and outlaws if she doesn't hang herself first.

September 14

D was too drunk to get his money's worth, but I told him otherwise and he didn't know the difference. He paid me three times over!

"Come on. Get the hell out of there." Cecil juggled the mattress, threatening to drop it, but Adam ignored him.

November 27

Who knew Abraham Lincoln was such a portly president? Sitting here at the end of the table like the king himself. Ragamuffin day and all the men come to the house thinking they're bigger than they are—John Bulls and Uncle Sams and the big man himself. Some of the masked fantastics made their way to our neck of the woods begging for pennies. Josephine was generous as always. We feasted on larded beef and mince pies to beat the band. Josephine always shows abit of class on the holidays, getting out her best dishes and fancy wines and whiskies. And Stanley bought me a bottle of perfume.

"Jesus Christ, get a move on or I'm going to drop this shit on you . . . What's so damn interesting?"

"It's nothing." Adam clapped the book shut and tossed it aside, not wanting Cecil to take an interest. "Let's get this out of here."

They hauled the mattress down the stairs, then returned to the room for the bedsprings and frame.

"Pretty fancy bed," Cecil remarked as they disassembled the frame.

"Must have been a pretty fancy person," Adam said, and Cecil laughed.

"She was good at her job." He shaped his fingers into a circle on one hand and jammed his finger on the other hand through it to gesture sex, and Adam laughed.

"Ever been with a whore?"

Adam shrugged.

"I almost did it with Virginia Pilling. She's a whore—though I don't think anyone pays her! . . . When I go in the army I'm going to have lots of girls . . . Are you going?"

"Yep . . . unless they stop the war," he said, though he didn't think so. He didn't see the appeal in making himself a target.

"Maybe they will."

They hauled the few salvageable pieces of furniture to the wagon while contemplating the immensity of the war, after which they did a sweep of clothes and trash and things too damaged to sell and piled it all in a clearing far away from the house. On one trip in and out, Adam picked up the diary and slid it under his belt beneath his shirt, thinking he'd study it later.

When they finished piling up the trash, Cecil threw a match on some kindling and lit it up.

"My dad says if Prohibition happens, the whole goddamn town will shut down. This place is dying. You ought to get the hell out."

"I am getting the hell out." Adam kicked at the leg of a chair poking out of the edge of the fire. A heavy, dark smoke rose from the flames.

"Join up. Say you're eighteen."

Adam laughed. "No one'll believe that."

"Hell, they will. They'll believe it because they want to."

"Maybe I will . . ."

"I mean it."

Adam could see that he did. Cecil was looking at him like he might give him a beating. Then he kicked a log and pulled it forward and sat down, and Adam took up another log. Cecil passed Adam some rolling paper and tobacco and they rolled themselves cigarettes.

"Did you hear about the Johnson family? Entire family got killed by the flu."

"I heard that."

"Eleven kids."

"Christ . . ."

"That's some flu . . ." Cecil watched the end of his cigarette as he inhaled.

"A bunch of cowhands were playing cards in White Earth. Next day, three were dead."

"Flu?"

"Yep. I heard they were bleeding all over the place. Out of their mouths. Their nose. Even their ears."

"Hell."

"Yep."

"Damn."

"I know . . . that's what I'm saying."

The two stared at the flames. Bits of burning fabric floated in the air above them, blinking like fireflies.

"Shit," Adam said. He turned his gaze to the house.

"Wish I'd seen it back then." He nodded toward the house

as an indication of when. Cecil shrugged, indifferent.

"Sometimes I see 'em."

"Who?" The ash at the end of Cecil's cigarette curled like a snake, then broke apart. He stomped on what fell with the heel of his boot.

"People."

"What people? Who?"

"From then."

"What the hell you talking about? You mean dead ones? Ghosts?"

Adam shrugged, and Cecil stared at him.

"No."

"Yeah."

"Really? . . . Shit . . . maybe they weren't buried right. That's what the Indians say. They stick around if they're not buried right . . . ghost sickness. I think. That's what I heard it called."

"You believe that?"

Cecil shrugged. "I don't know. Maybe . . . what do they look like?"

"I don't know . . . ghosts, I guess. People . . ."

"Damn . . ." Cecil ground out his cigarette. The smoke came toward them, so they moved their logs.

"My mom doesn't want me to go to the war. She's afraid I'll get shot . . . Neither does Mary. I'm going to marry her, you know."

Adam picked up a stone and threw it into the flames, then searched the ground for another, thinking that he'd like to have himself a girl. He picked up a rock as big as his fist and swung it into the fire, and the flames jumped.

"The old man . . ." Cecil said, and left his words hanging as if they didn't require any further explanation.

"Yeah," Adam agreed.

"He your grandpa?"

"Something like that."

"He's crazy."

"Yeah. Mostly . . . he's all right."

Cecil threw the stub of his cigarette into the fire. "I wish I had a beer."

CHAPTER 2

ALTA

What would Elizabeth do? Alta leaned back in the chair with the book on her lap and pondered the question. She would not be shy or intimidated, that's for sure. But *what would she do?* . . . What would Elizabeth Bennet do if she were to come upon a handsome young man sitting on a bench in the grand hall outside her father's office?

Alta was a fan of all things Jane Austen. And Emily Brontë and Charlotte Brontë and Charles Dickens, and really any writer or any novel she could get her hands on. Truly there was nothing as inspiring as a good Victorian heroine.

In terms of Elizabeth Bennet, Alta knew she would approach the handsome young man and introduce herself and say something both charming and witty. She wouldn't overthink it or plan it out—she was too self-assured and confident for that. She would certainly not hide away in the library or be intimidated.

The problem was that Alta's hero had been indifferent when she'd walked by, book in hand, looking for a place to plant herself. Of course, it was this indifference that was irresistible. Had he been old and rusting like the other men that visited her father, she wouldn't have noticed, but he was a slightly worn Adonis, with corn-colored hair, a shadowy jaw, and a gray suit jacket bursting around his broad shoulders. She couldn't ignore him or retreat—except to gather courage and plot an offense—any more than a cat could retreat from a snug box or patch of sunlight.

She stood up, took a deep breath, smoothed the front of her dress, and walked back into the grand hall. He was intent on the wristwatch he was twisting. Squeezing time like toothpaste from a tube, she thought, as he paused to presumably check the hour. He looked up as she approached, and his eyes sparkled like light off a lake, but they looked through her. She may as well have been a tree in a forest of trees and not a resident of the magnificent house of which he was a visitor. If anything, a flutter of irritation crossed his face—she was interrupting his watch flipping, or perhaps a hive of bees or hornets swarmed around the wisps of her hair. He looked at her like that.

"Good afternoon," she said. Not very witty or charming, she had to admit, but she was always polite to her father's guests, to any guests.

"Afternoon," he said, with a slight nod of his head. He flicked the face of his watch—pushing time forward. Probably he'd been waiting for a while. That would explain his impatience.

"That isn't going to make him come out any faster." Irritation erased the anxiety from her tone, so maybe it had a ring of witty. It was ridiculous how long her father made his guests wait. She was not sure if it was intentional—a display of his power—or if he was busy and preoccupied or he simply did not care.

The man clasped his watch in his fist and, finally, flashed her a smile. And then Alta couldn't stop it—she was smiling back. She sashayed past so he wouldn't see her blush and pushed open the heavy door.

The office was a cave, with curtains blocking all but slivers of light on either side, the dust suspended like souls in the radiant glow. It took her a moment before she could find her father behind his enormous desk, the umbra of a man, sharp angles with a pen in hand and a stack of papers before him. A shelf of leather-bound books towered behind him.

"What is it?"

Alta let her hand drop from the door. The dying embers of his eyes lingered on her, and Alta's fingers clutched the air. He had that effect. She approached slowly.

"There's someone waiting for you."

"I'm well aware of that."

"Well . . . should I offer him coffee or tea?"

Now her father set his pen down. She stood over his desk. Too close, really. He considered her like he might a butterfly for display—should he place her alone or with others in a shadow box on the wall? She eyed the cord that traveled from the lamp on the table to the chandelier on the ceiling, and for a moment wished she could scale it. She could, if she were a squirrel or monkey, she supposed. There was a hidden door directly above her, she imagined. An escape hatch.

"I could turn on the light."

"And why would you do that?"

"You could see your work better."

"I mean the coffee or tea." He never raised his voice—he didn't have to. His words pelted like lead.

"It's the polite thing to do . . . He's been waiting a long time . . ." She understood now that her mission was ridiculous.

"That's not your worry." Cadwallader turned back to his papers and released her from the spell. Her hand relaxed.

"Is that all?"

"Dinner. I came to remind you about dinner."

She lunged for the lamp, and he looked irritated in the flush of light. He tapped his pen.

"It's better for your eyes," she said in meek defense.

She pulled the door shut and rushed away from the encounter—her father left her depleted. She didn't look at the stranger, though she felt his gaze upon her back. She paused at the bottom of the staircase and took hold of the banister, gathering strength from the pillars and arches and finely crafted wood so that the elegance and grace and substance of the house moved through her like an aria. Restored, she ascended the grand staircase. Greta met her on the landing where a rainbow of light projected Golgotha on Easter through the Tiffany stained glass windows.

"Who is he?" Greta had taken note of the visitor tucked in the foliage on the bench downstairs. She made it her business to take note. Greta was only a couple of years older than Alta—the heiress's maid, and in this case, a paid friend. Already she'd imagined half a dozen romantic scenarios involving the stranger and Alta and a few involving herself.

"Who does he remind you of?" Alta asked.

"Mr. Cummings?"

"John Cummings? Certainly not." Alta wondered if Greta was soft in the head. Mr. Cummings was ancient and not the least attractive—unless an old man with faded skin and a disproportionately large belly that protruded like a watermelon was attractive.

"No? Then who?"

"Mr. Darcy. But with blond hair, of course."

"Mr. Darcy?" Greta was attentive, knowing she was about to be educated.

"Mr. Darcy was haughty, at least in the beginning. But it turned out he was a truly kind and generous spirit. And he loved Elizabeth."

Greta bit her lip. She couldn't remember which book Alta was referencing, though she'd certainly referenced it before. Alta was always trying to get her to read.

"Don't judge a book by its cover," Greta said, a useful

phrase that covered up her lack of recall.

"Exactly."

Greta took Alta's arm and guided her the rest of the way up the stairs to her room, where Alta dropped into a chair. Greta threw open the closet and disappeared inside, humming as she went through Alta's gowns.

"He was very handsome . . . Do you think he was handsome?" Greta's voice was lost to the gowns in the closet, but Alta knew what she thought—she didn't need to hear the words.

"I don't think he's from around here."

Greta stepped out of the closet, holding up a silk dress.

"He's very romantic, isn't he? It's like fate, don't you think?"

"No." Alta shook her head, and Greta dove back among the dresses and reappeared with an emerald-green satin gown.

"How about green? You look gorgeous in green."

Alta nodded, and Greta laid the dress across the bed, then waited for Alta, who was distracted, thinking about the stranger. There was something about him. She turned her eyes lazily toward Greta, then popped up.

"It could be fate," she said, coming to agreement with Greta, which made the young woman smile. Alta stood and stretched, then fell into the chair in front of her mirror.

Greta pulled Alta's hair back so they could both admire her jawline. She was pretty, she'd been told. With her looks and pedigree, she was guaranteed a fortuitous future. But Alta didn't think in such transactional terms. She thought in terms of an eighteen-year-old woman interested in handsome, eligible men. She would have romance and adventure—and true love, of course. That went without saying.

"Father's never mentioned him. I would recognize him by any description, I'm sure . . . He must be foreign."

"I can find out."

"You could? . . . Of course you could. Will you do that?"

"Of course."

Alta watched silently as Greta worked on her hair, wondering about fate and the man downstairs. It seemed about time that fate came visiting. She'd been paraded around to dinners and dances for a long time and met every eligible man in the city, it seemed. And tonight's gathering was most likely the same tired group of her father's business associates and their wives. She let out a long sigh.

"This awful dinner. Nothing but a bunch of old men talking about business."

"Will the girls be there?"

"No. They're away at school . . . I wish father would let me go away to school."

"It'll make you emotional and ruin your chances of marriage."

"Greta." Alta admonished her for her brazenness because she knew she shouldn't encourage it, but it was one of her qualities she liked. And in this case, Greta was repeating things Mr. Woburn had said. While all the young ladies from prominent families were sent off to prestigious boarding schools to live with their peers and get an education, she was held hostage in this enormous home left mostly to her own devices and periodically to play the role of mistress, when occasion demanded it. While she didn't mind hosting dinners, she was, in truth, bored, and it was easy to imagine she could spend her entire life trapped in this golden palace.

"He's old-fashioned," Alta sighed.

"Maybe the man will be there. From downstairs."

"Do you think so?"

"Maybe."

Alta ran her hands along the fabric. It was truly beautiful. Her father made sure she had the most beautiful clothes.

XXX

The Hill house was the largest house in the city, a masterpiece of design, and at one time, Alta had thrilled at eating in the massive dining room with its gold leaf ceiling and leather wallpaper. But with the Hill daughters at school out east, the Hill boys generally irksome, and the remaining company consisting solely of aged industrialists and their wives, the evening promised to be an ordeal.

Alta sat between Mary Hill and John Cummings, who made a point of brushing her hand too frequently for it to be an accident. To fend off the increasingly uncomfortable attention, she clasped her hands on her lap and turned toward the conversation on her left throughout the appetizers and soup—Kathryn had been married, Silvia had had a baby, and Lillian's prospects looked good, she learned. The party sipped wine from crystal, and the servants slid sirloin and mignon of lamb in front of the guests.

Mary Hill stabbed at her meat.

"There should always be a bit of blood in the middle," she whispered to Alta, splattering on the white tablecloth. "That's what gives it flavor."

"Sure is," one of the wives responded.

James Hill leaned toward their group. "Of course, they should be buying their meat from me."

Everyone laughed at his light-hearted interruption.

"That's true." Mary paused to taste her wine, giving the others at the table the opportunity to turn their attention to her. "We have a stock farm. James paid $5000 for an Angus bull twenty years ago, and you won't find better meat."

Alta nodded—she had no opinion about meat sources. At the other end of the table, several men argued about the price of flour and wheat and lumber and iron ore and what to buy and sell.

"How are the girls?" Alta asked Mary, hoping for more interesting gossip.

"Wonderful. Ruth is to be engaged," Mary whispered, since the news was not yet public. But of course, everyone at the table knew.

"She is!"

"He was a classmate of young James. A wonderful man."

"He is a wonderful man," a woman round and cracked as an egg interjected. "Very wonderful."

"Mr. Cummings is a wonderful prospect," Mary whispered to Alta, who responded with silence. Alta understood it was with the best of intentions that family friends wished to see her married—they worried about her lack of feminine guidance and wanted to see her taken care of. But their vetting process seemed to be limited to money and a beating heart. Alta wished they would include virility, character, personality, looks, and charm in their list of requirements for prospects. Mary, to her credit, caught Alta's disinterest and changed the discussion to the works of John Singer Sargent and then to the religious education of girls; all the while silver tableware clicked and scraped against the china plates like low-grade background percussion instruments.

"You look very beautiful tonight," Mr. Cummings said to Alta when she turned her head in his direction. Her neck was becoming sore from the hours of avoiding him. Staff cleared dinner plates and prepared the table for dessert.

"Thank you," Alta said. He plucked a thread from the fabric on her sleeve and held it up for her to see, as one might the feather from a goose or pheasant they'd shot.

"Do you know they call James the kingmaker?" Cadwallader boomed. Alta was certain her father was losing his hearing.

"His railroads have made this city," Mr. Mills agreed, because the guests always agreed. Every man at the table had accomplished great deeds, but none as great as James Hill. It was about impossible to quantify the impact Mr. Hill had had on the entire country, let alone Minneapolis-St. Paul and all the local industry with his railroads.

"Not one of the mills would be in business without him," Cadwallader continued. "No mills, no mill owners. I wouldn't be in business without him. And it's the Great Northern that is single-handedly populating the west."

"That's true," James laughed.

"How many folks do you think you're transporting in a day?"

"Oh, I couldn't say. But they're coming from all over the world."

Cadwallader twisted his glass and studied the ice cubes.

"Have you figured out how you're going to break the strike?" James asked.

"Business," Mary said, reaching to touch Alta's hand. "They never stop . . . You must be dreadfully bored . . . Your father. He's a good man, and he means well, but . . ."

"Oh, I'm perfectly fine."

"A young woman should be out dancing and going to the theater, not stuck talking business with a bunch of old folks . . . There's a wonderful production of *The Silver Slipper* in town. You really should see it . . . We'll arrange it! . . . The actor that plays Duval is quite handsome." Mary leaned in and whispered this last sentence conspiratorially.

"Oh, that would be wonderful!" Alta said, because of course it would be!

"It is a wonderful show," Mrs. Jorgenson agreed.

"I've got a young man who's going to help me castrate the union. Once you get a few to cross the lines . . ." Cadwallader had lowered his voice somewhat, but the mention of a young man caught Alta's attention.

"Well, I hope that's all it takes," James said.

"Really, James. We will be withdrawing shortly." Mary gave her husband a warning look, though she was really addressing Alta's father, and he understood the subtext.

"She hears it all the time. Believe me. If she were a boy, she'd be running my business."

"Be that as it may . . ."

XXX

Greta was waiting for Alta when she returned later that evening. She helped Alta out of her gown, and Alta gave her details about the dinner and the guests. Greta had an insatiable thirst for gossip, and the evening was always more pleasurable when replayed and filtered through Greta's eyes.

Alta had slipped into a nightgown, and now she sat in front of the mirror while Greta brushed her hair and Alta told her how she thought the visitor was hired to break the strike at the mill.

Greta paused with the brush in midair, and her mouth curled into a surprised *O*.

"So he's a hero. An adventurer?" Greta wasn't sure how to label him or where her loyalties should lie, since she knew many families of the workers who were leveraging for better conditions and pay.

"He's a hero," Alta confirmed, and Greta sighed with relief.

"Well, he's very dashing." Greta set the brush down and smiled at Alta in the mirror.

"Yes, he is." Alta stood up. "It's late. You should be going to bed."

XXX

By the next day, Greta had been able to interrogate multiple sources in the employ of Cadwallader—either at the house or mill—for information about the new strikebreaker, which she reported to Alta. His name was Stanley Olson. He was from a farm family in eastern North Dakota, and he'd come to the city to seek his fortune. He had quite a head for business. Most important, he was not married or engaged. "He's very ambitious, people say."

"He's going to make something of himself. You have to admire someone like that, Greta."

"Oh, I do!"

"He probably had a difficult childhood." Alta's imagination was exploding, thinking of the scenarios that had led him to this house. "Maybe his parents died. But he's worked hard and persevered. Just like Father. Father wasn't born wealthy. You know that, don't you?"

"Yes. Of course. You've told me this story. Everybody knows his story."

"And Stanley's just like Father. He'll probably be much more successful."

"Do you think so?"

"Of course. Don't you?"

"Of course I do." Greta knew better than to disagree about something so vital.

The romance was thrilling. After that initial meeting, Alta made it a habit to be in the vicinity on the occasions Stanley came to meet with her father. She was ubiquitous, passing by with a book or stitching or a vase of flowers to place in the library. Before long, Stanley began to take to the role of admirer, and their encounters became increasingly informal. On one such occasion, Mr. Woburn stuck his head out the door and found them seated together on the bench, their heads bent forward in conversation.

"Mr. Olson," he said, then addressed Alta. "Why don't you go see about dinner?"

XXX

The mahogany table was covered in damask with a display of flowers in the center cut so guests could see over them, an unnecessary detail on this night. Cadwallader sat at the end of the table, and Alta sat on the side near him so they could talk, though not much was said. They watched the servants carry out the soup and return with plates of sole. Cadwallader's silence was something Alta had never gotten used to. There was a tension to it, like he could boil over at any moment. He sipped his wine and ate his fish, and Alta gazed at the excess of dishes on the side table while she chewed.

"That fellow you were talking to today."

"Yes. Stanley."

"Mr. Olson . . . You need to stay away from him. He's not for you."

Alta set down her fork and fingered the linen napkin on her lap. "I can't very well avoid a man lingering in our front doorway when I need to pass through the hall."

"I'm not sure whether you've been passing through or you've set up camp."

"Oh, Father," she started, and was ashamed of the pleading note in her voice, so she didn't finish. He didn't understand love, which meant he would create obstacles for her and Stanley.

"I've hired Mr. Olson for a job. When I no longer need him, he'll go."

"Where will he go?"

"That's not my concern. Nor yours."

"He's a strikebreaker."

"That's right. The union's striking, so he's working and finding other men to work." Cadwallader leaned back in his chair. "He serves a purpose."

"Why don't you just hire him?"

"That wouldn't go over well with the union. And he lacks principles. Like I said, he's a strikebreaker."

"Maybe he needs the money . . . Principles are a privilege, don't you think?"

"Do you really believe that? Is kindness a privilege?" Cadwallader set his tumbler down slowly, as if some force were pushing back against it.

"Of course not. But maybe work, what you do to earn money is."

Alta cut her fingerlings into small bits and mashed them into her plate. She was afraid of her father, but beneath that, she was furious. If it was up to him, he'd lock her in her room and let her rot, or marry her off to Mr. Cummings or one of his other old industrialist friends.

She watched the potatoes rise up between the tines of her fork.

"There's honest work for anyone who wants it." The air in the room shifted, as if they'd sailed into the doldrums and her father had become something else. She stared at her glass of water and felt the blade of violence in his tone. She picked up the glass as if to draw strength. When she responded, her voice was shaky but defiant.

"I will not be impolite, nor will I be a poor hostess. It would be impolite if I didn't acknowledge a visitor to the house when I encountered him." She set the glass down.

"You encounter him quite frequently."

"Only because he comes by the house quite frequently."

"He's not a gentleman, Alta. He sees you and sees a stepping-stone into the upstairs office."

She glared at the velvet curtains and pinched her lips, clasping her hands in her lap. She was no longer hungry.

"Do you think it's possible that a man might find me attractive?"

"I'm sure he finds you attractive. He also finds your money

attractive. He looks pretty, he talks pretty, but there's not much else."

"That's rather cynical, don't you think?" She spoke to her glass.

"He's not like us. He's a peasant. Uneducated. He has nothing to offer you."

"He's exactly like you, Daddy. You're self-made. You say so all the time. Your parents were farmers."

"Do you think he's self-made? He hasn't made anything."

"Well, he will. He'll make something of himself. He says so."

"My God, girl. Have you gone mad? Do you love this man? Oh, if your mother were alive . . ."

"Well, she's not," Alta whispered, surprised by her own defiance.

"Go to your room," her father growled.

Alta pushed back from the table and did just that.

XXX

Alta was still furious with her father several days later when they attended the theater with Mrs. Hill and several friends. She sat in the box in a chiffon gown with antique lace, fanning herself. The auditorium was filled for opening night, and the air was stuffy, almost unbearable. Her father grumbled about the performance throughout the first act, which Alta thought was just fine. Mary sat on the other side of her, patting her leg reassuringly, which Alta found equally irritating. So she excused herself, along with Doris, another young woman who was part of their group, and made her way to the lobby for some fresh air during a break, which felt positively breezy. She paused for a moment at the bottom of the stairs to acclimate herself and study the crowd of St. Paul's finest clustered in various groups surrounded by brocade and gilt. The ceiling of the lobby was covered in gorgeous paintings with elaborate framing and the walls in velvet paper. Alta fluttered her fan appreciatively. Several ladies approached her to give her their regards, and then, before she knew it, it was time to return to their box.

She took Doris by the arm and was about to return up the stairs when she spotted Stanley across the room—she couldn't miss the gold crown of his hair. He was engrossed in conversation with a group of men and glanced up. Their eyes met, and then he was approaching through the crowd, dodging the swirl of elegant fabrics until he stood before her looking extraordinary in his tailcoat and pique shirt. He was, she saw, the most handsome man at the theater.

"What a pleasure to see you," he said, taking in her gown and the loose coil of her hair. "Are you enjoying the show?"

Doris smiled curiously, then stepped away to give them a small measure of privacy.

Alta said she was enjoying the performance and asked what he thought.

"It's not nearly as lovely as you." His smile was so charming her heart dropped into her stomach.

"Oh, you flatter me, sir," she said.

"I thought we'd agreed you'd call me Stanley."

"Stanley . . . whatever are you doing here?"

"I thought I'd see what all the fuss was about."

"It's quite good."

"And I heard you would be here."

"Oh. Well . . ." Alta was surprised, but it seemed rather romantic. "How would you know such a thing?"

"I asked your girl."

"Greta?"

"Don't be angry at her," he said, seeing something on Alta's face. "She was very reluctant, but I assured her I had the best intentions."

"Oh, I see." Alta would have to have a talk with Greta. She was too often imprudent.

Stanley pulled on his tie and shifted his feet—he seemed nervous. "I wanted to ask you if I could call on you." He saw a head coming toward them that looked a lot like Cadwallader. He glanced sideways at the crowd to see if it was thick enough, in case he needed to disappear.

"I don't think that would be possible. Father wouldn't allow it."

"Well, of course." He moved his tie side to side, then dropped his hand and bit his lower lip. "I've noticed many ladies go for walks in the park." He named a park. "On Sunday afternoons. Sometimes they sit on a bench near the pond and feed the ducks and geese . . . Your father couldn't possibly be upset if one Sunday afternoon at, say, two o'clock, you happened to be sitting on a bench feeding the birds and I ran into you."

"Those things do happen . . . wouldn't it be a surprise?" Alta's nod was uncertain. Stanley's proposal was odd or even inappropriate. Or else, one could see it as very romantic. Romeo and Juliet, after all, did not announce to their parents that they were meeting up. At times it was necessary that love be clandestine.

The intermission bell chimed, calling the audience back into the auditorium.

"What park did you say?" Alta asked before slipping away.

XXX

The following Sunday afternoon, Alta sat at her vanity, brushing her hair. She had decided she would take a walk in the park and maybe stop and feed the ducks, but Greta was taking forever to find a dress. Alta set her brush down and stared at the broken-necked rose, the one Stanley had given her, dangling over the edge of the vase. The petals were blackened and dry.

"It would be a strange coincidence if you ran into him today," Greta said from the closet. She came out holding a lovely blue dress.

"Strange indeed," Alta giggled. She stood up and took the dress from Greta and held it in front of herself in the mirror.

A little more than an hour later, Alta sat next to Stanley on a bench in the middle of a park, watching the birds dart across the half-frozen lake. The day was cold, but the sun was hot. Stanley talked about growing up in North Dakota and his plans for the future. He was going to be big, he said. As big as her father, once he started his business.

"What business?" Alta didn't know if her goosebumps were from the cold, the intrigue, or the thrill of having him so near.

"I haven't decided."

"Well, if you put your mind to it, I'm sure you will be successful," she said, and he smiled to himself, feeling understood.

"Have you ever been out west?"

"I've been east. To Chicago. New York. Never west."

"It's where things are happening. There's money to be made. That's what my uncle says. It used to be the cities, but now it's the west. People are moving west in the thousands to homestead, and every one of them is going to need services."

"I believe you're right. My father's friend owns the railroad. They're building towns alongside it all the way to the Pacific coast. The new farmers will keep the mills going. That's what Father says."

Alta and Stanley were fixating on a flotilla of geese honking and nipping at one another. She wondered how they didn't freeze floating on the icy water. She pulled her coat tight, thinking it a shame that she couldn't show off her pretty dress.

"Your father's a bit old-fashioned." Stanley took her hand. She'd removed her gloves, which now sat on her lap, and she welcomed his warm grip. She glanced across the way to see if Greta had noticed, but Greta was studying a squirrel with rapt attention as it scrambled around the base of a tree.

"I suppose he is. He doesn't like me to go out without Greta . . . I'm his only family."

"He's getting on in age."

"I suppose he is. It's not something I like to think about."

"What will you do when he's gone? Do you have any other family?"

Alta didn't respond.

"You must think about it."

"It's a morbid thing to think about."

"Some people would say it's practical."

"My mother passed when I was born, and Father never remarried. He still loves my mother. No one could replace her."

"Ain't that something?" Stanley squeezed her hand, and when she glanced at him, he gave her his sunniest smile.

"Do you mind if I kiss you?"

Alta's eyes flitted toward Greta, and her heart gave a leap—she'd never been kissed before! He pressed his lips onto hers, and her lips parted briefly. Then she pulled away and stood up.

"I really need to be going."

He grabbed her hand, and she spun to face him.

"I love you, Alta," he said, and she felt she might faint. The thrill she felt must certainly be love. Love at first sight! Or nearly. She wanted to rush to tell Greta she was living a dream! She said goodbye to Stanley; her smile, she hoped, was encouraging.

"Greta."

Greta rushed over and took Alta's arm, casting worried

glances at her mistress. When they were out of earshot, Alta giggled, and then broke into laughter.

"Alta, what is it?" And then Greta couldn't help it. She was laughing. She turned to make sure Stanley was out of sight.

"Oh, dear," Alta found a nearby bench and sat down. She needed to collect herself.

"It's nothing, Greta," she said when she could breathe. "I'm just happy, that's all. Isn't he wonderful?"

"Mr. Olson? Of course he is. He's so wonderful!"

"And charming?"

"Yes. Charming."

"He is, isn't he? A true gentleman."

"A mysterious stranger," Greta said with a sigh, which made Alta stop, surprised.

"Is he?"

"What?"

"Mysterious?"

"Well, of course. You know so little about him . . ." This seemed obvious to Greta.

"Like Mr. Rochester?"

"I'm afraid I don't know Mr. Rochester."

"He's the dark lover in *Jane Eyre*. The book."

"Oh . . ."

"But Stanley is not as gloomy as Mr. Rochester. Mr. Rochester was gloomy. And married."

"Married?"

"Well, his wife was a loony."

"Oh, dear." Greta was silent, processing this information. "Stanley isn't gloomy at all."

"Greta. Do you think it's possible that I love him?"

"Oh, I don't see why not. Oh, dear, Alta. Love!"

Greta was thrilled, being a devotee of love and romance, but she couldn't help feeling a little worried. Flirtation was harmless enough, but Mr. Woburn would not be happy about love.

"What about your father?"

"My father?"

"Well. Your father forbade you to see him, didn't he?" she asked, knowing of course he had.

"He is an old fuddy-duddy, don't you think?"

"Well . . ." Greta hesitated because this felt like a trap. Of course Mr. Woburn was a fuddy-duddy. But he was also her employer, and to say something injurious about her employer was dishonorable. So Greta didn't respond further to the question. Instead, she recalled that Cadwallader Woburn had given her strict orders regarding Stanley Olson. Alta was not to see him. Of course, Alta literally just saw him, but one could have called the meeting a casual coincidence. A run-in. Cadwallader couldn't blame her for a run-in. He was always telling her to get the girl outside and into the fresh air, and inevitably that meant she would run into people. But now love. Love complicated things.

"You need to obey your father," Greta said, without conviction. What else could she say? Her own heart leapt at the thought of love. She loved love!

"I'm a modern woman, Greta. I don't need my father's permission."

"He might become very angry." Greta suspected Mr. Woburn would be furious at herself as well as Alta. She wondered if she'd lose her job, and the anxiety gnawed like a rodent on the edges of her stomach.

Anxiety, however, was not enough to stop Greta from facilitating more meetings between Stanley and Alta. She was caught up in the intrigue. She was in service to Cupid.

After several weeks of secret meetings, Stanley proposed to Alta. He took a knee and slipped a ring on her finger. She clasped the ringed hand in the other and studied the single, delicate diamond.

"Aren't you happy?" Stanley asked.

Alta's face crumbled.

"It's small, I know," he stood up. "But I'll buy you a bigger one someday."

"It was the most beautiful thing I've ever seen . . ." Alta found her voice. "But Father won't allow it." She shook her head and brushed the back of her hand across her brow.

Stanley took her wrists in his hands and pulled her to her feet and against him. He was so tall and strong, she couldn't breathe. He lifted her chin so he could look into her eyes.

"It's not up to your father, Alta. It's your life. Our life. You're a modern woman, aren't you?" His hand stroked under her chin.

Alta nodded. Of course she was! She was doing her best not to cry, she was so happy! They were under a tree at a park near her house on a day that was particularly warm for this time of year. A goose moved toward them, plucking at patches of grass.

"I know what he thinks of me, and I'm going to prove him wrong. I'll make you proud, Alta. I'm going to make my fortune and build you a big house, and we'll have children, lots of children. You want children, don't you?"

"Four," she said, her voice nearly breaking. "Two boys and two girls."

"Four," Stanley laughed. "That's all? We can manage that . . . We don't have to tell him. We'll make it legal, then he'll have to allow it . . ."

He kissed her then, right under the cottonwood tree. His lips were warm and firm and she touched her palm to his chest and could feel his heart beating.

"I want you to be happy, Alta."

He wrapped his arms around her, and she closed her eyes and listened to the slow, steady beat of his heart.

When Alta told Greta later that day, her maid was shocked.

"But your father!" Her voice cracked in panic. She felt a

lurch in her stomach, like the rodent was in there biting down. It scratched and chewed, like it needed to fill up before the cold moved in.

"That's why we're going to a justice of the peace. I do hope you'll be there."

Greta knew she was damned. To serve her mistress was to betray the master, and vice versa. What could she do?

"Of course I'll be there . . . What will you wear?"

XXX

Alta had always imagined a big wedding in a church filled with hundreds of guests and a long walk down the aisle on her father's arm; but in some ways, she supposed, the courthouse was more romantic because it was more intimate. It was just the two of them and Greta, who'd come as their witness. Alta wore a light pink dress with cream beadwork and embroidery and held a bouquet of white lilies. Greta had made her a veil. Stanley wore a three-piece suit with a double-breasted sack coat. Greta wore her Sunday dress.

After the brief ceremony, they went to Alta's house to break the news to her father. They waited in the foyer while a maid retrieved Cadwallader. Greta had returned through a servants' entrance and slunk off to bed, all of them agreeing Cadwallader should not know of her role in the affair.

Alta clung tightly to Stanley's hand, now terrified by the thought of her father's reaction. She was sweating under her beautiful silks, not very becoming for a bride on her wedding night.

"He'll see how much I love you," Alta whispered to Stanley, as much for her own sake as for his. Stanley, for his part, had grown quiet. Looking down the long hallways trimmed in polished white oak and lit by crystal chandeliers, Stanley felt intimidated. He understood in that moment he was taunting a beast that could tear him apart with little effort. But then, greatness required a man to stroke the throat of the beast, tame it. This was a rite of passage. Stanley would not be pushed around or forced to cower by Mr. Woburn.

The clock along the wall ticked more slowly than usual.

"Oh, dear." Alta longed to sit down.

"What is this?" Cadwallader's voice boomed, and then he was striding toward them. He stopped in the hallway when he saw them shrinking like cornered prey.

"Mr. Woburn," Stanley said.

"Father."

"What is the meaning of this? What have you done?"

"Father." Alta's voice was pleading.

Stanley stepped forward to take charge of the situation because he was the husband, the authority, and he would assert his position and rights.

"Sir."

"I was talking to my daughter."

"Daddy," Alta fought the urge to run to her room and burrow under her quilts. "We married . . ." Her voice was a whisper.

She could see by the look on her father's face that they'd been hasty. For a brief moment, what was strong and fierce fell away like dead skin, and he was an old and broken man, and her heart split open. But then Cadwallader recoiled.

"Get out of here. Get the hell out of my house." He grabbed Alta's arm.

"You go to your room."

"But Father, we're married. He's my husband."

"Like hell he is. That will be undone. Leave!"

Stanley hesitated. This was not how he had envisioned this moment. Cadwallader should be respecting him—he was family now—not kicking him out the door like a stray dog. He wanted to hit the man, and had it been another man, that man would have been seeing stars. But of course, this was Cadwallader. Even with his bent frame and draped skin he was impenetrable and dangerous, and with his wealth, he had infinite power.

"You have no authority," Stanley said. It was all he could come up with. "Not now. Not anymore."

"You'll be gone by morning. If you're still in town when the sun rises, I promise you won't be here when it sets."

"Daddy." Alta reached for Stanley, and Cadwallader pulled her back. He pushed her into the hallway so she stumbled. "Get to your room. I'll deal with you later," he said. The two lovers exchanged looks.

"It's OK. I'll come for you," Stanley said. He nodded slowly at Alta, indicating that she should go. She burst into tears as she turned and lurched down the hallway. Greta met her at the bottom of the staircase and led her to her room.

"If I were you, I'd get as far away from this town as you can and don't come back," Cadwallader growled as he shut the door.

Stanley stuck his hands in his pockets and stomped toward the street. "God damn son of a bitch." He swung his arm at a low-hanging tree branch to whack it out of the way, and the branch ricocheted back and scratched him across the face. "Shit." He paused just outside the circle of light beaming from a streetlight. That hadn't gone at all the way he thought it would. Not at all like he planned. He watched a raccoon or a cat, or some small animal creep around the bushes in front of a house across the street. He was married. He let that thought sink in. To one of the wealthiest women in the state . . . He felt a swell of pride at the accomplishment. He'd done well. Really well. This Cadwallader thing was a hiccup. He'd get through it, figure it out. Damn. He tossed his cigarette on the ground and mashed it under his heel. A married man. He checked his watch, then made his way down the street.

CHAPTER 3

WENDELL

Two weeks after the bridge builders cut a hole in the barn to let in the car, Wendell heard the clatter of hooves and rattle of leads that announced the arrival of the Indian. The hole confirmed what Wendell already knew—the Good Lord was out to get him. It was not for him to know the time or day or, for that matter, the why. One early morning the bridge builders came up from the work camp with their tool belts hanging heavy off their hips and began tearing into the side of the barn, and since Wendell knew it was pointless to defy the Almighty, he abandoned his duties and rushed across the road to Tom's saloon for refuge—not his regular refuge—and a window seat to the devastation. Over a glass of cheap whiskey, Wendell admired how the men worked like they were arms of the same magical machine, tearing, trimming, and painting so quickly and efficiently he couldn't help but raise his glass in a toast. When he returned good and drunk to the barn, he ran his hand along the trim of the new opening and then slid in through the gaping mouth and into the belly of the monster's den. Or at least that's how he remembered it when he woke up tangled like a pretzel on the cold, hard dirt.

The car took some getting used to. It sat quietly in the stall that acted as a garage, and the horses pawed and snorted and shied away from it. Wendell thought for sure the animals agreed the place was going to hell in a handbasket, but then they got used to the car and it was part of the barnscape—except when Jake or Stanley came in and reanimated it with a roar. Then the horses jolted to the back of their stalls or out the stall doors, or they shook their heads and pawed at the straw.

"It won't last," Wendell said to a bay horse that was boarding for the night after Stanley blasted away in the automobile, leaving a waft of gasoline. He stroked the plush nose. "They'll get tired of it and be looking for good cow ponies. You just wait."

But to himself, he thought, it's not like it used to be, just as the bay's head went up. The horse whinnied and blew, and the approaching horses answered in kind.

Wendell went out to swing open the gate, and Smoke led a string of horses into the corral and released them. They tossed their heads and snorted and leapt around the enclosure. Smoke slid from his buckskin mare and, still holding the reins, took a seat on the top rail of the fence near Wendell. The two men sat quiet as potato plants studying the animals darting fish-like around the corral. The horses were small and stocky with heavy hindquarters ideal for bursts of speed, quick stops, and cutting—perfect cow ponies. Wendell tapped his fingers on the railing and Smoke spat into the enclosure. The palomino lifted his hindquarters in a halfhearted provocation of the sorrel mare. The sorrel nipped at the palomino and went back to scratching her neck on a railing.

"That palomino is thickheaded," Smoke said.

"That's a pretty little dun you have there," Wendell replied.

Smoke nodded, though Wendell wasn't looking at him. They both felt the perfect contentment that came with sitting on the fence in a splash of sunlight and watching horses. It was early in the season, but the past week had been unseasonably warm, and most of the snow had melted and dried up. Tiny green shoots poked through the dirt in places. It felt good to be out from under the heavy layers they'd gotten used to.

Jake strode into the yard and leaned his elbow over a railing on the fence.

"What you got here?"

He studied the horses and spat into the dirt and rubbed his face with his handkerchief. Wendell swung down and leaned over the fence next to him. Jake straightened up.

"Horses aren't selling so well these days," Jake said.

Wendell chuckled because he knew different. Smoke had the appearance of not hearing, but then he spoke.

"The bay over there is the fastest son of a bitch you'll ever see. Hot-headed, but it'll be a fine horse with a little work. The sorrel with the white sock up front is smart. She'll make a great cow pony. So will the gray. The mare with the blaze clear down her nose, she's the oldest of the five; a child could ride her. She's got good cow sense too."

"I tell you what, Smoke. I'll do you a favor and take the whole lot off your hands for a hundred fifty. Maybe I can sell them, maybe I can't. Automobiles. That's where it's at . . . Did you see my car?"

"That's dad-blasted larceny. A steal," Wendell said.

"What is?" Jake asked.

"A hundred and fifty for those horses."

"I don't recall asking your opinion, and I don't pay you to lean and run your mouth off. You need to get back to work."

Jake waved the old man away and took his rolling papers out of his pocket, which he laid on top of a post. Then he filled the paper with a line of tobacco. He offered Smoke a cigarette.

"These new folks, they're a different lot. Farmers . . . They'll want their plow horses. A few of them will. But they don't have any need for cow horses or riding horses, and it won't be long and they'll be using machines."

Smoke didn't know what to say. He'd been bringing horses to Jake for the past year and to other dealers in other small towns before then. He'd heard of farmers using engines for farming, and he'd even seen a real one, but there was no way in hell they were going to replace horses. As far as he could tell, Jake was talking crazy in order to rationalize cheating him on price.

Wendell came by with a wheelbarrow loaded with shit and dumped it in a pile off to the side of the barn. Then he tipped it over and banged it upside down louder than necessary, in case Jake hadn't caught on that he was angry. Jake glanced his way, and when he turned back to Smoke, Wendell right-sided the wheelbarrow with a crash.

"Four fifty sounds about right," Smoke finally said.

"There are a few cowboys and ranchers around buying horses. Maybe they'll pay you."

"All right," Smoke said.

Jake stood up. "You can go ahead and leave 'em here for the night. After that, I'll have to charge you. Wendell will throw them some hay."

Jake walked away, and Smoke stayed leaning into the fence, watching the horses. They'd settled some and were sniffing around the edges of the corral, picking at a bit of hay that had been pushed just out of their reach. The bay came over and jabbed its nose into Smoke's chest, and the Indian stroked its head. Jake was playing him—no doubt about it. Sometimes the man just had to fan his feathers.

As for Wendell, the feeling that Jake was bending circumstances to his advantage offended his sense of justice and left him in a sour mood. It wasn't that he was especially fond of the Indian—he liked him well enough, but he didn't know him all that well. When Jake was out of sight, Wendell directed Smoke to the tack room with his saddle, then he showed him up to the loft and told him he could nest there for the night.

Wendell pointed to the automobile entrance on the side of the barn, and the two talked about the car over cigarettes. Then Wendell offered Smoke a swig from the bottle he had stuffed in his sleeping roll, which he had the sense to tie up during the day, and the two men sat considering. Seeing Jake rain injustice on Smoke had Wendell wondering if the boss wasn't also raining the same on him. He wondered in what ways Jake might take advantage of an old hand such as himself. All the considering fueled a fury, which he directed to the bottle in his hand. Smoke, on the other hand, was considering how he might sell off the horses if it turned out that Jake was not just pulling his leg about price. Eventually, Smoke climbed down from the loft and trailed off to the bars, and Wendell got up to finish off his chores. He mucked out stalls and stole sips from his bottle, and he thought how he should be running the entire livery, not relegated to barn boy.

There was a crash in a stall, and Wendell turned to see Jake's silver stallion charging up and down, snorting and pawing and rushing the gate, and so Wendell figured one of Smoke's mares was in heat. He admired the enormous thoroughbred, of course. Who wouldn't? It was something to look at, all long legged, with powerful shoulders and hindquarters. When it moved, it floated—its hooves never seemed to touch the ground, and it was as fast as could be. But Wendell wondered if it wasn't too hot an animal for this part of the country. It was just like Jake, to buy the fanciest horse he could find in three states and call it an investment. Wendell pitched shit into a wheelbarrow and talked to the horse, and the muck was heavy. He stopped to take a drink, feeling worn out. And the truth was, he was getting too old for this type of work. But for the liquor, he wouldn't make it through the day. Even with it, he could feel the strain across his back and shoulders. It was just the way it was—every day, it seemed, the load was a little bit heavier. The muck was heavier and the hay was heavier and the water buckets—it was as if the air around him had become weighted, thickened around his body, or his own grave had risen to encase him, and he'd become stiff, calcified, a fossil of his previous self. Death had begun to work him over. It had come inside and locked the door and begun extinguishing bits and pieces of him—impatient bastard couldn't wait until he stopped breathing. He thought about the monster scientists had pulled from the dirt not too far away. *Tyrannosaurus rex* they'd called it, and he wondered if one day people would discover his own bones in the rocks and if they'd be as they were now, frozen with a pitchfork weighted with horse shit or a petrified lot of straw. He wondered what they'd call him—*Tyranoshit shoveler* or *Shoveler rex*, he decided . . . And then he thought it wouldn't be so hard to be dead. It's the living that's cursed.

Wendell pulled the stallion out of its stall and walked it to another empty stall so he could clean the one it occupied. The horse, he noticed, was favoring its right front foreleg. Wendell wrapped the lead around a railing, ran his hand down the leg, lifted the foot, and cleaned the hoof. The shoe was loose along the heel, and the hoof had been trimmed unevenly so that a crack was creeping up the wall. Wendell snorted in disgust. In his days as a farrier, he'd never done such shoddy work.

He retrieved some tools in the tack room—maybe he was nostalgic because he'd kept his tools. He pulled the shoe and felt around the edges of the hoof. The sole appeared bruised along the back wall. He pressed on the heel, and the horse pulled away. Wendell set the foot down and studied the horse. The animal snorted and turned toward the door and the mares.

Wendell pulled the flask from his pocket and took a swallow of whiskey. It wasn't his job, of course, to trim feet and shoe horses, but what kind of man would let an animal suffer if he could do something about it? It would be nothing to trim down the wall a bit so the hoof was even, and then Jake could get a hold of his fancy farrier who would strut around and brag about his East Coast schooling and charge an arm and a leg for work Wendell could do for nearly nothing.

The horse twisted toward the door and the hoof looked splayed in the muted barn light.

"What the hell?" Wendell said, picked up his nipper, and approached the animal.

He held the horse's leg between his own legs and trimmed carefully, horny flakes snowing onto the hardened dirt floor. The horse fidgeted and shifted and pressed its belly into Wendell's back and then cranked its head around to look at Wendell, tickling his backside with its warm breath. And then the stallion shifted its weight and leaned on Wendell like he was some sort of horse couch, and the old man had to release the leg and stand up for a breath.

"Jesus Christ, you son of a bitch. You still have three legs. What do I look like, a bescumbering stool!"

The horse blew out, and the man patted its shoulder and picked up the leg again, and worked his rasp around the edge of the hoof. Then, there was clatter and sputter and cough as the car bounced through the hole in the barn. The horse exploded. Wendell picked himself off the floor in time to see the horse nearly on its haunches pulling against the lead, and then the buckle snapped and the horse rolled onto its back into a stall, twisting. It ricocheted to its feet then burst over the wheelbarrow and out the door. Wendell struggled to his feet.

"Jesus Christ!" Stanley said, laughing as he lifted himself out of the car and lurched to the ground. "Did you see that!" He offered Wendell a hand. "God damn crazy animal!" He clasped the old man's shoulder, looking to where the horse had disappeared.

Wendell threw off Stanley's hand in a hailstorm of cussing.

"What the hell are you doing driving that dad-blasted

contraption around like a halfwit!" He rubbed his hand over the back of his head where a lump was forming.

"There's a goddamn potato growing on the back of my head."

"Settle down there. I was just parking the car. That stall belongs to that there automobile now. You'd better get used to it."

"You're scaring the living daylights out of the horses."

"They'll have to get used to it."

Wendell stood staring at Stanley, pushing on the growing lump on his head.

"I've got something for that." Stanley moved toward the car and Wendell glanced at the wheelbarrow on its side with the dirty bedding strewn across the aisle and the pitchfork flipped over like it was grabbing shit out of the air.

"Damnit to hell." He flicked his hand at the car as he left the barn.

"All right," Stanley said to himself, holding up his bottle. Seeing Wendell wasn't interested in taking him up on his offer, he went on his way, back through the car stall, sliding his hand along the edge of the panacea of glistening metal.

XXX

Outside, the horse was standing near the gate with his foreleg lifted, dangling. It backed away as Wendell approached, nearly buckling when it put weight on the leg. Wendell talked softly and circled, and the horse let him take hold of its halter. Wendell snapped on a lead and gently ran his hand along the stallion's trembling shoulder, then bent to study the gash mid-cannon and sucked in his breath.

The skin broke open into a thin mouth of uneven, leathery teeth spitting blood down the leg and into the dirt. Wendell ran his hand gently down the leg near the injury, and the horse whipped its leg back.

"Goddamn. Broke to hell . . . You're going to have to put him down."

"Damnit to hell!" Wendell hissed and carefully released the leg. He stood up and put his hand over his heart. "Why the hell are you sneaking around!"

Smoke was studying the leg alongside Wendell. Now he straightened up and took a step back.

"It's broken. Nothing you can do about it."

"Oh, come on. That's the best you got? You can see that from standing way the hell back there?"

"I can see fine enough. You're going to have to shoot it."

"Go to hell."

Wendell stared at the horse. It shifted its leg up and down and then let it dangle, its head hanging in a most pathetic manner.

Wendell rubbed his own head, and the lump was still there. He studied the inky red on his fingers and reached into his pocket with his other hand and pulled out a hankie to wipe off the blood. He was probably drunk. He shook his head and opened his eyes and nothing had changed—the lame horse, the Indian, and in the garage stall the piece-of-shit automobile. He could shoot the car. He'd enjoy that. Shoot out the tires and drill holes the entire length of the car's side. He pictured steam coming out of the holes and weeds eating at the rusting metal in some grassy grave.

The stallion snorted as the other horses bunched up on the other side of the corral, watching. It lurched toward the mares but jolted as its foot touched the ground, its neck recoiling like the loose handle on a water pump.

"I'd better go get the boss," Wendell said, feeling his shoulders cave just anticipating the rage.

Smoke nodded and took the lead from Wendell's hand.

"He's probably down at Josephine's," he mumbled to himself.

The rule was that Jake was never to be interrupted at Josephine's, no matter what, come hell or high water. Smoke had moved in and was stroking the stallion's silver neck, whispering words Wendell couldn't make out, and the old man stood at a crossroads. He thought of crawling into the loft and sleeping the day off or chasing Stanley down and beating the shit out of him.

"Goddamn," Wendell said, and he thought, this might just be the end of me.

"I'll be back," he said, leaving Smoke with the horse.

Wendell ran, though maybe you couldn't call it running. His arms pumped, and his legs lurched, and he stopped to catch his breath, then walked the remainder of the way to Josephine's house.

XXX

Josephine herself answered the door, and it was a matter of minutes before she had retrieved Jake, the big man tucking in his shirt.

"This had better be good," Jake said, smoothing his hair back with the palm of his hand.

Wendell explained and Jake followed him back to the livery, moving like a molten thing, burning through anyone or anything in his path. Wendell ran as if an animal, a bull, a mountain of dangerous flesh, was puffing at his heels.

The horse swung his head at the sound of footsteps, and Smoke, Wendell could see, was still talking in his ear.

"What the hell is he doing here? Was he fucking with my horse?"

"He's holding him."

Jake circled the stallion.

He ran his hand down the leg—he could be gentle when the circumstances required it of him—and the horse pulled back against the lead.

"What the hell were you doing fooling around with my horse?"

"I was fixing his feet. The dad-blasted foot was all messed up. That shit-ass farrier you got with all his fancy schooling fucked up his foot!"

"So you break his leg thinking that would fix the foot!"

Wendell had to admit it was a good point. "It was the goddamn car," he said. "It scared him."

"While you were playing farrier . . . You son of a bitch. I don't pay you to play farrier. I pay you to shovel shit. That's it. Do you know what this horse is worth? Do you?" When Wendell told of the incident later, he swore there were flames leaping from Jake's eyes.

"This horse was sired by the grandson of the greatest running filly in history. Jesus Christ . . . Get Doc . . ."

For the second time that evening, Wendell ran. Sharp jolts tore through his knees and hips, and his lungs screamed, but he ran to Doc's and came back several minutes later trailing a short bald man carrying a black leather case.

Doc specialized in humans but was known to have good horse sense, having grown up cowboying on local ranches, so he was often called to see to injured animals. Today, he set down his bag and walked around the horse, clicking his tongue. He decided immediately the injury was irreparable but didn't want to come across as rushed—Doc knew good medicine required a pinch of theater, so he allowed the tension to build before announcing his diagnosis, running his hand down the leg, bending down to examine the wound, all the time conveying the gravity of the situation with his clicking tongue. Then he stood slowly and cleared his throat.

"Cannon bone's fractured," he said, then took a deep breath and cleared his throat again. "In at least one place. Maybe two, I can't quite tell about this other spot."

"Jesus fuck," Jake said.

"I don't see that you have a choice but to put it down."

"Fuck!" Jake kicked a fence post, then walked up and down the length of the corral, thinking his thoughts, all circling toward a conclusion. When he finally settled on that conclusion, he spun around.

"You still got that rifle?" he asked Wendell.

"I got a rifle," Smoke said, not feeling satisfaction that his diagnosis had been right all along. "It's with my tack."

Jake ignored Smoke.

"Yep," Wendell said, glancing at Smoke.

"Do you boys know how to put down a horse?" Doc asked, not yet ready to transfer authority of the situation back to Jake. But Wendell was already on his way to the barn, and Jake didn't hear him.

"Goddamn," Jake said. Then he spoke to Wendell's back. "You go ahead and finish what you began. You take care of this. And then you're fired."

Wendell turned.

"Did you hear me? Can you manage taking care of that horse?"

"I can manage," Wendell said.

"Goddamnit." Jake spoke to Smoke. "There's going to be hell to pay. You know that, don't you?"

Smoke didn't respond but kept patting the horse.

When Wendell reappeared, Jake and the Doc were gone and Smoke was still holding the stallion's lead.

The Indian stroked the horse and whispered. He led the animal over to a fence post and wrapped the end of the lead around the post several times before tying it snuggly. The horse lifted its head only slightly when Wendell approached, pulling against the rope when the old man brought up the rifle. Wendell knew to aim in the center of the *X* that criss-crossed the forehead between the eyes and ears, and in his younger days in sober times he would have made a clean shot, but now his hand shook as he took aim, and it took several tries. He cocked the gun and took a shot. The stallion bolted back, ricocheting off the rope, and a dash of red rose above his eye. Cock, shoot, cock, shoot—Wendell fired again and again, sweating and gritting his teeth when he paused to reload; it took so much time. The stallion leaned back as if suspended. Another shot and the horse threw its head and bent sideways, and the whole mountain of it avalanched in slow motion to the ground. Smoke followed the stallion down, murmuring. In the corral, the other horses danced and shook their heads and ran furiously back and forth.

"Die, goddamn it," Wendell aimed once more for the forehead—he couldn't bear watching.

When the thrashing stopped, Wendell leaned the rifle against the fence, wiped his brow, and pulled the sweat-soaked shirt off his chest to let the air circulate, not really registering that he was burning up.

"I could sure use a drink," Wendell said as flies gathered on the battered, previously majestic headscape. Smoke nodded.

A farmer who had joined the crowd gathering around the morbid scene offered up his team to drag the corpse into a field for the scavengers. They hitched a rope around the neck and threaded the rope through the harnesses while the draft horses shifted uneasily, and then the horses pulled the stallion a quarter mile away from the town. The men unhitched it and rolled it into a gully to rot or be eaten by carrion.

"Well," Wendell said as he and Smoke walked back toward town, needing his voice to bookend the day's grisly events. "And that's that," he said, "that's the way it goes," though he certainly did not feel that was the way things should go at all.

"It's shit," Smoke said.

"Sure is," Wendell said.

They walked into the Tumbleweed saloon and ordered their whiskey straight.

CHAPTER 4

ADAM

Wendell wasn't around, so Adam went to his room and stretched out on his bed, and felt a thrill cracking open the diary. He wasn't much of a reader, but this could hardly be considered reading. This was a peep into the thrilling and exotic world of prostitutes and outlaws. He might as well be looking in the bedroom window!

Of course he'd imagined the whores' lives—in his fantasies, the house was still fine, with glittering lights and velvet on the walls. The women glided from room to room, spilling out of their dresses, smelling like cinnamon, taking the hand of cowboy or outlaw or maybe a wide-shouldered rancher. And then they'd disappear up the staircase. Picturing it aroused him. Of course he understood the mechanics of what went on in those rooms—he saw the cattle and horse and dogs going through the motions—but women were mysterious, and he thought there must be a working up to it all. Lola, he hoped, would clarify this complication. That was her name. Lola. It was right inside the cover of the diary in not-so-neat printing. She wrote an awful lot about the weather.

August 9

Hotter than hell today. It's a wonder the whole town don't burn down.

November 1

Wind tearing shingles off right and left. Jake's going to be mad as hell.

November 30

Weather seems to be keeping everyone home.

He flipped through the pages and found the part about Stanley. Was she talking about his father Stanley?

February 12

Stanley brought me flowers and rye. Alice says he's my opportunity and I'd better snag him before I lose my looks. I said he's married, and she said that didn't stop Madeline. Besides, she said, who wants to lie with a china cup? That made me laugh.

February 13

I said to Alice if things were different, I'd marry Stanley, and then she asked me, different how? I told her he had to ask. She wouldn't stand for that and she threw a fit. She yelled at me and called me stupid. She said to make things different. I said I will. And then she spit at me and said you'd better. Alice is like that. She spits at everyone when she's mad. Josephine said it's not ladylike, but that made her laugh. Alice said folks don't think sporting women are ladies. That shut Josephine up, and nothing shuts Josephine up. Alice had a baby once and gave it away, and people say that made her mean. I like her mean.

February 15

Alice said maybe he's just teasing me. I said if that were the case, I'd have his head. Or string him up. I won't be made a fool.

Adam heard Wendell in the kitchen and slammed the book shut. He didn't know what to think. He felt angry. Embarrassed. Dirty. It was his mom and his dad she was talking about. Or it seemed to be. He slid the book under the mattress so Wendell wouldn't see it. A book in the house would arouse all kinds of suspicion. There was a greater likelihood of finding a unicorn or a dragon hiding in the corner of Adam's room than finding a book, so of course Wendell would notice. And if he found it, he might try to barter it for a jug of something or other. A whore's diary, Adam was certain, had some value. He stood up and stretched, then went out to the kitchen to see what Wendell was cooking up for supper.

XXX

The next day was Sunday, but that didn't mean anything. Jake had a job for him, so Adam thought he'd get at it. Jake had recommended he carry his rifle. "When you're dealing with money, people can get crazy," he'd advised. "There's those who'd as soon blow your head off as hand over the few dollars they owe."

Jake had passed Adam a letter and slapped the horse on the backend, and now here he was, riding miles west of town looking for a small farmstead like one of the many that dotted the area. He could see a little tarpaper shack when he came over the rise, a black hole in the golden landscape. An old, swaybacked cow stood in the corral next to the house with nothing but dirt to nibble on. In the background were fields that looked like they had once grown wheat and corn, but now appeared to be nothing but stubble.

Adam kept the horse—Lady—to a slow trot, but still she was sweating in the heat, foam rising along the edge of the saddle blanket. She was a beautiful animal, a four-year-old palomino quarter horse with a sweet nature. She was easy to ride and responsive, and Adam probably would have taken the job without pay just to ride her.

He patted Lady's neck. A dog rose out of the grass near the house and charged him, barking. It was a small and dirty thing, and it circled the horse, baring its teeth. Lady lunged sideways, bucking.

"Hey there," Adam held tight to the reins to keep the horse's head up—a horse needed to lower its head to get a good buck in—and talked her down, stroking her neck the best he could with all the twisting.

"Rags!" An old woman rushed out of the house just as mangy-looking as the dog.

Rags got in a few more yaps, then retreated to circle the woman's legs, still eyeing Adam and the horse.

Mrs. Lund, he assumed, stood short and thick as an ancient tree trunk watching and waiting like she was expecting bad news. The dog growled like it needed to get in another word.

"Good afternoon." Adam removed his hat. He'd seen businessmen in action, and so he knew the moves.

"I'm here on behalf—"

"I know why you're here."

Adam reached into his pocket and pulled out the letter.

"Jake . . . he says that according to your previous agreement, you need to either sign over the patent for the property or pay what he loaned you, with interest of course. The numbers are all there."

"I don't have the money. Does it look like I have the money? . . . Where does he expect me to get the money?"

Adam looked around. It hadn't occurred to him that there would be questions.

"I don't know . . . He said he'll have to confiscate the property if you don't pay." Maybe she didn't get the seriousness.

"Where does he expect me to go?"

"I don't know. Why don't you go live with some family somewhere?" Lady stomped her feet and swished her tail—it's like she could feel his irritation. Or maybe it was the flies.

"I don't have any family. They're all gone."

"Don't you have a brother or a sister somewhere?"

Adam stroked the still-agitated horse. Most of the few horses Jake kept around were half dead. Lady was the exception. Jake fancied he'd ride someday and felt he required something fancy, which is why he had her. Adam didn't believe Jake was much up for riding. And Lady, he was certain, would throw him the second he put his foot in the stirrups.

Mrs. Lund turned to go back into the house.

"Listen. This letter says you have to go. Or pay." Adam found himself talking to the weeds sprouting on the roof of the house. He was embarrassed to be kicking a little old lady from her house.

He waited with sweat running down his forehead for her to come back and acquiesce. Lady stomped and pulled on the bit, wanting to graze.

"Hey," Adam called. And then Mrs. Lund appeared in the doorway.

"I know who you are . . ." Her voice was accusing. "I remember your mother. She was a nice woman. Classy. She wouldn't approve of what you're doing."

"I didn't make the rules. I'm just telling you," Adam said, and the words drifted here and there like cotton from a tree, seeming to miss Mrs. Lund's ears. Her face might as well have been carved in wood the way the look of disgust stayed unchanging. He studied her feet and could see, even in the shadows, that her shoes were torn to bits.

"Your father. He was something else. A real good-for-nothing. You're just like him, aren't you?"

Adam felt his face blaze. The truth was, he wasn't like his father because his father wouldn't sit here and let an old woman insult him. If there was one thing he knew about his father, it's that he hadn't put up with people arguing with him and standing in his way.

"I'll tell Jake you got the message." Adam turned the horse and pushed her into a lope to escape Mrs. Lund's scalding gaze. He didn't turn to look back until he knew he was well out of her line of vision, and then pulled the mare to a stop. He turned to confirm. The old lady and her dog and her tar-paper home had been washed away by the ascending horizon.

Adam spat into the grass and took off his hat and slapped it against his knee, then pushed the horse into a slow trot, in no hurry to return to town now that that work was done. He settled into the saddle and touched the stock of his rifle hanging off the pommel. He should have pulled it and showed Mrs. Lund who was boss and marched her across the prairie—that's what he should have done. The way she'd disrespected him. Belittled him even. She'd treated him like a child. Like he wasn't up to the task . . . He was up to the task . . . Stanley would have used the rifle, Adam knew that for sure. He kicked the horse into a run, faster and faster, leaning forward as the prairie gave way beneath him. The pounding and hot air rushing by felt good but didn't stop his thinking. And the more he thought about Mrs. Lund questioning him, the angrier he got. He slowed Lady back down to a trot. She wouldn't defy him again, by golly. That's for sure. He considered turning around and riding back to the house, but then there was the sprinkle of Mondak in front of him.

"Good girl, Lady," he said, patting the horse's neck.

Well. He wouldn't have to put up with that again because

he was getting the hell out of town. He sighed with relief at the thought of leaving.

Back at the livery, he unsaddled the horse and turned her loose in the corral and watched her trot away. She stopped to nibble on the grass along the fence line. He didn't hear Jake approach, but the big man was there when he turned.

"How'd it go?"

"Good. She got the message."

"Did she give you pushback? Don't let them give you pushback."

Adam shook his head. "She doesn't have any money." He turned away from the corral, thinking he'd be on his way.

"That's what they all say . . . I'll give her a couple days, then I'll send you back. If she's still there, I'll have you remove her. Can you do that?"

Jake's tone suggested he didn't think he could.

"Yeah," Adam said. No need to tell Jake he was leaving town to join the circus.

"Good." Jake looked him over, then reached into his pocket and pulled out a five-dollar bill and passed it to him.

Adam looked beyond to the bustle on Main Street. Everyone, it seemed, was out today. Adam grabbed his rifle, which was leaning against the barn.

"I'll need you tomorrow," Jake said, waiting as if for questions. Adam nodded, then turned away. He headed west of town, thinking the day was still young and he could shoot something for dinner. He kicked at a clod of dirt and watched it explode.

It wasn't long before he left the sprawl of Mondak and was marching through buffalo grass. The day had only gotten hotter, and the flies and grasshoppers were whirling like a dust devil. He wished he'd gotten himself some water back at the barn. About a mile out, some pheasants broke from the bushes and he got in a good shot. Several minutes later, he got in another. With the birds in hand, he walked the couple of miles back to the house, tired but feeling pleased with himself.

When he arrived, Wendell was home. This was becoming an unusual habit, so probably, he was broke, Adam thought, which meant he'd be in a sour mood. And he was—pacing back and forth like a caged animal. He walked around the kitchen opening and closing cupboards and mumbling to himself.

"Hey," Adam said.

Wendell mumbled something incoherent in reply, but then he saw the birds, and his face brightened. The two cleaned the birds, and Wendell cut and breaded the meat and warmed up the fry pan.

"Good job, son. I was ready for some supper."

"And here it is."

"Here it is. You're right."

Adam plopped himself into a chair, and Wendell stopped in front of the stove and poked at the birds, then continued his pacing. Adam glanced into the front room, which was nearly empty. "Christ," he swore under his breath. He'd forgotten Wendell had sold off the couch—for a few pennies, no doubt. He'd probably afforded himself a bottle of whiskey. The side table and reading lamp had disappeared weeks ago, and dust bunnies were piling where the furniture had been . . . When had he sold the rug? . . . Good luck keeping warm in winter, he thought bitterly.

"Want some?"

The question was redundant. Wendell plated the bird, then slid some in front of Adam.

"Thank you."

"Don't mention it."

Wendell sat down and then got back up for utensils, shooting a fork and knife across the table to Adam.

"Ever been to the circus?" Wendell's mouth moved side to side when he chewed.

"When would I have gone to a circus?" Adam wondered if he should tell Wendell about his plan to leave town—he was finding it hard to keep the secret. But then he decided Wendell would get all worked up and say something about his responsibility for the boy, that he was taking care of Adam because he owed it to Alta, or some such thing, and Adam would feel bad because he was cheating the old man of an opportunity to make good on a promise. But really, when it came down to it, Adam was pretty certain his absence would be a relief to Wendell. And it's not that Wendell did that much, if anything, for him.

"I went to Buffalo Bill's Wild West Show back in '87. I saw old Buffalo Bill himself. It was quite a show."

"It's coming here."

"Not the Wild West Show?"

"The regular circus."

"That's what I said," Wendell chewed slowly. "It's coming to town."

"You didn't say that."

Wendell glared at Adam.

"I saw the posters."

"Yep . . ."

They ate in silence for a bit. Adam finished his supper and was still hungry. He glanced around as if expecting to see some other food.

"Best goddamn show around . . . I'd like to see an elephant. Bill didn't have an elephant." Wendell was a much slower eater.

"There were elephants on the poster. I bet there'll be one."

Adam watched as Wendell sank into a reverie. Remembering Buffalo Bill, Adam imagined. When the old man let down his guard, Adam could see how dilapidated he was. Normally, he was so ornery that Adam sometimes forgot he was old. But now he could see he was thin and dusty, with loose, gray skin like long johns washed too many times—a straw man. He could stand in a field and he'd scare off the birds, Adam thought. Of course, when Wendell opened his mouth, his fierce temper overshadowed his physical fragilities. Adam felt a blush of guilt about his plan to leave—the old man couldn't care for himself. But then again, he didn't take care of himself the way it was. His descent into self-destruction was too far along for Adam to impact.

"You knew my dad," Adam said.

It was a rhetorical question, but Wendell didn't see it that way.

"Jesus Christ, kid. He was my nephew. Of course I knew him."

There was that glare again.

"You got something on your mind?"

"Did Dad ever visit the sporting house down by the river?"

Wendell gave him a visual grilling.

"Maybe. Some. Sure . . . he was a grown man, for Christ's sake . . . What the hell do you know about the sporting house?"

"Cecil and I cleaned it for Jake."

"You still working for that good-for-nothing cheap bastard? I hope he's paying you well."

"Well enough."

"Watch out for him. Cheap piece of shit. He just wants your money."

"I don't have any money."

"Your grandfather was one of the richest men in the country. Jake probably thinks you have a fortune socked away in your mattress. And if there's money around, Jake will find a way to get his hands on it. And he is willing to play the long game."

Adam was quiet thinking about this. He'd heard bits and pieces about his grandfather, but he knew even less about him than his parents. His grandfather might as well live on the moon. He'd heard Mr. Woburn had had a falling out with Stanley, and that's why there had been a rift.

"Did he kill her?" The question flew like a flushed bird from his mouth and Adam froze in surprise, not sure where it had come from. True, it had been on his mind. It was always on his mind, tucked into some crevice on the Outer Banks. But it wasn't a thought he gave any sunlight. Now, speaking the words made it seem like a possibility and brought with it a torrent of other thoughts and feelings, among them that he'd like to pluck the rot of his father from his own being.

"People say he did."

Wendell focused on cutting his pheasant in the most methodical way—long, even strips moving away from his person. He chewed slowly, staring at the wall. Eventually, he pushed his plate away.

"Did he kill her?" Adam repeated. Wendell stood up and carried his plate to the sink.

"No one ever proved anything."

"What do you think?" Adam put his hand on his thigh and realized his leg was bouncing up and down.

Wendell snorted. "Listen, son, Stanley was a son of a bitch. I hate to say it, but that's the truth." Wendell had never said so, but the boy should know about his people. The ones who made him. And who else was going to tell him?

"You think he did."

"Do I look like someone who knows something?" Wendell leaned back in his chair. He remembered there'd been something about that night. He'd come by when he'd heard the news of the birth, but Alta had been sleeping so he couldn't see her or the baby. Stanley had sat in a rocking chair with a pillow on his lap and a cold look about him, and it hadn't been just the weather. But was this a memory or just a picture he'd conjured up to illustrate Adam's words? And was this the same night? He'd been drunk, of course. Wasn't he always drunk?

He felt something drain from him.

"Listen, son. What he did or didn't do had nothing to do with you. You're nothin' like him."

Wendell stood up and threw open a cupboard, then turned to face Adam.

"Did I ever tell you about William Tell?"

"Many times."

Adam picked up the dishes and carried them to the sink.

"I got to be somewhere," Wendell said, and just like that, he rushed from the room and the house. Adam cleaned the kitchen, thinking about all the people that had gone before him. His people.

CHAPTER 5

WENDELL AND SMOKE

Wendell and Smoke spilled over their stools at the Tumbleweed saloon, each in their own variation of a foul mood, which the whiskey didn't brighten.

"Still thinking of that horse," Wendell said. "I hate to see something like that happen to such a nice horse."

"It was a nice horse."

"Too hot for this country. Of course it's going to have a conniption when an idiot drives a car into its barn."

Wendell couldn't get the image of the magnificent animal falling and its eyes emptying out of his mind. Smoke was more pragmatic. These things happened. He was thinking of the other horses still at the livery. The way it was going, he was losing money each and every day he didn't sell them, and so this moneymaking trip was costing him a fortune.

"We're going to have to pay for it," Wendell said, meaning the horse.

"I expect so," Smoke answered, thinking he meant the whiskey.

Smoke nodded to Clem to fill his glass.

"This is it," Clem said. "I'm going to have to cut you off until you pay for your drinks."

"Just put it on my tab," Wendell said.

"You don't have a tab."

"Well, why don't you start me one."

"Why don't you pay for your drinks?" Clem glared at Wendell to keep from coming across as soft, though in truth he was a bit soft for the old man. He was sufficiently entertaining and a bit of a lost cause, so Clem felt inclined to give him a break now and then.

"Well, now," Wendell said. He made a show of digging around in his pocket but gave that up when Clem drifted down the bar. He wondered how and when Jake was going to come collecting for his loss. Probably the scoundrel would string him and Smoke from a tree until their eyes bulged and their faces turned blue. Better to just drink yourself to death, Wendell thought, rubbing his hand on his throat.

On the next stool, Smoke had degenerated into something soft and lumpy, a pool of fingers and elbows with a rocky island for a head on the bar.

"You don't say much," Wendell said, himself feeling a little rubbery. Smoke replied that he said enough.

It's all because of a goddamn car, Wendell thought as he sipped his drink, and so that's what he said.

"It's all over a goddamn car. The goddamn automobile's going to mean the end of us."

"Maybe," Smoke bubbled, not so sure. Then, "I can't say I mind the car. I wouldn't mind riding in an automobile." He floated his head up to the level of Wendell's.

"You don't say!" Wendell thought about it. They could go fast, that was for sure.

"Loud sons of bitches," he said with authority. "I'll get you a ride."

"You can do that?"

"Hell yes." Wendell slurred. Tarnation! He ran the livery! The car was a livery car! He glanced at his friend. The black hair was sticking out all over the place like a scarecrow, and it hit Wendell like a rock to the head. He'd known that Smoke was native, but now he KNEW it.

"You're a goddam Indian!" Wendell roared, and Smoke slurred.

"Last I looked."

"You're an Indian!" Wendell repeated.

Smoke waited for whatever insight was about to be revealed.

"You must be good with a bow," Wendell said.

"You must be good with a lasso."

"Couldn't rope a longhorn if it was standing three feet in front of me."

"I once hit a rabbit from a moving wagon," Smoke replied. He didn't clarify that he hit a dead rabbit with the wagon as he drove over it—no need to suffer a story with details.

"You don't say!"

Wendell's mind was gearing up, he could feel it. He twisted in his seat as if to shake up the thoughts and then, by God, it was coming, a piece of fast-ripening fruit, and it was going to be perfect! Goddamn, the world was a crazy son-of-a-bitch place!

"Ever seen a Wild West Show?"

"This is one right here, isn't it?"

"Yes, sir, it is!" Wendell chuckled. "Yes, it is! . . . Clem, you sure I'm not good for another?"

Clem shook his head from further down the bar. "Pay for those."

"I'm about to do that." Wendell laughed, then turned back to Smoke. "Could you shoot a bottle off the shelf?"

"There's a hundred bottles on that shelf. A blind man could shoot a bottle."

"With a bow? What about an apple? Off my head?"

"Yeah, maybe. From here?"

"Ha! In the Wild West Show, they shoot an apple off a

man's head. You have a bow?" Wendell asked, because of course he must. And Smoke said he thought he had one back home.

"But there has to be one around here," Wendell was sure. The plan coming together was making him giddy, dispersing the clouds, but the plan required a bow.

"Clem, you got a bow?" He asked, and Clem said he did, in fact, have one around. Someone had left it or traded it for booze. The barkeep slid down the bar to face them.

Wendell clutched and unclutched his empty glass, and the world was looking bright again. At the very least, by God, he'd get himself some more whiskey.

Wendell waited for Smoke to have the epiphany—or Clem—but neither seemed to catch a glimpse of the beauty, the brilliance, which was so obvious.

"You heard of William Tell?" He asked, and they both said no.

"Well, William Tell. He shot an apple off his son's head . . ."

"Sounds like a bit of a gamble," Clem said.

"Why the hell did he do that?" Smoke asked.

"Because he won a bet!"

This all made sense to Smoke, and he thought about the last time he had shot a bow—had he ever shot a bow? Traditional weaponry had not been allowed at the mission school, and he hadn't had much reason to take one up in the years since—he used his rifle for hunting. But then Clem laid a bow across the bar. Smoke picked it up and examined it. The bow was made of scrub oak coated with glue from the hooves and tendons of buffalo, and the craftsmanship made Smoke about burst with pride. The arrows were long and straight from chokecherry, with the split feather of a hawk for fletching glued to the butt end. Smoke ran his hand over the flint tip. It was a beautiful weapon, the weapon of his people. Of course he could shoot it.

"Hell yes," he said. And Wendell slammed his empty glass on the bar to punctuate his enthusiasm. He slid naturally into the role of ringmaster. He turned and swung off his stool, lifting his arms, nearly pulling himself over with the momentum.

"How'd you like to see yours truly defy death right before your very eyes! Right here in this room, a reenactment of the American Indian Wars. A moment that demonstrates the terrible defeat of General George Custer!"

Folks thought he was feeling his drink and didn't pay him much mind at first. Wendell raised his fist and shouted, and then other men shouted; it was good fun. From then, it didn't take much to rally the crowd. Drinking and cards and fighting had become routine, and people were desperate for a new form of entertainment.

Smoke, for his part, didn't think Wendell should have invoked the humiliation of Little Bighorn. He worried Wendell would incite the crowd into some sort of retribution and felt like an obvious target, and so he considered making a quick exit. But for the Tumbleweed clientele, patriotism was circumstantial and tied to people's sense of Manifest Destiny and righteousness, and those that concerned themselves with such things were content that they were on the right side of history and the natives had been sufficiently whipped and contained.

"Damnit, people!" Wendell shouted. "I'm about to look into the eyes of Death."

"Death won't have you," someone jeered, and Wendell smiled, appreciating a good smart-ass.

"You won't want to miss it." Wendell pointed to a middle-aged cowboy and then to a young fellow from the work camp. He held out his hat. "It seems only fair that they pay for the pleasure of watching." He passed out the hat, and the patrons dug into their pockets, some reluctantly, and then they got into the spirit of the game and were slapping one another on the back and buying each other drinks. There was plenty of money to go around, since they were living in a boomtown in a boom time.

"How far is he going to shoot it?" someone yelled out.

Clem clapped his hands and shouted to be heard across the crowd. "All right fellows, let's take it outside!"

"A hundred feet!" someone shouted.

"Two hundred!" called another.

Clem leaned in close to Wendell and Smoke. "Maybe we ought to wait on this. Until everyone is clearheaded."

Wendell scoffed.

"Well, how far did old William Tell shoot his arrow?" Smoke asked Wendell.

"Well, I don't know. Maybe ten feet." His chuckle was nervous—he'd gotten himself into something. Clem might be right.

"If you wanted to kill yourself, it'd be a lot easier to just lay down on the tracks!" someone shouted.

And so it was, with a good bit of pushing and jostling, the crowd worked its way outside, pulling on coats to ward against the cold night air.

It was decided that Wendell would stand in front of the Great Northern Hotel in the state of North Dakota and Smoke would shoot his arrow from across the street in front of the saloon in Montana, from west to east, so the sinking sun was at his back and not in his eyes. The bars emptied onto the street as rumors spread of the death-defying performance about to take place. Clem pushed through the crowd holding out the hat, and it quickly filled. He dumped its contents into a bag and started over. Smoke stood on the steps of the Tumbleweed holding the bow, pulling the string back and then releasing the tension, thinking this mud show was a bad idea, but there was no getting out of it as far as he could tell. He took a drink of whiskey from his glass sitting on the railing, then bent his fingers to warm them up.

Smoke and Wendell assumed their positions, and the crowd hushed. Smoke placed the arrow in the bow and drew the string back, thinking this ought to feel natural, and there was probably a prayer he should be saying to some being, but none came to mind. Wendell stood swaying, waiting for the moment, then Smoke lowered the bow.

"What about the apple?"

The crowd shuffled, and a few people looked foolish thinking they should have noticed the missing target, and there were those who figured someone was hiding the apple, and who could it be? When no one brought an apple forth, folks became irritated and suggested alternative targets—an empty bottle or can. But Wendell was feeling superstitious, and substitutions seemed a way of pissing off God—keeping details as close to the way the original incident played out seemed essential to ensuring the outcome in which he didn't get shot. Hell, next thing you know, someone would want to exchange the bow for a pistol, and then some guy (himself) was going to wind up killed.

"Jesus Christ," Clem said. "Someone fetch Lew. He's got to have an apple over there in that store of his." A couple of fellows ran off, and more drinkers arrived and dropped money into the winner's pot.

Inevitably, Jake heard about the goings-on and pushed his way to the front of the crowd.

"What's all the hubbub?"

Lew himself appeared around that time with a bag full of apples. The apples were small and bruised, but Wendell found the largest of them, and Smoke gave it a look-over. They agreed it would do the job, but given its small size, they decided they'd have to shorten the distance a couple of feet.

"All right, let's move it back," Clem pushed the crowd to give a wide berth in case the arrow drifted off course.

"Any last words in the event they're your last words?"

With all the attention focused on Wendell—and being quite drunk—he felt generous, a little sentimental, and maybe it was best to get on with it, and so he said, "Goodbye. God bless you, folks. When the Good Lord calls a man home, there's not much to be done."

There were loud cheers, and Clem put the apple on Wendell's head and stepped back. Wendell swayed a bit as if blowing in a breeze, and Smoke drew the bow and aimed the arrow. The tension felt right, and his eyes were generally good—he had that going. He let the arrow fly. It whipped through the air, and Wendell went down. There was a scramble as the crowd closed in around the old man. Smoke dropped the bow and ran.

"Get the doctor!" someone shouted.

Smoke didn't make it far before someone yelled, "He's fine! Just a scrape!"

Cheers went up, and Smoke stopped running—he hadn't killed Wendell! He returned to survey the damage and collect his winnings. He felt a slap on the back and turned. "You shoot that thing like a white man," a yellow-toothed drunk leered.

Someone had wrapped a towel around Wendell's head, and it was soaked in blood. He sat in the cold dirt, patting his head and chuckling.

"Goddamn if you weren't trying to scalp me."

"If I were trying to scalp you, you wouldn't have a scalp," Smoke said, feeling done with the whole charade. He exhaled and watched a ring of breath rise in the darkening air.

"I thought you could hit a rabbit from a moving wagon."

Smoke snorted. "I ran him over. The rabbit was already dead."

"Wait a minute!"

"Well, now," Sheriff Courtney stepped forward, blotting out what remained of the sun. Jakob and Stanley stood on either side of him. The sheriff nodded, and Jake bent down to pick up the hat.

"What the hell!" Wendell jumped to his feet, grabbing for his hard-won earnings. The rag fell from around his head and dropped on his shoulder, and a small stream of blood slid down the side of his face. The sheriff stepped in front of him.

"It's all right," the sheriff said.

"Like hell it is!"

"I've been hearing about the horse you killed. It cost a pretty sum . . ."

"Killed?"

"Let's make this easy. I don't want to have to arrest you."

"We didn't kill a horse!" Wendell repeated.

"Didn't you shoot his horse?"

"Well, he told us to. It was lame. Ask the doctor."

"And who made him lame?"

"Jesus Christ! That goddamn car! And my godforsaken nephew . . ." Wendell lunged at Stanley. "He was driving the goddamn car!" Stanley grinned at Wendell's outburst.

"That horse would be just fine if you hadn't been fooling around with it playing farrier."

"You son of a bitch!" Wendell lunged at Stanley, but this lunge was less energetic than his previous lunges, more like a demonstration of a lunge, and the younger man easily dodged out of his way.

"Hey, you!" The sheriff whistled at Smoke, who slowly unfolded himself. Stanley and Jake watched him in a predatory way.

"I hear you got horses?" the sheriff said.

"Fuck that," Smoke grumbled. He knew where this was going.

"What the hell you grinning at, nephew?" Wendell glared at Stanley.

Stanley was smiling and working around the tobacco in his cheek. Much of the crowd that had come to watch the act had drifted away. The remaining clusters were watching the law being enforced.

"Just a couple of clowns," Stanley said. Wendell thought how much he'd like to yank his tie.

"Not anymore. They're Jake's now. To pay for that stallion you killed." The sheriff was addressing Smoke.

"You can't just take another man's property!" Wendell's face had steadily reddened during the standoff, and now he was sweating and rasping like a boiling-over teapot.

"Those horses aren't worth shit," Jake said. "Do you have any idea how much I paid for that stallion? How much I could have made in stud fees? He had bloodlines going back to Virgil, the sire of Firenze, one of the greatest running fillies in history."

"Probably stolen anyway," Stanley said, about Smoke's horses.

"How many times do you need to announce that?" Wendell crunched his face at Jake.

Smoke grumbled something incoherent and spat at Stanley's feet.

"Let's just get this settled," The sheriff interrupted. "My cells are full, and I don't want to have to release the bastards inside drying out." He turned to Smoke. "You're going to have to turn those horses over to Jake."

"Like hell," Smoke said.

"Better listen to the sheriff or he'll land your ass in jail. Or worse, send you down to Hiawatha. That's where they send troublesome Indians." Jake addressed Smoke for the first time in the conversation.

Now Smoke had heard of Hiawatha. All the natives had. It was called a hospital but run like a prison. People were sent there to disappear—no one admitted was ever heard from again. The few that had visited it described it as hell, with patients locked in their rooms or chained to their beds, stewing in their own feces. Smoke didn't know anyone with any personal contact with the hospital, and he sometimes wondered if it wasn't a tale people told to keep the natives in line. Maybe it was, but he didn't want to find out. So he kept his mouth shut.

"No one's going to jail tonight. I think I made that clear," the sheriff said.

"What the hell!" Wendell bellowed at Smoke as if he were standing on the other side of a river rather than right in front of him. Smoke took a step back.

"You really can't shoot a bow."

"I shot it, didn't I?"

Wendell nodded slowly. Technically, of course, he did.

"What about my mare? I need my mare. How else am I going to get back to the reservation?"

"He can walk," Stanley growled.

"Let him keep his mare," the sheriff, not particularly fond of Stanley, said to Jake. He didn't see the point in taking the Indian's riding horse. Jake hesitated, then agreed, thinking he had nothing against the Smoke going back to the reservation.

"Sons of bitches," Wendell said, reaching into his pocket for some tobacco.

"Jesus Christ, would you wipe that blood off your face." Stanley couldn't stand looking at his uncle's torn head.

"What's that?" the sheriff asked Wendell.

"I said you're all a bunch of sons of bitches. You going to tell me I can't have my say now?" Wendell took a swipe at his head but otherwise ignored Stanley. He'd about had it. Plus, he was beginning to feel a bit wobbly, so he sat down on the side of the road, and Smoke took a seat next to him. Wendell got out his tobacco and rolling paper so he could properly roll out his cigarette. His fingers weren't too steady, and the cigarette wound up misshapen, with tobacco leaking out of the end. The others stood watching, not seeming to know what to do with themselves.

"Jesus Christ," Jake finally said. He pointed at Smoke. "You'd better get that mare out of the stable by tomorrow or I'm going to think it's mine." He moved his finger from Smoke to the sheriff, then dropped it and walked away. And then without another word, the sheriff followed.

Wendell offered Smoke a cigarette.

"You shouldn't hate the car so much, Uncle. It's the future." Stanley was feeling generous now that everything had about gone his way. He stood over the two men, waiting for a reply.

"My ass." Wendell lit his cigarette and inhaled, letting the smoke unfurl inside his lungs.

"You should thank me," Stanley said. "Because of me, Jake is going to let you keep your job."

Wendell glared up at him. "Mighty thoughtful of you, nephew, considering I got you your job . . . I hope that wife of yours can keep you in line." Wendell turned to Smoke. "He says he got himself a wife, but I haven't seen one. Probably it's one of his stories."

"No siree. I have a wife, and she'll be here next week."

Wendell didn't look up to see Stanley smirk. He didn't feel in the mood to celebrate his nephew's good fortune. Stanley lost his patience and left. Smoke cursed something Wendell couldn't make out, and then he held out his hand. Wendell studied that hand while rubbing the place around where the arrow had sliced his head. Then he realized he was looking at cash, and he looked at Smoke and was amazed.

"Fast hands," Smoke laughed. "How about I buy you a drink?"

Wendell didn't need any convincing. He stood up, and they made their way back to the Tumbleweed.

CHAPTER 6

SMOKE

Smoke left Mondak in defeat the next morning. He saddled his horse in the front corral as the sky lightened. Wendell had already fed the horses and was hauling a load of manure out of the barn in the now inglorious wheelbarrow—the one implicated in the downfall of the gray stallion—and he stopped, almost flipping it over in the doorway to watch Smoke tighten the cinch on his saddle. Stanley and a small army of men had surrounded the corral and were watching with their hands on their holsters. A cold burst of air came at them from the north—the death rattles of winter not quite ready to relinquish its grip.

"Jesus Christ. What the hell do you need a bescumbering posse for?"

"It's nothing to do with you," Stanley yelled back.

Smoke paused to survey the scene.

"Just some assholes set on making trouble," Wendell said to Smoke.

"No trouble, Uncle. Not unless he's looking for trouble. Just making sure he doesn't have second thoughts about leaving the horses."

Stanley addressed Smoke. "You just get on your way, now, and there won't be any trouble."

Smoke didn't speak but walked over to the gate leading his horse.

"This is horse thievery," Wendell growled.

Smoke knew better than to get into it with this crowd. He mounted his horse and turned it out of the yard.

"You can't ride away like that. You let them win!" Wendell was furious that he hadn't put up a fight. And then he thought about how he was getting senile in his old age, sticking his nose into other people's business and getting all worked up when it was them that should be getting worked up. He glared at Stanley and the other men, thinking, among other thoughts, that it was ridiculous how Stanley insisted on wearing a tie, like he thought he was somebody, when he was nothing but a scoundrel. The other men were in various stages of rolling cigarettes, satisfied that they'd completed their mission. Wendell continued toward the shit pile, where he dumped the contents of the wheelbarrow. It was barely after sunrise and the day was already bitter.

XXX

Smoke, for his part, rode through the town straight-backed and poker-faced, past the townies standing in their storefronts and the farmers loading their wagons with supplies, giving no indication he was simmering beneath his calm demeanor. A cowboy stumbled up the street covered in oil from the dipping vat, glimmering like something fresh from the womb, cursing and grumbling and occasionally stopping to wipe the slickness from his face, and Smoke gave him a nod—thinking he felt a little like that, disgraced and tarred. But it was Jake waving from in front of the Triangle Building where he kept his office that really got him fuming. Smoke stared back, thinking obscenities and imagining himself sticking a knife in his overblown stomach and watching the shit-gas escape, leaving an empty hide on the ground for the horses and wagons to roll over.

He turned northwest and moved his ride into an easy trot, and he let his anger curdle into something small and tight, like a musket ball or bullet he could make use of later. Dealing with the whites was a game of chess, he'd long ago come to realize. And though he'd never mastered the game when it had been pulled from the shelf on the worst-weather days at the mission school, when formal studies were finished but assimilation continued, he had learned to appreciate the commitment to strategy. He likened his current situation to losing a few bishops and felt pride at the comparison. After all, he had his riding horse and a few dollars in his pocket, so he hadn't lost the game.

He pointed his horse toward the gray hills and thought how it'd be nice to get back to the reservation and his own people. He'd go hunting with his brother and go to Poplar in the evening and see if he could find himself a woman. And then he thought how Blue Dog would be waiting for him, wanting his money for the horses—because they were Blue Dog's horses that he'd taken to Mondak to sell for a slice of the profits. It was Blue Dog who had driven the horses over from the Blackfoot reservation where he had family that raised them. Blue Dog was mean as hell, and he wouldn't give a shit that Smoke had been cheated.

Smoke clomped through the tangle of still-dormant buffalo grass and took in a deep breath, his enthusiasm for returning home draining. He scanned the ground for gopher holes and stones that might trip up the horse and wondered what he'd say to Blue Dog when he ran into him. Maybe the other Indian would kill him—he wouldn't be the first victim of his wrath . . . Smoke concluded he'd have to lay low at his brother's— he couldn't show his face about town . . . He slowed his horse to a walk. He considered his options. He thought again about the injustice of Jake stealing the horses and how he'd like to have his getting even, and he thought about how he'd let the man chase him away like he was the thief. He wasn't a man generally prone to pride, but he'd had his share of humiliations, and maybe he'd lived among whites too long because the affronts felt like a blister rubbing on the inside of his boot. He stopped and dismounted and found a dry patch of grass and lay down and let his horse graze. When he spotted a rabbit, he pulled out his rifle and shot it, then skinned it and made a fire and cooked it.

He spent the afternoon smoking and pondering his predicament, thinking it was cowardly leaving the horses behind. It wasn't the way of his people—certainly not the great warriors and chiefs—to hand over valuables without a fight. Of course, he'd been vastly outnumbered and so cowardly was just another word for smart. But Smoke wasn't feeling smart at all. He thought a smart man might strategize, and he sure as hell could use a drink. That night, he set his saddle on its pommel and snuggled inside the curve of it, using the saddle blanket as a pillow, and he slept soundlessly until daybreak.

When he awoke in the morning, he sat on a rock smoking a cigarette, and his anger had become a dull thing. He thought that there wasn't much happening on the reservation, just Blue Dog and working for his brother and not making money. And then he thought of all the money to be made in Mondak. He could work for a bit and wait for an opportunity to have his revenge. In the meantime, he could make enough to pay the Dog and have a little extra in his pocket for padding. Of course, he knew he would be a target. He'd have to watch his back. But anywhere an Indian went he had to watch his back. And then he thought, really, except for the stallion and the bad deal with his horses, it had been a good time in Mondak. With that, he decided he'd take some time so things could cool down and then ride back to town. His decision made him feel fierce.

CHAPTER 7

ADAM

The circus train screamed to a stop in the still-dark morning, and it was like the birth of the world. The doors slid wide and people burst like cottonwood seeds from every opening.

Handlers appeared in the gaping mouth on the sides of the train cars with horses, camels, and zebras, which they led gingerly down the ramps, while wagons lurched and rattled across the crossover plates to the next flat and down long metal runs—a sort of train unrolling from atop atrain. Roustabouts unloaded iron polls and rolls of canvas from already grounded wagons and dashed across the prairie, and within minutes, the garden of tents was sprouting out of the dirt, growing to full bloom before his eyes. From the corners of the grounds came the echo of hammers pounding, the banter and yelling of humans, and the braying, neighing, growling, and trumpeting of every animal on the planet.

It must have been like this, Adam thought, in the beginning—a tempest rising from a long, twisted scar, leaving a wake of delicate flowers and infantries of trees and creatures of dust and shadows growing sharp edged in the ascending light. He was paralyzed, his senses battered. His slightest movement might shatter this tenuous world. He was witnessing magic, he knew, and felt a surge of possibility.

"Whatcha standing around like a goddamn rube!" someone growled, startling Adam. When he turned, he was facing a skinny man in a shabby suit. Stiff, Adam thought, because he looked like a dead man, and so that's what he called him. Stiff pointed to a train car, and Adam started toward it in a daze but stopped when an ostrich and a dwarf crossed his path. The towering bird curled its neck like a tube and nipped at the dwarf's shaggy mane.

"You look like you've never seen an ostrich." A middle-aged man with a burnt nose stood next to Adam, scratching his head.

"Well, I'll be damned," he said, looking Adam up and down. "Old Fox is hiring schoolboys. Can't be sideshow. You're too small to be a roustabout. What do you do? Or are you a rube?"

Adam was immobile, staring past the man at elephants descending from a boxcar, two by two, their trunks intertwined like snakes. Men on either side were guiding them with long poles.

"Well, there's no standing around. You better get your ass to work or get out," the burnt-nose man said and walked away. From somewhere above, the musky smell of animals and shit drifted with the scent of bacon, a siren's call, and Adam stepped toward it without thinking, but then changed his mind and followed the path of the ostrich. The bird disappeared behind a line of matching horses with feathered plumes bursting from the tops of their heads. They stomped their feet, their tails flicking away flies. Some of the wagons were loaded with caged animals Adam had seen only in pictures—bears, monkeys, big cats—and odd-looking creatures he couldn't identify. The circus people were equally odd-looking, some of the smallest and largest people Adam had ever seen, tattooed and scarred, and a few were leaping around and walking on their hands like monkeys. They swarmed the line of wagons and carts, bustling and chattering, digging in chests and boxes and fiddling with buttons, and one was juggling too many balls for Adam to count. Several women stood near a scarlet wagon at the back of the line. A pretty one, sweet-faced with golden hair, winked at Adam, and he turned a deep red. He walked away along the row of cages as if he had a purpose, and then he saw the tiger. It lay quietly in its cage on a red wagon with gold trim and turned to look at the boy. Adam stepped closer. He stared at the head as big as a bucket with its swirl of stripes and buttery eyes. The eyes gazed at him, through him. Adam had been anticipating the big cat, thinking about his mom's carved cat, about messages, and so probably he expected recognition, a transcendent moment when each saw a kindred spirit, as if the heavens would open and it would feel like home, and the hole that was in him would be flooded by something warm and golden. But the tiger flicked its tail and yawned and licked its foreleg. Adam felt water slipping through his rib cage. He jiggled the bars of the cage, and the cat didn't move, so he made growling sounds and then glanced around for something, a stone, a stick. He found a stick and picked it up. The cat's ribs jutted through his orange coat, ragged with what could only be mange—the tiger was not so magnificent after all. Adam twirled the stick near the tiger's paw and in front of its face, and when he couldn't get the cat's attention, he jabbed the stick between two ribs. The tiger turned to him and growled, and its teeth were thick and black.

"Hey! Hey!"

It was the dwarf who had been with the bobbing-headed ostrich. Adam dropped the stick and fled swiftly between the wagons and back into town.

Later that morning, the scream of the calliope preceded the parade, and the townspeople that hadn't already locked their doors and lined up along the boardwalk quickly did so. They jostled and elbowed for the best view as the clowns clomped toward them, kicking up dust with their enormous feet. A giraffe floated its head like a delicate balloon above the fray. There were jugglers and the menagerie in cages on the colored wagons, and there were ten elephants, including one that was pale and ghostly with a placard attached to its howdah that stated "Harish, the World's Most Sacred Only White Elephant from the Royal Kingdom of Siam."

Adam pushed his way to the front of the boardwalk and stared hungrily, thoughts of his escape flowering in his brain. A few horses tied near the street snorted and pulled on their leads or reins. Adam spotted Wendell watching the parade, wide-eyed and gripping a railing as if for balance. The old man didn't notice him as he practically skipped past, following the wagons with the bear and the tiger in their faded cages.

The parade route was short. The circus wound down Main Street and then looped into North Dakota and followed First Street back to the show grounds. Even this early in the day, there was the inevitable posturing of cowboys and farmers bored from long hours of work and tight living quarters, many watching intently while trying to appear disinterested. They tipped back their beers and pointed at the freaks and acrobats and laughed loudly, but they were in truth astounded by the light-footed athletes somersaulting in the air or gliding by atop six-foot stilts. Several well-lit men from the work camp were shouting obscenities, so the sheriff placed himself nearby and made a point of lifting his six-shooter from its holster to check the cartridges. Fewer in number but compensating in enthusiasm, the women clapped. Children pushed and shouted and jumped in and out of the street as the parade rolled by.

Adam followed to the corner where he watched the tiger get jostled away in its gilded cage, the animal gazing across the crowd, the tail rising from time to time in an irritated flick. It occurred to Adam that the cage was too small; the cat should be roaming. Stalking. Free . . . He felt a rush of sorrow. Then his view of the cage was blocked by stilt walkers followed by dwarfs leading dogs. A monkey in a laced vest and matching hat rode astride the front dog, sitting in a fancy saddle. The monkey jumped up and down and screamed a bone-chilling scream, and the children covered their ears and laughed. And then the parade was over, leaving a wake of glitter, confetti, and droppings in the street. The townspeople mingled and talked excitedly, and many drifted away.

It was several hours before the actual show, but there was too much excitement for business as usual. Wendell made his way to the Tumbleweed and Adam followed, feeling a bit nostalgic now that he was leaving. He had a knapsack hidden by the grounds ready to go.

"You have enough for admittance?" Clem asked as he slid Adam some cash.

"Sure," Adam said. But he took the money—since it was offered—thinking he could probably use it on his new adventure.

"He's been squirreling his money away, that's for sure," Wendell eyed him suspiciously.

"Saving for something?" Clem asked. He passed Adam a lemonade.

"Just saving." Adam shrugged.

They were quiet a bit, minding their business, Clem shining glasses and pouring beers. Adam and Wendell gazed into their respective drinks.

"You going?" Clem asked Wendell.

"Sure. Why not? I hear there's some pretty girls hanging from ropes with hardly any clothes on."

"I'm not sure your heart can take that much excitement."

"Probably not, but it's a good way to go."

"I'm closing up shop for the afternoon performance. No one's going to be around, anyway."

"You saw the elephants at the parade?"

"I did."

"They're big. Big animals."

"What about the camel?"

"Hell of a thing," Wendell responded. He finished up his drink and motioned for another.

"I never saw anything quite like that ostrich."

"Can't fly, but I hear they're fast as all getup."

It went on like that, Wendell and Clem going over the list of animals they remembered from the parade. Adam grew bored and slid from his stool, but climbed back up when Clem shoved a bowl of stew in front of him. He was always doing these things. The barkeep had a soft spot for Adam, felt sorry for the boy. He ladled up another bowl for Wendell and wiped the bar down while the two ate and the old man prattled. Outside the small square window, a family passed looking ragged and worn, with burlap bags slung over their shoulders.

"They're leaving as fast as they came," Clem said. He liked to make conversation. "Owing everybody, too."

"Where will they go?" Adam wondered.

"It depends . . . Some go west to Oregon or California. Some of 'em go back to the cities."

"Wendell said it's 'cause the Good Lord is angry.'"

Clem looked at Wendell, who was ignoring the comment, and laughed. "Wendell says a lot of things."

"He's selling off the furniture."

"What do a couple of bachelors need with a fancy table?" The old man had a defensive tone.

"Christ . . . You can always come live with me. I'm not much of a housekeeper, you know that. But at least I have some chairs for you to sit on."

Adam shrugged, feeling a rush of guilt about keeping his secret.

"They overproduced," Clem said, about the homesteaders. "'Food will win the war,' the government said. Now the prices for wheat are so low they can't hardly sell it."

"Will it?" Adam soaked up the last of the stew with a wedge of bread.

"What's that?"

"Win the war?"

"Who's winning the war?"

"Food."

"Oh. Right. Well, soldiers got to eat."

Later that afternoon, Adam watched the first show from the top row of the bleachers. He was bent over and tense with excitement. The elephants paraded around the ring swinging their trunks, then reared up on their hind legs as one climbed onto the back of another and the third onto the back of the second, and so on down the line in a long mount. A clown exploded out froma cannon into a net, and the aerialists flew and tumbled in the sky, swinging from a bar. Adam recognized the blonde girl from the morning, an angel all gold and light, and he couldn't take his eyes off her. She was the most beautiful creature he'd ever seen, and she was climbing up the ropes like she was walking across the prairie, like it was as easy as could be, and he supposed he would get to meet her. He clutched the knapsack, which he'd been keeping close, not sure when he would make his move.

After the show, he wandered around the grounds, making his way through the sideshow and the menagerie. He could work with the animals, he thought, because he sure as hell could shovel shit, and the circus looked like it could use some shit shovelers.

He recognized Stiff from earlier in the day. Stiff pointed him in the direction of the office, which was called the red wagon. "It's not actually red. That's just what it's called. It's got a sign on the front that says 'office.'"

Adam approached the office window and the man inside was sweating profusely in a woolen suit.

"Every kid from eight to twenty thinks they're going to run away with the show. What do we look like, nursemaids?" He laughed and waved Adam away.

The rejection clarified for Adam that jumping the train was the correct course of action, so he set about learning what he could about the planned departure, wandering amidst the tents. He paused occasionally to rest under a tree and nibble on popcorn and peanuts, listening in on conversations. Most of the locals had drifted away, and no one seemed to notice when he snuck into the backyard, where the players lived between shows. They had traded costumes for street clothes and were lounging on thin grass, flicking cigarettes or playing cards or practicing tricks on blankets in the shade of the trees. Adam moved in the shadows, picking up a sledgehammer or pitchfork or wedge of hay, as if he belonged. After the evening show, they would take down the camp and board the train, he heard, so he decided that's when he'd make his move. Eventually he fell asleep under a tree, so he wasn't aware there was a dustup brewing.

The grifters that accompanied the circus had been exceptionally active and successful following the first show. Though it had seen better times, Mondak had a reputation as a boomtown flush with cash that attracted an unusual multitude. They had swarmed into town on foot or horse or train, and probably some were part of the regular transient crowd stopping over for recreation. They were fast at work running fingers soft as butterfly wings across the pockets of merchants, farmers, ranch hands, and townspeople. One patted the shoulders of Ollie Ollipson while lifting his wallet from his back pocket, and another ripped off the editor of the *Yellowstone News* when he was interviewing a stilt walker. It wasn't just wallets and wads of cash the grifters were after. Several farmwives complained of chokecherry pies disappearing from kitchen windows where they'd been cooling. While the townspeople were used to some thievery, there were many among them and the visitors with a strong sense of justice. This bunch was hankering for excitement. They gathered in the bars after the first show and talked amongst themselves and concluded the acrobats and freaks were thieves. To make matters worse, the roustabouts with arms like thighs strutted around swinging their giant hammers like Thor's, taunting them, daring them to try to stop the stealing.

"What the hell's a clem anyway?" an old farmer asked Clem. Clem shrugged and said he thought it was a barkeep.

By evening, the air about town was charged. Men were clenching their fists and rubbing the blades of knives and spitting at beetles crawling across the boardwalk. Adam woke shortly before the second show oblivious to the darkening mood of the crowd. He stood behind a line of visitors filing into the big tent and watched a boy pick up a can and throw it at a whiteface clown that stood grinning in the tent opening. The can hit the clown in the nose and left petals of blood across his face.

"Look, it bleeds!" the boy shouted, and the clown disappeared. The father of the boy rushed his son to their seats.

The circus people were an intricate, organic machine linked by thousands of miles, close quarters, and their shared fate–the failure or success of the show. As blood streamed from the whiteface clown's nose and he rushed to clown alley to clean himself, the knowing moved like a bad odor through the ranks of the circus people. The clown reapplied his face paint while the ever-professional performers took to the rings. Acrobats managed a perfect loop-the-loop in the center ring of the big top, and the lions leapt through a ring of fire. In the stands, the father of the boy felt in his pocket for his wallet to pay the candy butcher who stood in the aisle waiting while the boy bit into an apple thick with caramel. The wallet, however, was missing, and the father, a well-respected judge, let several rows of seating know of his irritation. In response, other spectators checked their pockets, and several folks found them lacking. These people, along with others who had lost purses during the parade, joined one another in grumbling. As the hostile crowd left the tent after the show, words were exchanged between the spectators and the circus people. Inevitably the shout went out, the battle cry of the circus, "Hey rube!"

The roustabouts came running with their sledgehammers, and most of the locals fled the impending mayhem. The ones that stayed brought out their fists and knives. One man tore the sign from the Crossbar Saloon and used it to lash at anyone with a painted face. The echoes of the battle could be heard for miles across the prairie.

The tents came down more quickly than usual; first the sidewalls and the tops were dropped and stretched, and roustabouts carried the tent rolls to waiting wagons that rambled onto the train while the fighting raged along the edge of the lot. Adam, meanwhile, had been hanging out in the menagerie tent waiting to make his move. Handlers were moving the animals, stacking cages onto wagons, and driving the wagons to the trains. Adam was behind the tiger's cage watching the aerialists and acrobats a hundred yards away loading trunks onto another wagon under the light of a kerosene lamp, and the blonde was among them in street clothes, a shadowy dress. She reminded him of moonlight, and he couldn't avert his eyes. When she turned, she saw him staring. He could have sworn she winked, and he thought of the diary and the whore, and he thought of lovemaking. The thinking made him blush. Of course the aerialist couldn't see him, but he imagined she'd read his thoughts, and he retreated back into the clutter of cages. A handler glared at him, and roustabouts loaded another wagon as the walls of the menagerie collapsed. A handler appeared holding horses and hitched them to the wagon, which rattled away, and another wagon came to take its place—the circus was like that, Adam saw, finely tuned, thousands of moving parts working in a symphony of efficiency. Even as he turned, the sidewalls were rolled and loaded, and nearby the performers packed their costumes and equipment into trunks and onto wagons, and the wagons rolled back to the train and up the runs and onto the flats and along the crossover plates between flats, one after another, pulled by horses and men. The stock cars swallowed the horses as they were unhitched from the wagons. Not even a raging battle could slow the circus's retreat to the train. Roustabouts pummeled the townies between pulling up stakes, pausing to dab at the blood from their noses or the gouges on their cheeks. The chaos and speed of the deconstruction made Adam nervous, and he darted between the few remaining rows of cages, not sure where to go.

He was startled by the whoosh and resounding thud of the big top coming down. It lay like the skin of the moon in the center of the lot. And then just like that, the roustabouts swarmed it, rolling and folding, and an army of men slung it across their shoulders and carried it to a wagon. The lot emptied like a receding wave with the last few workers and wagons draining into the train, and Adam panicked, thinking they were leaving without him. He was behind the tiger's cage, among the few remaining cages, and once again he saw how the beast was starving and the cage was filthy, and it was a tight fit. Too tight for such a big animal. He didn't think about it, but flicked the latch. He urged the gate open. In another row, there was a grinding of heavy metal and the opening and slamming of gates. A deep voice ordered animals to git or move back or yaaa! The tiger growled and looked toward the sound, then sniffed the open gate. Adam stepped behind the heavy bars and the cat leapt easily to the ground and sniffed the air before trotting over a roll of canvases and disappearing into the darkness.

It took Adam a split second to realize what he had done, and then he too, with much more urgency than the tiger, fled into the dark.

He'd barely reached the tree line surrounding the circus grounds before he heard the shout, "Tiger! The tiger's out! The tiger escaped!"

The news of the escaped cat reached the town nearly as quickly as Adam. He stood shakily watching men pour from the bars and leap onto horses or into trucks, and he realized that the cat's chances were slim. He carried his knapsack back to the house and sat on the porch listening to the sounds of the hunters and the departing circus. Eventually, the night waned into silence. Adam retreated to bed and crawled under the mountain of covers, where he lay not sleeping.

CHAPTER 8

ALTA

Alta arrived in Mondak on the morning train—late in the afternoon. As the train slowed, she leaned out the window to see if she could spot him in the throng of people and horses and wagons bumping about. The wind was freezing, so she shut the window and stared through the frost at the remaining patches of filthy snow. The low-hanging clouds cast the town in a muted palette of mostly gray.

She spotted him as the train lurched to a stop, the only splash of color in a blue suit and boater stroking the red shell of a car, the only car in the lot. People were parading by to gaze at the automobile or to touch or run their hands along the shiny surface or along the edge of the interior, and she could see they were asking questions. The train screeched, and he pulled a handkerchief from his pocket and bent; she gripped the arm of her seat as his head was crushed in the mandibles of a giant glistening insect. Dear Lord, she said under her breath, but of course he had simply dropped from view behind the car armored like a beetle, odd and angular amidst the strutting cowboys and the railroad men loading crates onto wagons.

How silly, Alta thought and squeezed the locket Stanley had sent her as a wedding present, twisting it so the chain pulled on the back of her neck. Stanley was looking now as the train released the passengers. He moved toward her with his quick-stepping stride, searching the windows, and she felt a flood of relief—all her fears were vanquished. She stood and brushed her skirt and picked up her bag and—holding the back of the seat to keep from tumbling because she felt like she was still moving—it's starting, she couldn't help thinking, their life together was starting. There was a surge toward the door as the children of homesteaders from all places east pushed and shoved for solid ground after days or weeks of travel, and then Alta found the door and he was flesh. She sank into him and nested her head against his chest and felt the slow-train rhythm of his heart. Home.

"Here you are!" he said.

"Yes," she said. "I'm here."

Stanley pulled away and gestured with an air of ownership toward the station and the nearby stockyard, where a whorl of cattle ready to load onto the next eastbound for Chicago stood in a bunch. Not too far away, cowboys edged their horses along a fence driving a separate herd down a ramp into a black pool, and the cattle sank until all but the mounds of their flared noses or a bit of their heads bobbed along while men with long sticks poked and shouted and stirred the soup of them, and then farther along, the cattle lurched, tarred and matted, up a recovery ramp and pooled along the far end of the corral.

"Dipping vat. It kills ticks," Stanley said, as he steered Alta through the crowd of circling passengers moving to and from the train, tickets raised like bidding paddles. Her shoes were inappropriate—she could feel the mud and slop soaking through, and it was glorious, really. No Greta rushing with towels and clean shoes prodding her inside, away from the crowd. She was a real-life Dorothea Brooke—though maybe not so serious. More likely she was the impetuous and light-hearted Catherine Morland—the comparison made her smile. Well, this certainly is an adventure! she thought. Here she was, in the Wild West. And truly, it was wild.

A wagon rattled by and sprayed her skirt with a veil of mud, and she turned away into the lashing tail of a passing horse. Near the depot, several men were leaning on a crate, smoking and openly leering.

"This is the beginning of an empire," Stanley explained.

Alta was amazed to imagine this rather small beginning, barely a town and positively filthy, growing into a Rome. But then, every empire started with the equivalent of sodbusters herding their animals down rutted streets and men with pistoled hips, and children dashing about in rags and some without shoes. Of course, an empire had to start with something.

Stanley opened the passenger side of the car and let Alta sink into the leather seats, then went to retrieve her traveling chest, which a porter was loading onto a cart.

"It's a beauty, isn't it?" he said after he saw to the loading of the chest. He climbed into the car and leaned forward to stroke the front panel.

"Yes, it is. I didn't know you had a car. Business must be going so well!" Alta had seen her share of cars—her father had several. But still, she was impressed.

"Well, it's Jake's car. My partner, really. I take the car out whenever it suits me . . ."

A fight broke out as passengers clambered onto the train. Alta was surprised to see the conductor jump into the midst.

"Tickets," Stanley said. "There're never enough." He turned the car onto the main road and they bounced and lurched over the ruts. Buildings were lined up on either side facing off like opposing armies, with wagons and horses jostling in the no man's land between. Occasionally a horse shied at the puttering engine as it approached, having never seen an automobile.

"North Dakota," Stanley said, pointing east. And then he pointed west. "Montana. This road is the border." He let go of the wheel to wave his arms up and down in line with the road.

"Montana is a drinking state, and North Dakota is dry. People walk across the street from North Dakota and get their alcohol. It's our whole reason for being. Jakob Steel. Jake. He's a genius and visionary, and he saw right away there was a fortune to be made satisfying North Dakota's thirst, and so begot . . ." Stanley gestured in a grandiose way that took in the cluster of buildings and the patchwork of gray snow and green shoots under the low-hanging aluminum sky that extended into eternity, then went on to explain how in just over a year, the people had built six saloons, two storage houses, several breweries and distilleries, a bank, two mercantiles, a post office, a school, a church, a newspaper, a land office, two hotels, a depot, and two liveries. In addition, Stanley didn't mention that there were several houses, including one down by the river, that were doing a staggering business entertaining the glut of lonely men.

"It'll be bigger than Minneapolis someday. You just wait. This is the land that feeds the mills. Someday, we'll own the mills." He smiled, and it was almost a smirk.

Alta clutched her basket on her lap. She wondered if his blustering meant he was still sore with her father.

"Don't you worry about Daddy," she said, leaning against him. "He won't bother us. He doesn't even know where I am . . . We don't need him." Stanley flashed her a look that might have been concern, and she noted his chiseled chin and thought him quite handsome, though he was different too, than she remembered. With sharper edges, as if he'd been drawn in thinner ink.

She took a breath of the fresh air and yes, she could see the potential—the sprouts of a city in a sea of black loam ready for seeding with homes and shops and schools and theaters.

She smiled to herself, thinking she had arrived at the beginning into the steel arms of destiny.

The ride was short. Stanley parked the car in front of a house.

"Our house," Stanley motioned to the slapped-together boxy thing, "is on the North Dakota side of the street." He pointed to the swing on the front porch. "Just as I promised," he said.

Alta followed her husband up the two steps to the front porch. Stanley swung open the door and followed her through the three rooms and watched her reaction as she took in the tufted couch and side table with legs thin as birds, nearly identical—though less fine—to the furniture in her father's house. It was obvious, his effort to please, in the way he'd tucked the quilt into the mattress of the four-poster bed and swept the floors and put fine plates on the table in the kitchen.

"It's small, I know," Stanley said. "But when I start my business and make a lot of money, we'll get a bigger house, you'll see."

"Oh, it's darling! So quaint. It's like a dollhouse!"

Her eyes landed on the monster of a thing taking up an entire wall of the kitchen. The stove. Foaled, she imagined, by the rattling black beast that had delivered her through the eternity of overcast sky and melting snow, an iron altar dedicated to domesticity.

Stanley ran his hand along the edge of it as he had the car, drawing her attention to the water reservoir and the warming oven.

"I ordered it straight from the Sears catalog," he told her. His collar was tight beneath his chin. "Along with the complete kitchen furniture assortment," he added.

"It looks suitable. I'd like to meet the cook."

"Well, I thought we could do without, being it's only you and me. You can do the cooking."

"But I don't cook."

"Of course you cook."

"I don't know how, Stanley." Alta had never imagined cooking. Occasionally she'd snuck a slice of bread from the warming oven, but to make a meal . . . "I really have no idea how to go about it."

"It's all right. You'll learn. How hard can it be? You'll need something to keep you occupied." He put his arms around her and kissed her neck.

"Yes, of course. It'll be fun. How hard can it be?" Alta took a moment to pull her eyes from the stove before turning around and wrapping herself in his arms. A proper heroine, she knew, was always resourceful. She brought her lips to meet her husband's, and he showed her to their wedding bed.

XXX

It was a dissonant feeling the next morning after Stanley left for work. Alta lay in bed under a mountain of blankets. The quiet stillness was unexpected after the weeks of subterfuge. It was not only the messages from Stanley she and Greta had hidden from her father and the rest of the household. All the preparations for Alta's escape to Mondak had been done without arousing suspicion. Greta had squirreled away items of clothing in her brother's home—after he'd accepted a significant payment for his silence—which included day outfits, afternoon dresses, and evening dresses, as well as outerwear and shoes and hats, not to mention an assortment of clips and combs and brushes for Alta's hair and, of course, her wedding trousseau. Alta had purchased the train ticket herself so that Greta could not be coerced into giving away the final destination. And of course, Greta had prepared a basket of lunch for the journey and found an appropriate travel costume. On the day of her departure, Alta had slid from the house while Greta was immersed in other duties, so the young maid would have an alibi and, hopefully, escape any suspicions that she had been an accomplice.

So now, here she was, in an unfamiliar role in an unfamiliar house. The truth was, Alta had not thought beyond her journey and immediate arrival. She had no idea of her role and expectations beyond what she'd read about in books.

"Goodness. I might as well get started!" She kicked the covers off with forced enthusiasm. What she really felt was a flash of panic. The books had not prepared her for the small room of this tiny, empty house. In the light, she could see the painting had been sloppily done, with the white from the walls bleeding onto the wooden floor. And there was no rug on the floor. When she crept across it to the wardrobe where she'd hastily hung her dresses, it was cold and dust stuck to her feet. She picked out a smart blouse and navy blue gored skirt while wondering if Greta had thought to pack slippers.

Standing in her own kitchen a few minutes later did nothing to alleviate her panic. She gazed at the monster of a stove and felt a rush of homesickness.

"Oh, dear," she mumbled, as she approached it with the slow care one might a wild animal. I can do this, she thought to herself as she opened doors and turned nobs. She found the fuel box, which had some kindling in it. Probably she could just throw in a match. That thought felt like a victory. But where were the matches? She looked on the shelves and lifted some towels, and wondered where one would keep matches.

There was a percolator on the stove, and when she shook it, she could tell there was coffee remaining—Stanley must have made it before he left. She poured some into a cup. It was cold and bitter, but it gave a boost; then she searched through the cupboards to familiarize herself with her new home. She would learn how to run her kitchen, she told herself. She would conquer this challenge, which is what one must do. And really, this was not much of a challenge—think of the trials of poor Jane Eyre!

The kitchen was quaint—white walls with no decorations or frills whatsoever. The red pump in the sink was the only jolt of color. There was not even a curtain to cover the window—well that was something she could easily fix. She'd noticed a store on the drive through the town the previous day—it hadn't looked like much. Probably she'd have to get in the habit of ordering from the city. And there must be a seamstress and cook in the town. Of course, she would have to convince Stanley of the necessity, but he should understand a successful businessman couldn't expect his wife to waste her time in the kitchen. There was just too much to do when managing a household and a family. Alta felt pleased with herself at how well she was already planning and organizing her new life and her day.

She sipped her coffee slowly—it really was terrible—and listened to the low drone of activity from the road outside. She wondered how her father was doing, how he'd reacted to her disappearance. She wished she could ask Greta.

There was a knock on the kitchen door that led to the side yard, but before she could get up, an old man burst in and then stopped in his tracks.

Alta jumped out of her chair, spilling her coffee.

"Oh! Goodness." She put her hand on her racing heart. "Can I help you?"

"Where is he?" the old man bellowed. He was thin and bent, with a tumbleweed of thinning gray hair and a sunbaked face. She got a whiff of something and wondered if it was drink. He looked ready to fight, then seemed to recognize she wasn't a threat. He tore off his hat and held it clasped in his hands.

"I'm looking for Stanley," he said, his voice now sheepish.

"And who are you?"

"Wendell. I'm his uncle. Wendell."

"Stanley's uncle?"

"You've heard of me then." He seemed pleased with this revelation, so Alta didn't see a point in correcting him.

"You must be the wife." He bound forward and clasped her hand; then, seeming uncertain, bent down and kissed it. Alta had to hold back a laugh.

"Stanley's been bragging about you to no end. I didn't believe him, to tell you the truth. But here you are, a pretty little thing."

"Well, thank you." Alta felt her face flush at the compliment. "You can probably catch him at work."

Wendell didn't pick up that she was asking him to leave.

"Nah. No. I can catch him anytime." Wendell and Alta stood facing one another in some sort of stalemate; she didn't know why. So she motioned to the coffee pot. "Would you like a cup?"

"Don't mind if I do!"

"It's been sitting a while . . . I'd warm it up, but I'm afraid I don't know how to work this." She motioned to the stove.

"Makes no difference to me." Wendell took a seat. "I should have brought flowers. Had I known you were here, I would have brought flowers."

"It's quite all right."

"The only thing blooming is crocuses. They don't make much of a bouquet." Wendell picked up his cup and his hand shook. He looked around the kitchen. "Well, now . . . The boy did all right for himself."

"You've not been here before?"

"We're not on the best of terms."

"Oh . . ." Alta wondered if she should have allowed him into the house.

"We had a falling out . . ." Wendell clucked and shook his head. "I'm the one who got him his job."

"Well, then, I should thank you. We should thank you."

Wendell looked embarrassed. "Jake was looking for him. He needs him to do some driving, it seems."

"Of course," Alta said. Wasn't that where Stanley had gone this morning?

"It's very nice to meet you." Wendell took his cup to his mouth. A bit of coffee dribbled onto the table. "You'll have to excuse an old man" He swiped at the spill.

"I wouldn't be surprised if he didn't mention me. You know, I didn't see that boy for years. After his father—that would be my brother—died, he took off for the cities. You'd know that part of the story . . . Then one day he came wandering back into Williston looking for work. I myself was hooked up with old Jake, and so I made the introductions. Don't let him say I never did nothing for him." Wendell pointed his finger at her and it shook, so he wrapped it around his coffee cup to steady it. That set the cup to rattling on its saucer, so he set the whole business down.

"Well, I'm sure happy you stopped by, Wendell. Our home is your home, of course." Alta stood up to walk him to the door, but he didn't notice.

"That's mighty nice of you," he said, and gazed into his cup. She waited expectantly, then sat back down.

There was something strange about her, he was thinking as he watched her. He couldn't quite place it, just sitting there at the table drinking coffee. And then it hit him—just sitting there, drinking coffee—no woman he knew of had time for sitting and drinking.

"So," he said. "How are you finding Mondak?" He glanced around the kitchen again half expecting to see a dozen maids, since she seemed like a lady of leisure, used to such things, and Stanley had said she was from that ilk. But of course, there weren't any helpers. The kitchen was fancy, with a new cookstove and shelves filled with pots and pans. No doubt about it. Stanley was getting to be a big shot.

"Just fine, thank you. From the little I've seen."

"Is that there a pump right in the sink?" He jumped up and went over to lift the handle and set his hand in the stream of water.

"Yes, it is," Alta laughed.

"Will wonders never cease . . . And look at that cookstove. That's a nice looking cookstove."

"Yes. I suppose it is."

"Nicest one I've ever seen. Must make you proud."

"Well, yes, it does," Alta said, unconvincingly.

"Something the matter with it?" Wendell was running his hand along the edge of it.

"Not that I know of. I'm sure it's plenty nice."

Wendell prided himself on his sensing, and right now he was sensing something not quite right, and then he realized.

"Ah, hell. You're probably used to fancy stoves. Hell, you probably had two or three in your kitchen."

"I never paid much attention, to tell you the truth. I really don't have anything to compare it to. I don't know how to use it. I've never laid hands on one of these." Alta wasn't sure why she was confessing so much of her personal life to Wendell, then concluded he wasn't the type that would (or could) use it against her. And he was endearing, in an odd sort of way.

"Well, that can't be right. Are you pulling an old man's leg?" Wendell felt a little put out, like she was making fun of him, but then he saw she was serious.

"Well, goddamn. Christ Almighty! How do you eat? . . . You've been eating?" Then he covered his mouth. "Pardon me. I shouldn't talk like that in front of a lady."

"Well . . ." Alta was too embarrassed to notice the language. She didn't want to say she hadn't been eating. That made her seem helpless.

Wendell circled the room, surveying the kitchen like a

rodent scanning for hawks. He poked at the kitchen furniture on the shelves and sniffed at the sack of flour while Alta watched warily.

"How about I teach you to use that thing? I can't make fancy stuff, but I can turn the stove off and on and show you how to cook up some hotcakes."

Alta didn't respond. She wasn't sure this was appropriate. But Wendell seemed harmless enough, and she was famished. Plus, she thought, if she could learn how to use the stove, Stanley would be very pleased.

"Well, if you could teach me to turn it off and on, that would be wonderful!"

"No trouble at all. I've already fed the horses, and I can use a little something myself."

Wendell pulled what he needed off the shelves and showed her how to mix up some batter and light the stove and oil the griddle, chatting up a storm the whole time so that Alta decided he was a Character, and she rather liked him. He made a stack of hotcakes and put them on two plates, and they sat down to eat. She decided they were the best she'd tasted.

Afterward, she told him she could clean up—he'd made quite a mess. And he said he had to get back to the horses.

"I work down in the livery. Do you know where the livery is?"

Alta shook her head.

"It's down the road past the White Horse. East of the station. If you ever need anything, you can count on me."

With that, he left. Alta cleaned up the kitchen, and when she was finished, she took a walk down Main Street to see about ordering some material for curtains.

CHAPTER 9

ADAM

Adam woke at some ungodly hour to the old man banging around the kitchen. He sat up and reached for his clock, but it was too dark to make out the face. Anticipating the old man's antics made him reluctant to rise, so he sat listening.

When he finally made it to the kitchen, Wendell was well agitated, opening and closing cupboards and the closet and darting from the kitchen to the front room and back into the kitchen.

"It's not in there," Adam said, watching him go through the closet one more time.

Wendell spun to face him.

"Dad-blasted! You scared the living daylight out of me!"

"Sorry," Adam said, but he very well wasn't. Scaring Wendell seemed like justice done for the crime of waking the boy at a godforsaken hour.

"How do you know it's not?

"You already looked there. Twice."

"Where is it?" Wendell asked.

"I don't know what you're looking for."

"Then how the hell do you know it's not there!"

Adam enjoyed watching Wendell's fury, the way it came over the old man like a giant wave and transformed him from a frail weed to a raging beast. His lips quivered and his jaw clenched, and he lifted and dropped his fist like he was hammering something. When he spoke, he spat his words. Adam could tell he was drunk, so the boy guessed he had not been to bed yet.

"There's a goddamn tiger on the loose! A tiger! How the hell did a tiger get loose!"Wendell stood in the middle of the kitchen shaking with rage.

"I heard about that. It's fled the country by now."

Wendell ignored the sarcasm. "There's a three-hundred-dollar reward for the guy who shoots it!" He turned and shuffled through the cupboards. "Where the hell did I put my rifle? It's not on the rack."

"Well, you wouldn't find it in there anyway . . . You sold it. Along with just about everything else."

Wendell spun and scratched his head, then sat down at the table, drumming his fingers.

"Where's your rifle?" he finally asked.

"Maybe you should get some sleep, go look for it in the morning," Adam suggested.

Wendell too seemed suddenly tired.

"You're not going to find it in the dark."

Wendell sighed. "Damn cat," he said. "You should get some sleep," he said, waving Adam away. For once, Adam didn't argue.

XXX

He woke up the next morning later than normal and stared at the familiar four walls of his room and felt a heaviness. This was the first time he allowed himself to think that he'd blown his escape. And now here he was. He'd lived in this room his whole life, and to the best of his memory, it had never changed, besides growing more faded and dustier. The bed was the same four-poster frame with scrapes and scratches, the bureau had nicks and bruises, and the floor was worn.

This morning, the fixedness of the room felt like a trap. He had the terrible feeling he was here to stay. He stood up and turned, feeling restless. He flicked the bedframe and then the edge of the bureau. Then he spun and grabbed the diary from under the bed and sat down, determined to get his mind off his predicament.

August 1

Won't be long before Josephine sends me on, and I don't blame her. She's got a business to run. But I won't be no Hazel . . . Hazel was a fool. She didn't make plans, which is why she ended up strangled in some house over in Butte. The way I see it, I either start my own house or marry a farmer. Last year, old Dixie married a farmer. He wasn't much to look at, and she's a swaybacked old mare with a horse face and bones sticking out all over the place, but he made her decent. And I'm prettier and smarter. That's not bragging, that's the truth. I can read and write and I know my numbers. I wasn't born into the business.

"Stupid," Adam tossed the book back under the bed. It wasn't helping to distract him. "What is she even talking about?"

He stood up and opened the top drawer, staring at his mother's trinkets, which he'd stared at a hundred times—empty perfume bottles, scarves, and hair combs. He had kept them as they'd always been, in the basket on top of the bureau or tucked away in the drawer. They were a comfort to him, and Adam didn't need much room for his own things. He picked up an empty bottle, then let it fall from his hand, giving the top of the bureau a light pump with his fist.

"Now what?" he said to himself. "What am I even going to do now?"

He picked up Alta's hand mirror, searching for a trace of her all gossamer and light beneath the dull puddle of glass. His own reflection was streaked from the mirror's wear, and as he gazed, he thought he could see her. The eyes were pitch, but with the high cheekbones and slightly upturned nose—it was his mother looking. He'd seen her picture. She whispered something, the shape of sounds echoed in his head, and he dropped the mirror and it shattered. She broke into infinitesimal shards.

Fuck, he thought. He kicked the bureau and had the urge to get out of the house. He grabbed his rifle from where it was leaning in the corner—how had Wendell not searched this room?—and thought he'd go search for the tiger.

At the grounds, the only evidence that the circus had been there was a scattering of trash and wagon tracks on the seascape of prairie grass. A new layer of posters covered the barns and buildings, offering a reward for slaying the tiger, and it seemed everyone in town was out searching. Businesses were boarded up and the taverns were deserted—the hunt was keeping people from the day-after doldrums. Most of the men who could shoot a rifle had joined the few circus people who had stayed behind, and they all went out searching for the big cat.

Adam went through the motions of searching. He took his rifle to the river bottom and walked for miles. In truth, he didn't want to find the tiger. He didn't care about the reward. And he didn't want to shoot it, but then he thought, he'd rather it be him than someone else, that would be the right thing. What he really wanted was for it to escape, to run off to the mountains in the west where it could hide and hunt and live out its days.

When he arrived back in town at the end of that first day, he was relieved to learn the other hunters had been unsuccessful. And they were unsuccessful the second day and the third. There were sightings, flashes of color in the distance or out of the corner of an eye, sudden movements in the grass, and for a couple of weeks, people were jumpy and carried rifles whenever they left their homes. But then the big cat was part of the ambience, a quiet rhythm playing in the background of the workings of the town. Officials from the circus abandoned the hunt and left to catch up with the show, and the farmers and ranchers returned to their livestock and fields. Adam, however, continued to walk the coulees and river bottom with his rifle, and that's how he happened by the river on the morning Don Nelson pulled the car from the water.

CHAPTER 10

SMOKE

Smoke pointed his horse for the Tumbleweed, where he figured he could ask about work and a place to board the animal—a place other than Jake's livery—casting about for anyone he thought might be an adversary. When he spotted the woman across the street from the Tumbleweed beating the ground with a hoe, in a dress much too fancy for gardening, he slowed to watch. Her hair was stacked high, and she was long-limbed and elegant, and she didn't seem to be making even the slightest dent in the ground. The incongruity of it was like some grand joke, a fancy white lady trying her hand at farming, completely useless by the look of it. He thought she must certainly be crazy. He slowed his horse to watch and was glad to see Wendell making his way toward him from the saloon—the old man was sure to see the humor in the scene.

"Where the hell have you been?" Wendell shouted when he saw Smoke, confirming what the Assiniboine man already believed—the bastard was hard of hearing. And it was a redundant question because Wendell knew exactly where Smoke had been.

"Away."

"I know that. What the hell you been doing?"

"Hunting."

"What were you hunting?"

"Whatever I ran across."

Wendell had reached him and now grabbed hold of the reins. He worked his lips as he considered.

"Catch anything? . . . Probably not if you shoot a gun like you shoot a damn bow." The horse snorted as if of a similar opinion, and Wendell patted it affectionately on the shoulder.

Both men laughed when Smoke lifted the jackrabbit that had been hanging from the side of his saddle.

"Well, what do you know."

"I've only been gone a few days."

"Weeks. A few weeks."

Smoke nodded toward the woman, wanting Wendell to get a look and see the situation as he saw it.

"Oh, hey. Why don't you come meet my niece?"

Wendell called Alta his niece because she was married to his nephew, and it was easier to say than "my nephew's wife." And it could be there was another word for the relationship, but the word didn't come to his mind. In addressing her as such, he left out the vital information about her being Stanley's wife. But then, if he had thought about it, he'd have assumed everyone already knew.

"Your niece," Smoke said, raising an eyebrow.

"Pretty little thing, isn't she," Wendell said, as if deserving credit.

Wendell walked across the road, and Smoke followed, still on his horse.

Alta straightened and greeted Wendell and smiled at Smoke. Smoke could see her eyes were intelligent, which made him uncomfortable—he'd been enjoying the story he'd told himself about how she was crazy. For her part, Alta saw Smoke sitting up on his horse, exotic and wild-looking, dressed like a cowboy in a work shirt and scarf, but with his hair like pitch, uncombed and chopped near his chin. His eyes were steady and dark. He reminded Alta of Heathcliff, if Heathcliff were a Native American.

Wendell introduced the two.

"Jesus Christ, you're a terrible gardener . . ."

"You think so?" Alta wasn't put off by Wendell's criticism, which embarrassed the old man. While he'd never been a self-conscious person, being near a pretty woman made him feel uncouth and clumsy. That she was someone born of wealth and status didn't help the equation. Now here he was listening to the words that came out of his own mouth.

"No offense," he said, taking off his hat.

"It's quite all right. I'm well aware of my limitations. I was planning on hiring a gardener. Do you know anyone who would be interested?"

"Hell, yes. This one right here is looking for work," Wendell said, feeling heroic. "Jesus Christ. Get off that horse and help the lady out. I'm too old for this shit."

Smoke generally wouldn't let the old man order him around—he supposed he'd lost his good sense along with his horses—but he found himself obeying. He slid off the horse and passed the reins to Wendell, giving the old man what could be interpreted as a mean look. He had a bad feeling about the situation.

The look gave Wendell an itch, though he couldn't say why or where.

"What the hell, you need work," Wendell griped.

"Well, this is wonderful." Alta couldn't be more pleased. She was proving herself adept at managing the household, she thought, as she handed over the hoe.

"That husband will pay you for sure," Wendell said, and then he realized exactly why he'd been feeling that itch—because that husband was Stanley and he was an ungracious son of a bitch, not to mention it seemed Stanley had taken a dislike for the Indian. No, not seemed, Wendell thought, scratching his belly.

Wendell watched Smoke tear up the dirt—that Indian sure knew how to hoe, he had to admit. He wondered if he should let Smoke know that, technically, he was getting himself into a situation with Stanley by getting into a situation with Stanley's wife. But then, it didn't make sense to get the Indian all riled. Right now, everything was working just fine.

The horse, which until that moment had been standing—head hanging, foot cocked, tail flicking—stepped toward Wendell and sniffed the back of his shirt, as if he'd tucked in a sack of oats or alfalfa hay. Then he was nuzzling the collar of his shirt and it tickled Wendell's neck.

"Goddamn it," Wendell stepped back. And then, hell, he thought. Stanley's gone for the day, driving folks around and whatever else it was Jake wanted him to do.

"Why don't I take this thing down to Lew's for the night," he said to Smoke, nodding toward the horse. Really, he was feeling quite pleased. The day was working itself out. He'd accomplished his good deed. He might as well get on with his evening. "He owes us both a favor after all the money we made him last month."

Smoke didn't answer but looked up and nodded.

"I'll have Phyllis cook up that rabbit for the both of us," Wendell said, as he led the horse away. Phyllis was the wife of Clem, the barkeep. She often would cook up game that Wendell caught.

XXX

Alta felt awkward standing there watching Smoke work with nothing for herself to do. She rubbed the blister that was forming on her finger then stood clasping her hands. It was a warm spring day, though occasionally a gust would remind her that it was still early in the year.

"Do you have a shovel?" He hardly looked up from his work.

Alta shook her head.

"You should really have a shovel." Smoke felt irritated. All this digging would make a bit more sense with a shovel. People moving up and down Main Street threw curious glances in their direction.

"I could go and purchase one."

"I can make do." Smoke paused to wipe his forehead.

"What are you going to plant here?"

"I don't know . . . I've never planted a garden." Alta was embarrassed. She wondered if he meant the entire plot when he said "here" or if he meant the particular place where his hoe was touching down.

"A person usually knows what they're planting before they start digging in the dirt."

"Well, I'm new here. This is all new to me. And whatever I plant, I need to prepare the soil, don't I?" She had read this somewhere, probably in a novel.

"Sure," Smoke said, not being one to argue. He studied the plot. He knew a little bit about farming from his brother.

"How about some corn? Beans? . . . maybe some tomatoes? They like the sun . . ."

"OK. That's what we'll do . . ."

"Do you know how to plant seeds?"

"It can't be that hard, can it? Just throw some seeds in the ground . . ." She was becoming exhausted from focusing on details she knew nothing about. "Would you care for some lemonade?" She'd purchased lemons and was proud that she had learned to make such a refreshing treat.

"All right." Smoke had nothing against lemonade, and he was certainly thirsty.

Alta went into the house to prepare a batch and when she was ready, she called to him.

"Oh, do come in," she said when he hesitated at the door.

"I'll just take it out here."

"Oh, no. I won't have it." Hosting and the treatment of guests was something she took seriously. Generosity was a sign of good breeding. And as a friend of Wendell's, Smoke was almost family; he certainly deserved the respect of a chair.

Smoke stepped inside and stood in the doorway thinking no good could come from being alone with a white woman in her house.

"Sit, please." Her first guest in her own home—she didn't count Wendell since he'd taken her by surprise, and she had been unprepared. She wouldn't make that mistake again.

Smoke took a seat, and she poured him a glass and stood over him while he drank.

"It's very good, isn't it?" she said of her accomplishment.

"Yes. It is." He finished quickly and pushed his chair back to leave.

"Oh, please. Have another!"

Alta poured him another glass of lemonade, and he drank it, more slowly this time, since he was no longer thirsty. And so he was sitting at the table with a glass of lemonade in front of him when Stanley burst through the door.

"Stanley! Darling! . . . I didn't expect you . . . Would you like some lemonade?"

Stanley, for his part, paused just long enough to observe the domesticity that was the Indian sitting at his table and his wife serving him lemonade before he rushed Smoke.

Smoke was out of the chair with his hands in the air, as if to surrender, and then was gone through the front door before Alta had time to register the incident. She turned with a glass for her husband, and the room had shifted.

"Get the hell out of my kitchen!" Stanley was shouting from the front room.

"Stanley . . . goodness." Alta came up behind him, wondering what Smoke had done to offend him so. Had he taken something without her seeing?

"What the hell was he doing here?"

Before she could answer, he was on her. He grabbed her by the throat and shoved her against the wall. The glass of lemonade shattered on the floor.

"You're choking me," she rasped.

"You're damn right I'm choking you. What the hell are you doing with an Indian in my house?" He gave her an additional shove when he said "Indian."

"Stanley," Alta could hardly squeak his name. She didn't recognize the face twisted in rage leaning over her. When he finally released her, she bent over, heaving, catching her breath.

"Stanley," she repeated. She pulled herself into a chair. "How could you? He was helping me. In the garden."

"That Indian is no good. No good at all," Stanley said, coming toward her. He was calm now—a forced calm, like a window shut against the storm of him. "He could hurt you . . ." He took her chin in his hand and gazed down at her, but there was no warmth in that stare. "You stay away from him."

"Of course," Alta said, because what else could she say? Stanley nodded and dropped his hand then took up pacing like he was looking to pounce. "He's dangerous." He picked up a porcelain figurine from the mantel and studied it like it was the most interesting thing in the world.

"I have to go," he said, setting it down. "Jake's expecting me."

"Do you want some lunch?" Alta whispered as he walked out the door.

"Nah . . . I'll just eat at the White Horse."

Alta was shaken after that. She'd seen her father rant and shout, but she'd never experienced violence before. How dare he, she thought, sitting down at the table to gather her wits. She should report him, but then, too who? He was her husband. She let that thought swirl around for a bit and wondered if she should leave. But where would she go? Home? she thought cynically. To her father? He probably wouldn't allow her back. And then, she thought, she had let a strange man into her home. Maybe Smoke was truly dangerous. She knew nothing about him. It could be Stanley was protecting her. That had to be it. She closed her eyes and took a deep breath. He was protecting her, of course. That was his job. She stood up slowly to pick up Smoke's empty glass to wash it. He was protecting her, and yet, she didn't feel safe.

CHAPTER 11

LOLA

Lola set down her pen and studied the page. She had beautiful penmanship, her teachers had always said. And she had a gift for words. She wished there were someone she could show her entry to, but for obvious reasons, that was impossible.

She wrote a new line beneath what she had already written and underlined it: *I will marry a farmer*. She let out a sigh, as if the deed had been accomplished. It was as good as any contract; she couldn't fail. She studied her reflection in the mirror, which was hanging with boas and necklaces and every number of glittery, shiny accessories. She didn't like what she saw—the lines on the edge of her mouth like fish gills—but she didn't allow herself to turn away. Repulsion was inspiration.

She thought about the girl again and felt ill. The girl had arrived in the doorway with a bag and a wrap and the sun circling her head like a halo. Josephine had looked her up and down the same as if she were buying steers at an auction—you have to know the stock. She'd been working her jaw, doing the numbers, adding up to a fortune, no doubt about it. Lola had taken it all in, going about the parlor picking up glasses and empty beer bottles, running her own set of numbers. She'd been surprised when Josephine changed her mind.

"This place ain't no velvet," Josephine had said to the girl.

"You'd better get yourself some other work. I don't have time to babysit."

The girl said she was sixteen, but Josephine wasn't having it. Besides, that was too young.

"And I'm a French nun," she'd said. "You go on home to your family."

"I ain't got no family."

"Listen, honey, why don't you go on over to the hotel. They're always looking for someone to clean the rooms. Like I said, I can't be babysitting. If you're still looking for work when you're eighteen, you come see me."

Josephine had closed the door on the girl.

"You did the right thing," Madeline had said. It wasn't so much the competition as that someone so young made the rest of the women appear older. And Madeline, Lola had thought a little smugly in the moment, had much more to worry about than most of them since she was practically growing a beard. She shaved her chin every day with a razor and hand mirror in her room. Fortunately, there were those men that liked her hairy chin.

"I must be getting old," Josephine had said. She'd looked tired leaning against the door, and she never looked tired. So maybe it was Josephine looking tired that got Lola feeling the things she was feeling. She had excused herself to go lie down.

Now she picked up a pen again.

> *The girl was a beauty, no doubt about it. Fifteen at the most. With yellow hair, violet eyes, and a thicket of lashes. Her skin was smooth as glass. She stood in the doorway, and I saw her whole life right there. Sometimes I can see things like that—a young girl looking like an angel, and twenty years from now she lies beaten in a crib in a dusty miners' camp,*

> *looking old before in her time. Truth is, women like us don't have much time. Too young, too old. Twenty years is the blink of an eye. Used to be I made men's heads turn. Used to be men would fight over me. They'd pay me a fortune for a smile. Now I'm all crow's feet and my neck is slipping down like a stretched-out stocking.*

Lola studied her reflection to see if it was true, and it was. She closed the book, as if doing so would hide her flaws, then stood up and pushed back the bed. Most of the women couldn't read, but they could find someone who would, and Lola wasn't taking chances. She lifted a slab of wood that had come loose from the floor and slid the book into a crevice, then replaced the slab, finally moving her bed back over the top of it. Just writing the words had made them true. She would marry; maybe not a farmer. But she had someone in mind.

CHAPTER 12

ADAM

Don Nelson bought himself a new Fordson tractor in the spring of 1918. It was the first tractor in the county, so of course he was looking for an opportunity to show it off. He drove it up and down Main Street several times, which brought the crowds running—everyone wanted to touch it, and the kids wanted to climb on it—but parading didn't demonstrate the tractor's enormous power, and a few people accused him of being a dandy. And then one day, not long after the circus fiasco, he was rounding up an old cow that had wandered off by the river when he saw the water swirling around what could easily be some rocks or tree trunks. He had to peer closely to make it out because the river had done its damage. The thing rose like some ancient kelpie, with weeds and branches waving from the tangle of it like a windblown mane in the current and several slashes of red paint along the top like scars where the water rarely reached. The small island that had attached to it was the result of lodged logs trapping sediment. Don let out a whistle—the remains of the old car, the bane of riverboat pilots. It was an inspiration for a farmer looking to show off the power of his new tractor engine. People had been trying for years to rescue the old Winton from the river's clutches—farmers had hitched their most powerful horse teams to the axle or bumper or some part of the car, but no one had managed more than a budge. Inevitably, the current had pulled the car back into its cold, wet grave. And so the car had taken on a mythical quality, an automotive Excalibur, and as Don rose in his saddle to gaze on the island of metal, it seemed like God himself was calling to him, showing him his destiny. He and his machine would accomplish the impossible—they would rescue river travelers from the dark knight that ruled the riverway, the automotive death trap. He rode home with his horse nipping the heels of the old cow and planned the rescue.

Don announced his plans later that night while drinking in Bert's bar. He mentioned his plan to Bert, and since the saloons were the central nervous system of Mondak, anything newsworthy that happened or was discussed in one was known almost immediately discussed in all of them, and so the news made its way to the town's extremities. Almost immediately, everyone wagered on the rescue, and the following Saturday morning most of the citizens of Mondak gathered in the weeds along the riverbank for the Challenge of the Century. The crowd picnicked on boiled eggs and slabs of bread as they waited for the tractor, jumping to their feet when they heard it rumble down the road toward them with Don sitting atop it waving and smiling, wearing his Sunday best like fancy chain mail. At the river's edge, Don made a show of turning the tractor around in a complicated back and forth, and then he leapt from his seat and stood on the bank and stared at the brown water. The river was high this time of year, especially after an enormous snowmelt in the Rocky Mountains.

"Looks cold," someone observed, watching him shift.

"Christ," Don said. He hadn't thought about the fact that he'd have to get in the water to tie the car to the tractor.

"Hey, son," he pointed at Cecil, who was standing in the

crowd nearby. "Want to earn a couple bucks?"

Cecil took the end of the rope and the crowd watched him step into the river, leaping a few times until he got used to the cold.

He bent down and submerged all but his face to loop the rope around the car's rear axle. Don tied the other end to the tractor, a monster of a thing—all tanks and valves and rods and levers. He took his seat and waved to the crowd, then shifted the gears around. The enormous wheels churned and dug into the mud, and the car lurched and sucked. Some in the crowd laughed and cheered, and those that had bet on the tractor stood stock still waiting for the river to relinquish its grip. But the river didn't release its hold on the car. The tractor wheels dug into the bank, and after a while, it became clear the machine wasn't up to the task. Don stopped the tractor and jumped to the ground and took out his tobacco, stuffing a pinch along the inside of his cheek.

"Well then," several farmers came over to give the tractor a look. "Probably shouldn't have sold your horses," someone laughed.

"It's probably sunk halfway to hell," someone said.

Don responded by calling old Harry Teasdale over and mentioning that maybe Harry should go get his Belgians, because surely the enormous horses would tip the power struggle between the river and the tractor in favor of the citizens of Mondak, and since they were all standing around on a Saturday, they should relieve the river of this wreck.

People stood along the banks talking, and some were spitting tobacco. Adam and several other boys watched as a frog settled on the surface along the edge of the river. The boys clutched rocks in their hands and launched them in a burst.

"Got it!" one of them chuckled.

Eventually they heard the rattle of harnesses and clomp of feet, and the horses came around the curve with their blond manes glistening in the sun.

The horses shied several times as Harry guided them along the edge of the river, but eventually they settled enough so he could hitch the team to the car. Harry got behind the horses, and Don sat down at the tractor. The horses heaved and the tractor flung mud and rocks from its iron cleats, and the ropes creaked and cracked and crept ever so reluctantly up the bank. The butt end of the car lifted out of the water like a small whale. The water rushed off the fins and sludge fell in clumps from the rusted body.

"Oh, my goodness!"

"Well, I'll be."

"Just look at that!"

The exclamations came from everywhere in the crowd, and people repeated variations of the origin story in which the car came to rest at the bottom of the river. There was a surge, and the river released its grip in a hurl of water and the car lurched onto the bank. The horses stumbled forward in their harnesses and the tractor jumped, in so much as a tractor can jump, and the crowd clapped and cheered.

"Well, what do you know!" someone said.

"Well, I'll be!"

Harry unhitched the horses from the car, feeling every bit the hero he thought he would be for leading the charge against the river.

Snags old and new stuck out of the car's wheel spokes and fenders like wiry hair or whiskers. Jake, who had arrived at some point during the rescue, circled the wreckage. Folks watched for his reaction. Everyone was always watching for Jake's reaction, Adam realized. He'd seen this before, of course, but now he really saw it. Jake stopped and stared at the car, and he might as well have been performing some magical feat. People talked about the bank robbers and outlaws or maybe it was drunken lovers who had pointed the wheel of the

Winton toward the water, but they were tuned into Jake, waiting for him to issue some directive from on high.

"It was that murderer," someone whispered into Adam's ear. "Before they caught him. They hung him right on the Main Street."

Adam couldn't help but look in the direction the man pointed, but he was thinking about power and being in charge, about the fact that a man could suck up the attention of an entire community while doing nothing but standing. Adam stepped away from the voice to get a better look at the car. It was hard to believe it had been as fancy as folks were saying.

Jake came over to where Adam was standing. "I have a job for you and that friend of yours," he mumbled, not turning his gaze. "Tomorrow."

"Yes, sir," Adam said. He watched Jake thank Nelson and Teasdale for their efforts before driving off to town in his Model T. Most of the crowd soon followed, abandoning the car on the river bank.

Adam walked back into town, picking up a rock and tossing it. He wandered along the boardwalk, peering beneath it or else kicking at clumps of weeds along the side. At the far end of the street, men from the distillery were loading barrels onto a wagon.

Adam sat down on the steps in front of the hotel and pulled up a blade of wheatgrass and wound it around his finger.

CHAPTER 13

ALTA

Alta's worlds collided in the backroom of the White Horse Tavern. She was a guest of honor for a dinner party hosted by Jake Steel, Stanley's boss and one of the founders of the town. It was a courtesy, she supposed, extended to the brides of associates.

Jake greeted her and Stanley at the door, an enormous man with cheeks like risen dough.

"Good evening, my dear, you must be Alta!" He clasped her hands, his own large and sweaty as undercooked eggs.

"You're just as pretty as Stanley said. It's a pleasure to meet you."

He took her by the arm and inched her toward the cluster of the guests at the back of the room, pausing every step or so to gesticulate or emphasize some point he was making about the pedigrees of those she was about to meet, beginning with himself.

"You're looking at the son of a New York City butcher. In what other country would the son of a New York City butcher be building a town!" He stopped and faced her, giving her the opportunity to size him up, see what a builder of towns looked like. She wondered if he wasn't ailing, with his labored breath like a dying animal. He grabbed hold of her arm and took two more steps.

"Lew is married to Beverly," he nodded to the couple. "You'll meet Beverly shortly . . . Lew runs the mercantile, so you'll get to know him well. And then there's Clem and his wife Phyllis. Clem owned tracks of land next to the railroad's grant, which he sold to the railroad. Then he bought up the Tumbleweed saloon and a distillery in town. He supplies most of the saloons." A few more steps. He was moving at a tedious pace. Alta had the urge to pull him along. At this rate, they wouldn't reach the back of the room for hours. Alta eyed their destination and noticed a woman in the group wearing black satin and lace. Her bearing was familiar. It was several moments before Alta registered that the woman looked like Mary Hill. She had the same short stature and dark hair lined with gray. Alta's breath caught in her throat.

"Oh, dear child! Whatever are you doing here? . . ." It was Mary. She had spied Alta and was rushing toward her, but then she stopped as if colliding with an invisible wall. She stood motionless, looking Alta over as she might a stray cat, and she didn't care for stray cats. James appeared next to her, and Mary's language returned.

"Oh, I can't believe it! We didn't know what had become of you. Your father is beside himself!"

"Mrs. Hill . . . Mr. Hill . . . What a surprise!"

"Indeed!" They went about complimenting one another on their appearances as a way to buy time while Jake stood aside and beamed down on the group like they were pots of honey.

"You know one another?" he asked, when there was a lull, though he knew they did. Stanley had not held back details of his marriage into the peak of society. It was why they were all here. Jake had built his success on recognizing opportunities. Stanley had useful qualities, one of which was that he was charming to women. Here, Jake was capitalizing on Stanley's talent—hiring him for anything that needed doing, giving him a title while waiting for him to come into Alta's money, which

Jake would funnel into whatever moneymaking venture he could get Stanley to sign up for—and ultimately the big man's own pockets. This was Jake's magic—his ability to see money and bring it home. Alta was an access road to two large rivers—her father, if Jake and Stanley could clear the debris, and now James Hill. Already Alta was lending status and legitimacy to tonight's huddle. Her presence was priming Mr. Hill.

"Well, of course. James has been in business with Alta's father for years . . . Whatever are you doing in Mondak, my dear girl?" Mary repeated, her voice accusing. Cadwallader had been vague about Alta's disappearance, even with his closest friends.

"Well, I married." Alta glanced toward Stanley, who was standing next to her waiting to be acknowledged. He bowed slightly in confirmation and flashed Mary his most charming smile, which she didn't bother to return. She knew a rapscallion when she met one, and she'd heard the rumors about Stanley.

"Your husband . . . well, then." Mary took Alta's hand between her two. She felt conflicted, torn between feeling protective toward the girl and angry with her for her poor choice and disloyalty to Cadwallader. But then, what could one expect from a motherless child? Of course Alta had turned out impulsive and headstrong. She must, however, realize that she had made a terrible mistake in defying her father before there was any chance of forgiveness.

"He was very angry." Mary leaned in to Alta to whisper, though her voice was loud enough for the others to hear. "He says he has no daughter."

"No daughter. What does that mean?" Stanley's brows clutched like caterpillars undulating across the dry bark of his forehead at a possible breach in his ambiguous plan. Jake too, felt an angry jolt.

"He was very angry," Mary repeated. "As would be expected."

"It's a small world," James said, changing the subject. He'd been shuffling next to Mary, half listening to the conversation, eyeing the pictures and trophies on the wall. The personal tone of the women's conversation made him uncomfortable. And this one had grown heavy and dark.

Jake noticed the mood change and stepped forward to redirect James's attention to a more comfortable subject. If Jake could gain his support, the dream of Mondak was a guaranteed success.

"So, what do you think? Are they going to keep coming?" he asked about the settlers moving to the prairie.

"In ebbs and flows," James said.

"Mostly in flows from the way you've been packing those trains," Jake replied. "You are almost single-handedly expanding this great country."

Just then the back door opened with an explosion of sunlight, which was almost immediately blocked. There was scuffling and chatter, and then an enormous white bull draped in flowers was shoved into the room. The bull stopped just inside the doorway, seemingly startled to find himself at a dinner party. The crowd parted ways for him oohing and ahhing.

"Ladies and gentlemen . . ." Jake stepped toward the animal and opened his arms wide, then swung around to face guests. "Let me present this great white bull, honoring the strength and power and virility of our new and wondrous city. Mondak!"

He took a bow and everyone clapped and shouted, and the bull stepped forward tentatively, his shoulders quivering. A front hoof pawed the floor. The guests backed away, worried he might charge, and then the bull's handlers swarmed him, turned him, and both lured and pushed him out the same door he'd entered.

"Oh, does he have to go?" someone laughed.

"He's not housebroken," Jake quipped as the door shut

behind the bull.

The guests were worked up after that. Having the conventional order of the evening upended left them feeling full of possibility.

"He is just wonderful, Jake," Mary said, and James clapped him on the back.

"That was something," Clem laughed.

Waiters directed the party to their seats and poured drinks and served up littleneck clams.

"Courtesy of the Great Northern Railroad," Jake flattered his most prestigious guest—the ask had already been spoken in multiple languages—economics, business, patriotism.

"We have a unique opportunity here," Jake continued, mostly to James. He explained how the cheap (and free!) land coupled with conflicting state alcohol laws ensured Mondak a particularly promising future, and he explained how he had gathered together the investors and was personally running the land office, where he acted both as an information broker and was in charge of the plat. He would ensure the town was developed properly, with a mix of merchants and farmers in a way that would best benefit the railroad.

"You get them here, and I can keep them," Jake boomed, and motioned for a waiter to bring tumblers of whiskey.

"They're reworking how to parcel out the reservation. There's a lot of land wasted on the Indians that will be available."

"That's a few million acres to plow and plant, and all that grain will need shipping," Ollie added. Ollie Ollipson was the least involved of the founders. He'd given up his authority over the direction of the town's development when he'd sold his land to the Mondak Townsite Company, but he was free with his opinion.

"So I've heard," James said. He was in the business of knowing.

"I'm not so sure about all this dry-land farming," Lew addressed James. He seemed less enthused than the others about the development plans for the town.

"It's going to change this country. It locks in the moisture. Rain. Rain just washes all the nutrients away . . . We have conferences to educate farmers. You'll have to come to one of them . . . you'll see what I mean," James assured him.

"The more you plant, the more it rains," Jake said. "That's science."

Mary signaled the waiter for wine and passed a glass to Alta.

"Here they go again," she said. The women had been segregated to one end of the table, so the men could speak business. It was an unconventional dinner party in that way, one that would not stand in civilized society, Mary thought to herself. "Welcome to the Wild West. No one has any manners. You'll be running shoeless before you know it."

"Oh, I don't know about that," Alta laughed, though she didn't feel light. She was grateful to talk about anything but her father.

"It's not all that bad." Beverly was a graying and thickening woman with a pragmatic, competent air. "It can be rough, it's true, but I assure you, we wear shoes."

"I've seen plenty of migrants without shoes," Mary warned.

"There's a lot of knife fights," Pearl said. Pearl was Ollie's wife and reminded Alta of a squirrel. She was small and darting and distracted.

"Well, there are those," Phyllis agreed.

"Oh, dear," Mary said.

"I'll stay away from those." Alta felt homesick.

Mary reached across the table and patted Alta's hand, feeling more inclined to mother her now that the girl had seen the error of her ways.

"Your father will come around. It'll just take some time.

It's not just his heart that's been broken. His pride is injured. Sometimes pride takes the longest to heal, but we'll work on him." Her voice was conspiratorial. "James will talk to him. He has his ways. Just be patient."

Alta nodded, unable to meet Mary's gaze.

"You just need to direct them. Orchestrate," James boomed, so the women had no choice but to listen. "You're the bandleader. Find all those migrants a place to land, show them where to dump their grain, and we'll move it . . . We're going to have to build an elevator . . ."

Jake was pleased with James's use of the pronoun *we*. "We wouldn't be much of a town without an elevator."

"Absolutely," James puffed. "That's what I mean."

"One sure thing," Stanley piped in, "is once they're here, they're going to need the railroad."

"Ain't that a fact." James pointed at Stanley.

"I've got flyers at the printers right now that we'll send out all over the world, calling on the ambitious, the romantic, the adventurous . . . That sort of talk appeals to all those folks needing a little incentive."

"Well, it's a rare opportunity, no doubt about it," Clem opined.

"Oh, dear," Mary sighed. "Whatever do you do here, dear?" She resented being drowned out. She was struggling to understand how anyone would choose to live in such a remote, dirty place. "You are going to be bored to death . . . There's just nothing. No theater . . . No culture. You know what I mean. If you're used to living in a big city," she addressed the women. "If you don't mind my saying, every town can use a bit of culture. Poetry, music, theater . . . Maybe you can host salons . . . It's a bit of a thing," she whispered to Alta.

"I've been to a few."

"Well, then. You know what I'm talking about. You could be a salonniere. Like Isabella d'Este. Or Madame de Rambouillet and her blue room. You are familiar with the Marquise de Rambouillet?"

"I'm afraid not."

"Oh, dear . . . Well, Madame de Rambouillet would gather all the brilliant minds of her time in her blue room—called so because it was blue—in Paris, and they would discuss important matters. Literature, philosophy. . . . The salons were incubators for ideas . . . She was just a wonderful, inspiring woman . . ."

"A salon?" Phyllis was working the idea over. The people of Mondak could do with a little culture or intellectual stimulation, that she didn't doubt.

"Of course," Mary said. "Who better to bring culture to Mondak than this young lady?"

"I'm sure Alta will find plenty to keep her occupied."

"Well, I think it's a wonderful idea," Beverly said. Alta had a good feeling that Beverly would turn out to be an ally.

"I don't think the ladies around here have much use for the fancy arts, but they're always up for a chicken pie social," Pearl broke in.

"Oh, you poor thing," Mary said, taking Alta's hand. "You'll have to make a trip to Williston or Bismarck or one of the bigger cities. Don't let Stanley keep you all to himself . . ."

"Of course."

"What about staff? Do you have good staff?"“

"I'm learning to cook."

"Oh, my," Mary put her hand over her heart. "I won't say such a thing to your father."

"Have you never cooked?" Beverly was stunned.

"I'm learning," Alta said defensively.

"Goodness gracious, this child has never lifted a finger in her life . . . She's built of something different, completely . . . Where is this husband of yours?" Mary spun around.

"Oh, no," Alta said, grabbing hold of Mary's arm; the

thought of Mary confronting Stanley did not sit well with her at all.

Beverly patted Alta's hand. "I'll teach you everything you need to know."

"You'll teach her?" Mary looked at Beverly expectantly.

"Of course."

"Poor Ed Ellingson," Pearl broke in. Alta had no idea who Ed Ellingson was. Seeing Alta's questioning gaze, Pearl continued. "He got run over by the Fast Mail," she whispered loudly.

"He just didn't see it coming," Phyllis said, joining in from further down the table.

"Gracious," Mary said.

"I don't like to hear that," James piped up, having an ear for train talk. "Of course, the train's business is bigger than a single man. But I still don't like to hear it."

"I don't see it, how a train can take a man by surprise," Stanley said.

"It happens more than you'd think," James replied. "But usually it's a case of someone wandering onto the tracks in a drunk. When that happens, we call it a case of separating the wheat from the chaff."

The men chuckled and the women looked stern.

"I don't know how someone's misfortune is a laughing matter," Mary said.

"What do you think of that car?" Jake was walking around the table and paused to lean down and whisper to Alta.

"Excuse me?"

"My car. Didn't Stanley meet you at the station with the car?"

"Oh, yes. Yes . . . It's very nice."

"Have you ever been in a car?"

"Yes, I have. But yours is very nice."

"Wonderful machines! We're going to make a fortune driving folks to Williston and back—some people don't want to wait on the train . . . Don't let on to old James," he winked, then straightened and returned to his seat.

The Diary

February 17

I talked to the girls about banking their money and they laughed. Most of 'em spend it faster than they make it, borrowing for stockings and fancy soaps. Bunch of fools. Bette called Alice a fool for planting roses in my ear. She said Stanley is no more going to marry me than Widow Jones, who's ninety years old with cataracts. He's got feelings, I know that. It's just a matter of getting the wife out of the picture.

February 20

Did I say he brought me perfume! It must have cost a fortune! He's a gentleman, not like these other drunks. The girls are jealous.

CHAPTER 14

ALTA AND SMOKE

Her brief time in Mondak had changed Alta. There was an urgency to her need for success in her new role. She didn't want to displease Stanley, because she feared the consequences of failure. And with that, the town itself no longer wore the glitter of a fairy tale. It was a strange and hostile space, the platinum sky like the face of an anvil. Her house, previously quaint and cute, transformed into something small and ordinary, and the kitchen appliances spoke an unfamiliar language. The growing pile of laundry curdling over the sides of the basket in the corner took on an ominous quality. She considered sending it out—of course there was a laundress in town that would appreciate the work, but if Stanley found out, he might be angry. She struggled to find enthusiasm and energy for her tasks—her inability to conjure a Jo March or Jane Eyre to inspire her to tackle her work was a sign of how far she had fallen. Her usual heroines remained stranded between the leather covers of books.

The local women paraded to the house bearing pies and cookies and pots of roast, and Alta was grateful for the food and company. And some of them seemed sincere and friendly. But with others, she had the feeling she was being scrutinized, like an oddity at a fair, and that her failure was something to be discussed at church socials or afternoon teas. And so, she decided to make her way to the Mondak equivalent of Oz—the Mondak Mercantile—thinking there might be some magazine or book to advise on housekeeping questions. Of course, Beverly had offered to help her, but they hadn't talked since the dinner, and Alta didn't want to put the other woman out. Plus, she'd found Lew, Beverly's husband and the owner of the mercantile, to be a kind man with the magical ability to find solutions in the many jars of powders or cans on his shelves.

Alta took her basket and shut the door and stood outside on the porch watching what was a great deal of activity in front of the jail. A fight, she figured. They were commonplace, and already she'd learned to tune them out.

Across the street, Smoke was leaning on the railing on the boardwalk outside the Tumbleweed; Alta was sure it was him. He was carving, it looked like, flicking a knife around something in his hand. She felt a jolt of anxiety after the events in the kitchen and Stanley's warning. But then her good breeding overcame her. He was a friend of Wendell's, and Stanley hadn't paid him for his work but had, in fact, treated him poorly. She started toward him, thinking she'd make amends.

"The sheriff's been shot!" a voice bubbled out of the wash of people heading south, and the knowledge seemed instantaneous and ubiquitous. The doors of the saloons flung open, every one of them, and patrons blew out with their hands on their holsters shouting, leaping over railings and down steps and into a river of people rushing toward the sheriff's office, forking around Bert Steel's Crossbar Saloon, which sat on skids in the middle of Main Street—Bert had decided to turn the building into a bank, which was an east-side-of-the-street business. Large beams poked from the overhang of the saloon, and the sign dangled from a single nail like a tattered flag, rattling in the occasional gust of wind.

Details percolated up from the road. Sheriff Courtney and

a deputy had been shot and killed outside the offices of the Union Bridge and Construction Company. Courtney and his two deputies had received news from down south that a fugitive was working with the crew that was building the bridge across the Missouri River near Snowden. The sheriff and deputies had gone to the construction company office in search of the man—Jessie Collins. Tom Wilson had gone inside and Collins was there, waiting. Collins confiscated Tom's gun, then walked out and shot the sheriff and Sam Bermeister, the other deputy, before disappearing into the woods.

Now, men were saddling their horses, and a posse was barreling toward the river.

Stanley blew past Alta and into the house—she didn't see him approach—then back out in a matter of moments, tucking his pistol into his belt.

"What are you doing?" Alta grabbed his arm.

"Catching a murderer." He shook her loose and bounded into the crowd.

Alta stood motionless on the edge of the road, not sure what to do, feeling shaken. Yet it was business as usual for many folks. Smoke was still on the boardwalk lounging and carving, and farther down the street, men from the distillery were loading crates onto a wagon; and then, beyond the tightly packed hub of the town, workers were scurrying along the yellow beams of the school holding hammers and saws, like sailors on the spars of a ship dressing the bones of it with muscles of wood. Did they know? Alta wondered. They must have heard—they must have noticed the pandemonium.

There is nothing I can do, she told herself. And with the entire town on alert, the main street must be safe. Plus the mercantile won't be busy. I can pick Lew's brain and purchase some soap and tubs. This was how she rationalized her decision to head north past the drunks slung over the railings like drying sheets. She felt shaken knowing there was a killer on the loose, but that the danger was tangible rather than existential gave her clarity—she clutched her basket, ready to swing at the first hint of an attacker. And oddly, the danger made the town more tentative and dear. She studied the locked doors of the shops she passed, with their foggy windows and some with closed shades, and thought fondly of the shopkeepers who'd run off to join the fray.

Inside, the mercantile was dimly lit, and it took Alta a moment for her eyes to adjust. Once they did, she made her way along the counter, dodging a harness that was about to fall from the ceiling hook and pausing to look at the glass beads and jewelry in a showcase—nice enough pieces. Lew was helping another customer, so she looked over the books and added a copy of *How to Make Good Things to Eat* along with two magazines and some cans of chicken and tongue and veal—she would master the art of making food.

A garishly dressed woman was staring at her from over by the fabrics. She wore a low-cut dress she looked about to fall out of, and Alta had the urge to throw a shawl over the front of her. She looked exactly as Alta imagined a lady of the night would look, with rouge on her cheeks and lines under metal eyes—Alta was fascinated, in a morbid way. The women's hostility, however, was perplexing. Courtesy, she thought, is the best way to gain control of the situation.

"How do you do?"

The woman ignored Alta and turned to the counter. She paid for plug tobacco, rolling paper, and silk stockings, and then brushed by Alta, knocking her shoulder in what could only be a purposeful action. Alta watched as she sashayed out of the store.

"Goodness," Alta said as she turned to Lew.

"Lola," Lew said. "She usually sends someone to do her shopping, but I guess the murder has everyone a bit mixed up today." Lew wiped down the counter as if wiping away evidence of the woman's presence.

"He killed a lot of people, is what I heard, before he shot the sheriff and deputy. Cold and calculated, he is. The whole world's gone crazy."

"That's terrible. Will they catch him?"

"You bet your bottom dollar," Lew said confidently.

"I need washing supplies," Alta said, getting back to business, and Lew asked what in particular. When Alta didn't respond immediately, Lew had the grace to offer suggestions. He knew of her predicament.

"I'll send my boy with the washing supplies in the morning," he said. "He's off hunting that killer this afternoon."

"That would be wonderful," Alta said. And then Lew made another suggestion.

"I have a new style of tub. Not many women are familiar with its workings. Why don't I talk to Beverly and have her give you a demonstration?"

The subtext was clear, but Alta was grateful for his prudence in not bringing it up, and she said so.

"I would be very grateful," she added.

The town seemed more charged when she left the store. The streets had cleared, so Alta walked home much faster than she had come, listening for the thump of rushing steps behind her. As she approached her house, she saw Smoke in the place she had left him, looking unfazed by the day's events, and for some reason this made her angry.

"The sheriff's been shot," she marched toward him, the implication being he should do something about it.

"I heard." He scraped at a small piece of bone with a knife.

"There's a murderer on the loose."

Smoke didn't respond, but kept at his work.

"Aren't you going to do something? . . . There are hunting parties. Don't you think you should help look?"

"I don't see that it's my business." His look implied neither was it hers. But of course it was. It was a matter of safety.

"Of course it's your business."

"How's that? The sheriff was no friend of mine."

"He may not have been a friend, but he was the sheriff. The law. And now with the murderer loose, we're all in danger."

Smoke gazed at her like he could see the skin and bone and thoughts of her, and she felt herself blush from the intimacy.

"The entire town is out looking for him." He didn't know why he felt the need to reassure her, but he did.

She hesitated, waiting for something more; she couldn't say what.

"You should go back to your house and lock your doors."

"What about you? What will you do if you see him?"

Smoke shrugged and glanced around—after the episode with Stanley, he didn't care to have anyone see him talking to Alta.

"What are you working on?" Alta gestured to the small carving in his hand. He'd sheathed or pocketed his knife; it was no longer visible.

Smoke wasn't keen on revealing his handiwork, but for some reason, he relented and held it up.

"May I?" Alta took it from him and examined it. It was a small, delicate tiger, the stripes cut into the bone.

"It's beautiful. You made this?"

He nodded. She looked him in the eye and could see he was pleased by her compliment.

"Well, it's beautiful work . . . Is this a religious item?" She asked because she'd heard some Native American stories, and they were loaded with symbolism. So of course a tiger must be significant.

Smoke shook his head.

"Does it mean something?" She wasn't sure if he understood the question, but of course he did. He didn't feel the need to say that the tiger wasn't in the cultural pantheon of his native tribe, or that among native people, the big cats were as likely to be demonic as they were warriors and leaders. He didn't say that the most notable of the big cats on the reservation where he grew up was the lynx—which helped to bring summer to the Assiniboine people. He liked the tiger because he knew it was fierce.

"Why a tiger?"

"I saw one once. In a circus."

"Well, I've never seen one." Alta passed it back.

"You keep it." He took her hand and cupped it around the carving. His hand around hers was warm and strong.

"Are you sure?"

He hadn't been, but then he was, and he nodded.

"Oh, thank you. I will treasure it." She thought she should say something else, but there was nothing to say.

The brackish crowd in front of the jail caught both their attention. There was a good deal of shouting and pushing, and when the crowd moved just so, they could see a line of men with rifles standing guard. Both Alta and Smoke understood the fugitive had been captured.

"No good can come from that." Alta felt afraid. The gathering violence was palpable.

"You should get home," Smoke said, himself feeling an urgent need to get beyond the range of chomping teeth.

"Yes. And thank you," she said about the tiger. She turned, then spun back to face him.

"Wait," she said, digging in her basket. She pulled out some dollars and held them up.

"I forgot to pay you . . . for the gardening." She pressed the money into his hand and then hurried the short distance across the street. Once inside, she locked the door and closed the curtains. For his part, Smoke retrieved his horse and rode off to spend a couple of days on the prairie, away from the mob. Neither Alta nor Smoke were there when later that night, the riflemen walked away from the jail. The mob broke through the doors and hauled out Jessie Collins. Alta could hear the subsequent celebrations from her house and occasionally glanced through a crack in the curtain, but she didn't see when several men looped a rope around Collins's neck and tied it to the back of a spring wagon. Once secure, the men jumped into the wagon, and the driver drove up and down Main Street, pulling Jessie Collins by the neck until he died. The wagon passengers shouted, and onlookers shot off their guns, and men and women rushed into the street to spit on the corpse, and when everyone got bored and thirsty Jake broke open a barrel and offered free drinks. Musicians set up on the boardwalk, and the town fathers oversaw the hanging of Collins's body from the bowsprit of Bert's Saloon. People tossed rocks or beer at the corpse of Collins, and a few walked up and punched it. When Alta pulled back her curtains, she saw the bouncing lights and a mass of people. It must have been half the town, and there was dancing and laughing and shouting. She huddled inside her house, thinking it sounded like a wedding, but the union was dark.

In the morning, Alta woke to the smell of coffee in the kitchen. Stanley's side of the bed was undisturbed, and she hadn't heard him come in. Maybe he'd just come home. She gazed at the bone tiger so small and elegant on her dresser.

Stanley was cleaning his pistol when she walked into the kitchen.

"We got him," he said, and Alta pulled her wrap a little tighter.

"He had it coming."

Alta turned and fumbled at the stove, firing it up. "You must be tired," she said. "Do you want some breakfast?"

"Yeah," he said. And then he was behind her, wrapping his arms around her waist, and she moved as if he was not.

"You look pretty this morning," he said. She asked if he wanted his eggs fried or up.

"My eggs can wait." He turned her around and she pulled away.

"Please," she said. She moved to a corner of the kitchen.

"Where did you find him?"

"Past the fort. In the brush by the river."

Alta poured them both some coffee and sat down.

Later that morning, Alta took a detour by Bert Steel's Crossbar Saloon. The body was there, a grotesque thing dangling like an enormous eggplant or the purple stump of a tree from a beam hanging off the front of the building. The hands were tied behind the back, and the head bowed as if the corpse was studying its own feet. The skin was grated and bruised and hanging in places like fringe on a coat. What remained of the man's clothes was filthy and shredded. Alta gazed for nearly a minute before she turned around toward the mercantile, suddenly grateful for the distraction of household chores, a place she could retract into, like the shell of a turtle.

CHAPTER 15

ADAM

Unable to sleep, Adam rose early and made coffee, and sat drinking it at the table. The diary and the old car had him thinking about the old days an awful lot. They seemed like colorful times. He'd heard the stories, but they were just that, stories. He wondered what his parents had really been like. What they would have thought of him. He liked to conjure pictures of himself as part of a family, with them doing family things—sitting around the dinner table talking about the day or driving into the country for a picnic. He imagined chopping wood with his father, hunting geese or pheasant, or fishing in the hot days of summer. Stanley, people said, had been mean. But probably people didn't understand him. If he was mean, it was because it was part of the job. Adam could see that. You couldn't be a pushover and do the job Stanley had had to do. He would have been a good father, of that Adam was certain. And his mother. She would have made cookies and breads—Adam could never get enough of baked goods. In his imaginings, she was full of light and good cheer. Sometimes he let himself believe they were coming back. They'd been gone a trip, and any day a car would stop in front of the house and they would jump out, and he would walk out the door and they would be shocked at how much he'd grown and how fast he was becoming a man, and they would say how they were just so glad to see him, and they would rush him with hugs and kisses, and he would be restrained and a bit embarrassed by their devotion and attention.

Wendell rattled into the kitchen, startling Adam out of his reverie. He looked worse than normal, yellow-skinned and bloated, with a lingering cough that shook his entire being.

"You look like hell," Wendell coughed, then stopped to scratch the wiry matting on his chest, and Adam thought of insect legs.

"You're not so pretty yourself."

"I look as good as I'm ever going to look, until you scrub me up and lay me in my coffin."

Wendell poured himself some coffee, then launched into a monologue on the destruction of civilization and the damn Germans while cooking breakfast. "We ought to just blow up the whole damn country," he said, stretching bacon across the fry pan.

"How long you think the war's going to last?" Adam asked, though he wasn't really interested in Wendell's thoughts on the subject. Keeping gas in a car is how he thought of his attempts to distract the old man—the ramblings were the bubbling up of whatever life remained, running through the petrifying bones. Adam clung to these brief moments of clarity and near competence. If the conversation stalled, Wendell was certain to become preoccupied by drinking. By nightfall, he would be an eidolon sweating whiskey.

"Hell if I know." Wendell flipped the eggs.

"I found a diary," Adam blurted, deciding Wendell might be helpful.

"You don't say." Wendell shoved a plate on the table in front of him and a second plate on the table for himself, then stood planted over Adam like a flag pole.

Adam picked up his fork and stabbed the leaky hearts of his eggs.

"In the whorehouse."

Wendell grunted and stuffed a piece of bacon into his mouth.

"It was one of the ladies'. She wanted to marry Stanley."

"They're a conniving bunch."

They ate in silence for a moment, then Wendell paused and stared at the boy. Adam dropped his eyes, uncomfortable.

"You need a haircut," Wendell said, and Adam didn't respond. Wendell kept staring so that Adam started fidgeting and bouncing his leg. He's too pretty, and that's the damn truth, the old man was thinking, with that hair slick and black like a raven's feathers. The boy looked like his mother, but for his hair and his eyes.

"Where the hell did you get those eyes?" Wendell lifted his mug slowly so the shaking in his hand didn't become a jiggling, and the liquid lap-lap-lapped at the rim of his mug. He tilted the mug to drink, and the coffee slapped his upper lip. He set it down in a lurch, and it splattered the table.

"Goddamn," he cussed at the coffee. The kid was staring at him like a circus freak. And the truth was, if the kid hadn't been watching, he would have spilled. That was for sure. "Goddamn! What are you doing here? Don't you have school or something?"

"It's summer."

"Are you sure? Don't you have work? Aren't you working? Goddamn lazy piece of shit," he said, though the boy was far from lazy. But he still had to say it. "Lazy piece of shit."

Adam glared until Wendell turned his attention to his eggs with their yokes bleeding into the rubbery white, as if they might offer a revelation.

"Lola was her name. She wanted to marry Stanley." Adam repeated the line because Wendell didn't seem to be finding the urgency in it.

"They were always after someone."

It turned out Wendell wasn't so hungry—he stood up and picked up his plate. His hand trembled and shook the fork off, and it clinked onto the floor and rattled in his head. He walked the plate to the sink with two hands. And then the shaking was different. Lola. He knew that name! She'd been a bit more worn than most of Josephine's girls and wore her hair piled high. Picturing her brought back something else.

"That Lola was no good," Wendell said. He wished he had a drink. He looked around the room wondering if he had a bottle hidden somewhere.

The conversation wasn't going anywhere, so Adam took a different approach.

"Maybe Stanley was kilt. By the murderer."

Something clicked for Wendell. He could feel the churning of wheels and the dancing. Stanley was dancing, and he flew into the train and the immense sea of prairie fell silent in the wake of the iron beast. And he recalled the laughter and drone of voices carrying on with no regard for the train.

"Stanley was killed by a dad-rat train. Tossed like a rag doll. You know that. Why would you think he was murdered?"

"Who tossed him?" Adam smirked as if he'd found a loop-hole.

"What the hell are you talking about?"

"You said he was tossed. Who tossed him? He couldn't toss himself."

"Jesus. That's an expression. Anyway, it doesn't matter. They're all gone."

It mattered to Adam, though he couldn't say why. It seemed a matter of justice. And that Wendell didn't see it as significant was maddening, so he kept prodding.

"They found his car."

Now he had Wendell's attention.

"The murderer's," Adam said, as if Wendell was an idiot, because he was beginning to think he was. But Wendell still looked at him as if he didn't know what in the hell he was talking about. Wendell, for his part, was wishing the boy would stop rambling.

"Christ, kid. Anyone ever say you talk too much?"

Thinking about it, Wendell could feel the liquor burning down his throat and spreading warmth to his limbs. He sat down and held the edge of the table, trying to capture that feeling, make it stick, to quiet the ringing in his head. He glanced up at the clock on the wall. Too soon. He had hours to kill. He wondered again where he had a stowed bottle.

"They pulled it from the river yesterday. Old Nelson brought a tractor. He just bought it."

Wendell stood up and opened the cupboards and slid the cans around—there was really no place to hide a bottle in an empty kitchen. He looked behind a shelf of empty jars blurry with webs of flour and dust. And then it occurred to Wendell that maybe he had hidden the bottle from himself, and this seemed profound. He turned and reached for his coffee cup on the counter to keep his hands occupied. The liquid splattered as he lifted it to his mouth, but he managed to get a sip. He walked toward the table.

"You don't say . . ."

Setting the cup back on the table felt like a victory lap after a hard-fought race. Wendell and Adam both stared to see if a final wave would wash over the edge, and then Wendell sat.

"Said the murderer stole it and drove it into the river. Probably it was his getaway car. Maybe he murdered Stanley."

Wendell dug through his cavernous memories for a car and then the picture was there in full color.

"You talking about the Winton?"

"Yeah. Jake's car."

"It wasn't a murderer that stole the car." Wendell's mouth moved upward into a smile as he flipped through the pictures.

"They hung him up."

"The murderer? Not for stealing the Winton . . . It wasn't no murderer who stole the Winton."

"That's what people are saying. They pulled the car out yesterday. He stole it a long time ago."

Adam nodded and Wendell's mouth gaped open and a big bellow came out, something alive, and then he was hunched over holding his belly, and he was rocking and laughing. And then he was coughing. He laughed and coughed and coughed. Adam sprung forward to pat his back and Wendell gasped for breath, then went back to chuckling. Adam couldn't help but smile. The old man hit the table with his fist and the coffee leapt, and he hit the table again.

Wendell let out a gasp and straightened up."What?" Adam asked.

"Well, I'll be."

"What?" Adam repeated.

"It wasn't the murderer that drove the car into the river."

Wendell nodded up and down, still echoing with laughter, and Adam waited expectantly.

"Who stole it?"

Wendell burst into laughter again.

"Oh hell," he said, finally coming up for breath. "That was a hell of a thing."

"What? What thing?"

Wendell held up his finger to stop Adam, who was still pushing eggs around on his plate.

"Me and Smoke, we thought we'd take it for a ride. I'd never driven a car before. Didn't know the difference between the brakes and the gas!"

"You were driving?"

"Ah, hell," Wendell said. He dropped his finger in the coffee pooled on the table. "We were going like a bullet by the time we hit the bank, and then we were flying. Jesus Christ, we must have scared the birds. Next thing we knew, we were in the river. You never knew a car could fly, did you, kid?"

"*You* drove it into the river?"

The question pushed Wendell into another round of laughing.

"Did Jake know?"

"What? . . . Jake . . ." Wendell unhinged himself and stood up, teetering to the sink to pick up a rag.

"Jake's a goddamn son of a bitch. Jake had his getting even . . ."

"How do you mean?"

Wendell grasped onto the counter, as if for balance, and then lurched over to the table, swinging the rag.

"What he do?"

"Jesus Christ, kid!" Wendell couldn't land the questions that Adam was asking. His thoughts were flushed grouse, darting skyward.

"How'd he get even?" Adam flipped his eggs with his fork, and they tumbled in a gelatinous piece. He stirred the coagulated yolk.

"Jesus Christ, kid. Don't you have to go to school?"

"You already asked me that."

"What'd you answer?"

Adam stared, and Wendell swiped at the coffee so there was a thin oily trail across the table, and then he made his way back to the sink to drop in the rag, all the while struggling to remember.

"Did Jake know you were driving? How'd he get even?" Adam was looking at Wendell as he poked at his plate. The motion seemed to matter.

"What's this your business for?"

That Wendell was reluctant to say piqued Adam's interest.

"How'd he get even?" he repeated.

"Jake always had it in for Smoke . . . That's a fact."

Wendell stared at the boy, and the boy stared back, and

something of the old days, not so long ago, appeared in the line of his chin, the slight curve of his neck, and the eyelashes long and dark framing those tarry eyes. Those were his eyes. Goddamn! He'd never thought it. Sure, there'd been all sorts of rumors swirling in those days, but then again, everything had been swirling, and sometimes Wendell couldn't remember what was real and what was fiction. The fingers drumming on the table, grasping and releasing the fork, those were his, no doubt about it. Goddamn, he'd never thought it. He shook his head, but he couldn't stop staring at the boy.

"Jesus Christ."

"What?"

"What!" Wendell growled.

"You look strange."

"Funny thing," Wendell said. "You look a little like him . . . If I didn't know better . . ."

"Who? What the hell are you talking about?"

Wendell shook his head, because the idea was growing into something solid in his head. It lodged there like a stone between his ears and then it was the only thing, the only truth.

Wendell turned, remembering the broom closet just off the front door—he remembered sliding a bottle in it once, for a rainy day. He opened the door and the bucket was rusting, and the handle was broken and there was no bottle.

"There's nothing in there," Adam said, but the old man didn't hear him. "I threw it out."

Wendell stopped and stepped toward Adam. "Son of a bitch!"

He stepped toward Adam with a raised arm and the boy sat as if to dare him.

"Have you seen yourself? You don't look nothing like a Viking."

"You're drunk," Adam hissed. He waited for a blow, but it didn't come. Wendell kicked the wall, then slumped in a chair as if the whole epiphany/revelation thing was too much. He felt around in his pocket for money. He pulled the change out and let it roll across the table. There was a dime and several pennies. He looked at Adam expectantly.

"Smoke was a decent fellow. Had a way with horses," Wendell said to the table. "And good at carving . . . did I ever tell you about William Tell?"

"You really are crazy." Adam left, slamming the door.

CHAPTER 16

ALTA

Alta didn't want to wait around for Beverly, so she began working on the laundry just as soon as Lew's assistant dropped off the supplies. She'd never handled a washboard, though she'd seen them in use. She propped the board up in a tub of warm soapy water and gripped it with one hand and used the other to scrub shirts. It was awkward business—the loose cotton repeatedly came unbound, so Alta banged her knuckles on the lumps on the board. She paused to shake the pain from her hand—dear Lord, this was terrible work, she thought—and wondered for the hundredth time if she shouldn't just send the laundry out. And then she glanced up and Beverly was standing in the doorway watching her.

"Oh, goodness," Alta jumped up. "I didn't hear you come in."

"Good morning." Beverly stepped into the house holding out a pie.

"How nice to see you."

"I'm so sorry I haven't been by to welcome you sooner . . . I had to rush out of town for a bit . . . parents . . ."

"Of course . . . Thank you so much for coming." Alta stood up and wiped her hands on her apron, and Beverly set the pie on the kitchen table. "My famous chicken pie."

"It smells delicious."

"It is," Beverly laughed.

"Would you like some tea?"

Alta filled a pot with water and turned on the stove.

"Oh," Beverly said. "You have a pump. In the house!"

"Yes."

"Do you mind?"

Beverly ran her hand over the red cast iron spout and lifted and pushed down the handle. A stream of water splashed into the sink and disappeared down the drain. Alta laughed at her enthusiasm.

When she'd finished testing the pump, Beverly walked around the stove, running her hands over the nobs and edges, then turned to the shelves and cupboards.

"Look at this kitchen. Stanley thought of everything. That's a fact." She picked up the eggbeater and turned the handle, then set it down. Alta poured the tea into cups and sat at the table, watching the other woman.

"What a mess that was last night . . ." Beverly said about the lynching. She sat down and toyed with the handle of her cup. "I didn't see the point in dragging him through the street. Five wagon loads of fellows from Medicine Lake got here before the new sheriff. That's when the deputies walked away from the jail. It was that or be killed."

"Asphodel."

Beverly looked at her, confused.

"From a book, *The Odyssey*. Near the gate to the underworld. Odysseus was swarmed by the dead. It reminded me of that. The lynching."

"Well. I don't know if I'd call it a lynching. He was a murderer. He had it coming. He could have killed any one of us."

"Of course." Alta adjusted the handle on her cup so it was exactly perpendicular to the edge of the table, then pulled it several inches closer.

Beverly turned to the tubs of water, anxious to change the subject.

"Did you soak it?"

"I'm sorry?"

"The laundry. Did you soak it?"

"Oh . . . No."

"You should soak it overnight. It loosens the stains . . . I hope you don't mind . . . I'm quite an expert," she laughed. "With Lew in the business he's in, I have access to the most up-to-date equipment and knowledge. And you were raised different from most of the ladies around here. That's nothing to be ashamed of."

"Well, I would certainly appreciate your help and advice." Alta watched the dregs float along the edge of the liquid at the bottom of her cup.

"You need to organize yourself, my dear." Beverly stood up and started working her way around the kitchen. "Towels next to where you do the dishes." She moved the stack of towels to the shelf next to the sink.

"Of course. That makes perfect sense." Alta nodded enthusiastically.

"Pots on the shelf by the stove. Save your steps. And set up a schedule." Beverly stood in front of Alta with her hands on her hips.

"This is important. Cleanliness is next to godliness, you know. And a wife has certain responsibilities . . ."

"Of course."

"Organize. Everything has its day . . . Prepare your laundry on Monday. Sort and soak." Beverly then showed Alta how to adjust the dampers and flues and kindling on the stove properly to heat up water, something she'd been doing less adeptly. "You have to work twice as hard at scrubbing if you don't soak. Soak on Monday, wash on Tuesday, iron on Wednesday, clean your house on Thursday . . . You can learn this."

They emptied the tubs and refilled them with warm, clean water, and Beverly showed Alta how to drain the water off the soaking clothes and cover the clothes with hot water and soap, and then transfer the washing to another tub with hot, sudsy water where she would scrub the clothing and linens and then ring out the washing. If there were remaining stains, Beverly showed Alta how to soap up and scrub the stains, then boil and stir the washing on the stove, then rinse the clothes, and then she must blue the whites, then dip the washing that needed starching into starch, and then wring the washing out and hang it to dry.

They worked for several hours, and Alta was hot and tired and her back ached and her hands were sore, and she supposed she should be pleased with her progress but didn't feel it at all.

"It seems silly, doesn't it?"

"What?" Beverly poured a bucket of foul water into the sink and watched it disappear, just like that.

"All this for clean skirts."

"Well, they're not going to clean themselves . . . It takes the time it takes. The work it takes."

"There are just a few items that would be better in the hands of a professional . . . Don't you think? And probably those ladies need the money or they wouldn't be offering their services."

"I don't think that would hurt at all . . . You poor thing. Whatever did you do with your time growing up?" Beverly seemed genuinely curious.

"Lots of lessons," Alta quipped. She didn't feel like talking about it. "More tea?" Alta filled the kettle from the pump. "I appreciate the help. I do . . . I have seen futures destroyed by a stain on a dress."

Beverly was tired too, at that point, and happy to take a seat.

"How is that possible?"

"A woman, Eva, was to appear at a Christmas ball where the young man she was to be engaged to also appeared—he was the son of flour baron, a friend of my father's—very handsome and successful. They had been courting for months, and she'd turned down numerous proposals expecting to marry Henry. That was his name. Everyone expected an announcement any day. On the night of the ball, Eva wore her most beautiful gown, a gorgeous green velvet that perfectly matched her eyes. But as she was drinking a glass of punch early in the evening, someone bumped her. The punch spilled all down the front of her dress, so of course she had to leave and change. By the time she returned, in a not-so-beautiful gown, the young man had taken up with another woman, the daughter of an industrialist who was visiting from out east. Henry ended up marrying this other woman. Eva was a little bit older, and the suitors she had turned down had married other women. As far as I know, she never ended up marrying. She's an old maid."

"All because of a glass of punch."

"A glass of punch."

"That was potent punch," Beverly said, and then laughed, realizing she'd made a joke, because she rarely joked. They sat in the afterglow of good humor, and the kitchen felt lighter.

"Mary was right," Beverly said, noticing how Alta held her teacup so delicately and how she sat with her spine so straight. "You should organize something for the ladies. We could benefit from some culture."

"A chicken pie social? I'm not sure . . ."

"No. Of course not. A salon, like she said."

"Oh, I don't know . . . The women I've met don't seem so interested in literature . . ."

"Maybe not. We could use a little culture . . . Lew told me Mrs. Olson bought a copy of the *Ladies' Home Journal*. And I can tell you that Frances never bought a magazine before you came into town. That's a fact. You've inspired them. And every one of them could use a little livening up. They'll come, because they won't want to be left out. And maybe they'll learn something. It never hurts anyone to learn something new."

"I will think about it," Alta said. Thinking about the idea brought back some of her usual enthusiasm.

"I could help you . . . I am good at organizing."

Alta laughed.

"I know you are." She gestured to the finished laundry, and Beverly laughed too.

XXX

Several weeks later, Mondak celebrated the Fourth of July with a dance. This was an event Alta had been anticipating—it was the biggest social event of the year. She and Stanley arrived early, and they were the most fabulous-looking couple on the dance floor, by all accounts. She wore a layered violet gown Greta had ferreted into her traveling chest, and he wore a double-breasted waistcoat. All eyes were on them when they floated into the ballroom of the Mondak Hotel, which pleased Stanley. He felt it appropriate for someone of his growing status. The two had been there only a few minutes before he noticed a gathering of businessmen near the beverage table and excused himself to make his presence known.

"I'm going to get some punch."

"Is everything OK?"

He didn't respond but left Alta in a chair along the wall, and he didn't stop at the punch table but went out the door because the businessmen were going across the street to Montana. Alta waited for what seemed to be a long time in the sweltering ballroom, but then her dress was sticking and she could hardly breathe in the stagnant air, so she accepted a cup of punch from the punch table and made her way to the boardwalk. There was a crowd outside of each of the bars along Main Street and a stream of people flowing back and forth between them and the hotel, but she didn't see Stanley.

She walked north enjoying the sweetgrass breeze and the long light casting off the bejeweled sky—it was late, but the days were forever this time of year. She paused at the end of the boardwalk to gaze upon what seemed to be the edge of civilization, buildings scattered like tossed dice on the waves of gold-crowned grassland; roads and paths snaking between and around rises of earth too small to be called hills; and beyond that, an eternity of space. A warm gust rippled the grass and felt good on her skin. She hadn't realized she was tense, but she was. Here, however, she could breathe. She closed her eyes and inhaled and her lungs filled with the warm smells of summer, and the tightness started to leave her body. Here, she thought, opening her eyes and looking across the starlit prairie, is where the wind lives. The wind and time, she supposed—though she would never have previously thought this—would wipe this slate of prairie clean and scatter the remains of the town like leaves, and who would remain to mourn the loss? The wind didn't give a damn for either the living or the dead. She too, would one day be a scattering of dust. She would sink with the township, and the wind would blow and the grass would grow. She felt a ripple inside herself, like she too was wind. And then she chastised herself. These were morbid thoughts, not worthy of someone like her. And when had she become so serious?

She turned to go back to the dance where people were clustered like tomato vines. From the corner of her eye, she saw someone break away and switch back toward her. Smoke, she noted as he came closer. He was good and drunk and his face had softened into something like pudding. He wore a big, loose smile—had she ever seen him smile? It was a warm and mischievous look and made her heart leap.

"Hello. How are you?"

He pointed his finger at her.

"White Duck," he said. "Little White Duck."

Alta turned around to see where he was pointing.

"You," Smoke said to clarify. He was standing in front of her now. "You're Little White Duck." He'd seen her standing there, at the edge of the world, like she could take flight, and he needed to convey this to her, but she thought it was an insult.

"I don't think name-calling is necessary."

Smoke could see he hadn't made his point and was searching for the words.

"It's a good name."

"I don't see how it could be."

"There are stories. Duck raises the world from the bottom of the ocean." He smiled and knew better than to mention that there were stories in which Duck was a fool. And he didn't mention Duck was the name of his brother—he wasn't naming her after his brother. He was acknowledging something about her. Her displacement, which made her seem familiar.

"Well, then, I thank you." Alta walked toward the hotel, and he walked beside her.

He must have had more than he thought to drink, because he was flirting. "You look pretty . . . Were you at the dance?"

"Yes. It's nice. You should come in."

"You think so?"

"Well, only if you want to, of course."

"Would you dance with me?"

"Well . . ." she said. Of course she couldn't. Stanley would get angry. She gripped the railing to keep her balance.

"You think I'm a dancer?" He did a little jig and she laughed.

A hand clamped Alta on the arm, squeezing hard, causing

her to jump.

"What do you think you're doing?" Stanley hissed into her ear. Alta tried to pull her arm free, but he was squeezing too hard.

"I was talking, Stanley," she said. "Let me go. You're hurting me!"

She glanced toward the now-empty street as Stanley pulled her violently back to the dance hall. They stumbled inside and pasted on their most charming smiles, and Alta did her best to appear normal.

"Could you get me some punch, dear?" she asked in a syrupy voice loud enough for the ladies nearby to hear. "I am so very thirsty."

Stanley was still gripping her arm, but at her request released her—he didn't want to make a scene. Alta rubbed her arm and watch him charm the women at the punch table, feeling a wave of fury and indignation at the injustice of his behavior. He returned with her drink. "We should go," he said, and once again grabbed her.

"She's not feeling well," Stanley said to Beverly and Lew, who were standing by the door as they exited.

"Oh, dear," Beverly said. "Is everything all right?"

"A bit of a headache," Alta said. "Nothing some rest won't cure."

"Well, I do hope you feel better soon."

Stanley kept his grip on her, and when she stumbled into the dry, rutted street, his grip kept her from falling.

"That Indian is up to no good. That's a fact," he said. "He's a goddamn lying, cheating son of a bitch."

"You're hurting me."

"You're goddamn lucky I don't hurt you," he hissed.

They passed several men talking about heading down to Josephine's. Stanley couldn't make out all that they were saying, but he heard one of them mention Lola, which distracted him.

"You don't want to be seen associating with that Indian," Stanley mumbled, straining to catch the men's conversation. "You have to think of your reputation." He squeezed her arm for emphasis and repeated that the Indian was up to no good. "Give him an inch, he'll take a mile," but he'd lost interest in reprimanding his wife. He was picturing Lola slipping out of her dress like she was sliding through water. And then he pictured her standing with her breasts hanging heavy, and he could feel the weight of them in his hands. He had a premonition—one of those assholes screwing her, and he thought, no fucking way. He imagined the blanched moon of Lola bent over the bed and his hand sliding to the warm place between her legs as he rushed Alta into the house. He nearly shoved her through the door, so she stumbled and almost fell but caught herself. She turned around, expecting him to launch at her. Instead, he stayed in the doorway.

"I have something to take care of," he said, and yanked the door shut as he left. It vibrated long after his feet receded from the steps.

Alta sat on the couch shaken and relieved, then had her own premonition—about Smoke. If Stanley found him, he would harm him. Kill him, even. He just might.

CHAPTER 17

ADAM

Wendell is a crazy son of a bitch, is what Adam thought later that morning when he was saddling up Lady. The horse bloated a bit, so he paused before tightening the cinch to give her a moment to relax. He felt a resolve. He was off to visit Mrs. Lund again, and he was going to prove to Jake he was up to the task. He was not going to be pushed around by a little old lady. And more than that, he wasn't going to be pushed around by Jake.

Adam rode away from the livery with the rifle strapped across his saddle, going over what was coming in his mind, thinking of all the possible scenarios. Mrs. Lund would be ready for him this time. She was old, but she was fierce. That she'd shown. And she was wily. They all were. These old ladies could see inside you and read your thoughts. But he wasn't going to let her get to him.

He moved Lady into an easy trot. Maybe she'd gotten a gun. She'd use it, no doubt about it. That he could tell. He could see her standing in the doorway, barrel aimed at his head. Well, then, she'd give him no choice. He picked the rifle off the pommel of his saddle and aimed it at some bushes.

"Bam!" he shouted, then pointed it at another clump. "Bam! Bam!"

Of course, there was the chance she wouldn't aim a gun at him but would just refuse to move. What then? He couldn't physically drag her out of the house, could he? Is that when you shoot? He wasn't certain of the rules. This last bit was complicated. He chewed on the inside of his mouth and scanned the horizon for the tiger—you never know where it could be. There hadn't been a sighting in days.

It was hot, even this early in the day, and he lifted his hat to get a breeze on his sweaty head, then set it back and wiped his forehead. When he came over the rise, the house was smaller and more dilapidated than he'd remembered. He approached slowly. He wasn't going to fail in his mission. It was her fault she hadn't kept up the loan payments. She'd broken the contract. He was just enforcing the law when it came down to it. The thought made him feel riled. By God, he would see her off the property. Probably Jake would make him his right-hand man. Just like Stanley had been. He'd practically promised it. He had other jobs, he'd said, if Adam got this right. Good-paying jobs, not the shit jobs Adam had been doing. The thought of it made Adam proud. Everyone in town would know who he was. They'd stand aside when he walked down the boardwalk. Adam pictured it all, the men nodding their heads, the women smiling shyly. He'd be somebody.

He thought again about the fact that Jake had always relied on him. Jake must have seen something in him from the beginning. The thought made Adam sit up taller.

Just like the last time, the dog came charging out of the house followed by Mrs. Lund, looking small and old. She didn't have a gun. She just stood in her filthy dress with her thin gray hair blowing around her sodden face.

"I knew you'd be back," she said in a drooping tone that disarmed him and made him feel small.

"I'm just doing my job," he said defensively.

"I know you are." She dipped into the house and came back

with a halter, then slid between the bars of the corral to put it on the cow.

"Jake said to leave the cow."

"He did, did he?" She didn't look at him and went about her business. "You might consider getting yourself a different job," she said, once the halter was on. She slipped through the fence and back into the house and came out with a bundle, which she strapped to the cow.

Adam watched nervously, not sure what to do. She was supposed to leave the cow, Adam was certain of that. Collateral, is what Jake had called it. But she clearly intended to take it with her. This was a conundrum. He wasn't going to be Jake's right-hand man this way.

"You need to leave that," he said again. His voice was pleading, but she went right about her business. He couldn't very well shoot her, not like this. It would be different if she had a gun pointed at him.

"You need to leave the cow," he said, but she didn't seem to hear. He felt in his pocket. He had some money. He carried it with him because it wasn't safe in the house. Wendell would find it for sure and drink it down. He pulled out the wad of cash and counted it out. Thirty-seven dollars and forty-three cents.

"I'll buy it." He flashed the fistful of cash.

"Give me a hand," she said, pulling the railing loose from the corral. She didn't have a real gate. She just tied the railings up over a section with twine string.

"I'll buy the cow," he said. He had dismounted and was thrusting the cash at her.

She looked at him, startled.

"What's that for?"

"The cow. I'll buy the cow."

"That's too much money." Her face had softened. "It's an old cow."

Adam shook his head and pushed the money into her palm. It was more important to get the job done to Jake's standards. He couldn't go back a failure.

She took the money and handed him the lead, and then she gathered up her bundle.

"Rags," she said, and the dog followed her as she walked back toward town.

Turned out Adam was going the same way, so he took the cow's lead and mounted Lady and followed Mrs. Lund toward Mondak. She was faster than he'd have thought, and the cow matched her pace, so there was no way around walking together, which was awkward. Adam got fidgety thinking of something to say.

"Where you going to go?" he asked. It was the only thing that came to mind. Then it occurred to him that she might really have no place to go. She was too old and broken down to do much work. A horse or dog in her condition would be shot, put out of its misery. But here she was, tromping into Mondak with thirty-seven dollars and forty-three cents and a bundle of clothes.

"I don't know. Maybe Williston."

"Do you have family there?"

"A nephew. Maybe he'll let me stay."

"Well, you hold on to that money. Don't let anyone know you have it." It made him feel grownup saying such a thing, even though she didn't respond.

"When did you last see your nephew?"

"About two years ago."

"Do you know he's still there?"

"No."

"Well, what if he's not there?"

She dropped her bundle and Adam dismounted to pick it up and hand it to her.

"What will you do if he's not there?"

"I'll worry about that then," she said without turning to look at him.

She really was a frail thing, probably a hundred, he realized. Maybe older. The skin on her arms was like tissue paper, covered in spots. Gosh, if she got poked by a tree it would tear. An old lady like that should be living with her family, drinking tea and making pies, not starting a new life in a city with some nephew she hadn't seen in two years, Adam thought, and the thinking made him depressed.

They split ways as they approached town. She walked to the train station and he to the livery. He turned the cow loose in the corral and threw it some hay before unsaddling Lady. Jake came by as he was brushing out the horse, looking pleasantly surprised.

"Everything went OK."

Adam nodded.

"Did she give you much trouble?"

"Nah. She was fine," Adam said. He felt irritated with Jake; he couldn't say why. He stood behind Lady, slightly to the side to avoid potential kicking, and combed through her golden tail.

Jake reached into his pocket and pulled out a five. He studied it a bit before handing it to Adam.

"I thought she'd give you some trouble," he said.

Adam shrugged and stuffed the money into his pocket, tossing the tail comb into a basket.

"Thank you," he said, figuring he had to start acting like a right-hand man. But he couldn't look the big man in the eye. He opened a stall and led Lady into it, shutting the gate after the horse while Jake watched, then he hung the lead on a hook on the wall and nodded. Jake was watching him. He hadn't moved.

"See ya," Adam said, then stuffed his hands in his pockets and clutched the five as he walked from the barn. Sure, he'd lost thirty-two dollars and forty-three cents, but it was an investment, he told himself, as if he needed convincing.

He walked back down Main Street and picked a whiskey bottle from the railing of a bar, thinking what easy targets the cowboys were once they got to drinking, then made his way back to the livery with the bottle and climbed into the loft, knowing Jake would never catch him because he was too fat to climb up. Adam lay back in the hay and had a drink, thinking how he'd shown him.

CHAPTER 18

SMOKE

Later in the evening the night of the dance, Stanley's mood had lightened. He rattled down Main Street on the way home from Josephine's, the steering wheel throbbing in his hands—Goddamn this car was a remarkable machine! Jake had it all, no doubt about it. Several oil lamps lit the boardwalk, and the few farmers and trainmen and workers from the camp that still roamed had taken to shouting and occasionally throwing their fists in the street—it was that time of night. Lola had been in good spirits—she was really something—thank God for whores, he thought to himself. Lord knows what would become of men if they were stuck with nothing but wives. Now Alta . . . innocent is what she is, he thought, feeling generous. He'd called her a fool to Lola, but you could say anything to a sporting woman. It didn't matter. And Lola had liked hearing it. She was jealous of Alta, which made Stanley chuckle. A jealous whore was a hardworking whore . . .

Alta was probably wondering where he was. Let her wonder, he thought. She was a good-looking woman, no doubt about it, but damn if she wasn't dumb as a post when it came to the way things were. This marriage thing, it made him wonder. Of course his marriage would pay soon enough—Alta's father wasn't going to live forever; he was already ancient. Any day he'd cease and she—meaning Stanley—would inherit his fortune. There was no way Cadwallader would keep Alta from it—he had no one else, and he wasn't a monster, completely. It was just a matter of patience. But what the hell was she doing flirting with the Indian? This thought charged up from somewhere and stuck in his throat like a thundercloud, and he had to pull the car over to dislodge it. What the fuck was the matter with her? Spoiled, that's what she was. He'd have to teach her, that's what he would do . . . one thing at a time . . . He was thinking these thoughts while his eyes drilled down on a horse standing with its hind leg cocked and its head hanging, though he wasn't really seeing the horse. He was seeing rage. And then, low and behold he saw him, holding onto a railing like he was holding on for his life. Drunk as hell, that was for sure.

"Well fuck me," Stanley mumbled to himself. "It's as if God answers prayers." He drove the car up the road a bit more, then shut it down and got out.

For his part, Smoke had a picture of the livery stuck in his head—he'd been sneaking in at night to sleep there even though Jake had outlawed it, because it was warm and comfortable and Wendell often had a bottle of something or other to share. So he was walking and grabbing at the railing because the road kept lifting up beneath him, and the sky was shaking, just a little. He stumbled and straightened himself up, and he heard the rattle but didn't pay it much mind. A light bounced on the road coming from behind and landed just in front of his feet, and he thought it a most amazing little sun. As for the shouting and scurrying, these things were part of the texture of evening and so didn't penetrate his thoughts. Instead, he focused on the road. And then his arms were yanked. They grabbed him beneath his arms and lifted him, he couldn't see who, and they pulled. He kicked like hell and twisted, and they were carrying him somewhere, he couldn't tell where. His head was pressed into someone's chest, and he could hear a heart thundering and smell several days' work. And then they pushed him upright and shoved him down a ramp and he stumbled and fell, sinking into a lake, cold and greasy. He couldn't breathe. He kicked up from the bottom gasping, and it was oily and smelled like shit or garlic and tasted like metal. His foot connected solid on the bottom and he could stand. He was in the dipping vat, he saw when he straightened up and wiped the sludge from his eyes. Several men stood looking over the edge at him, looming shadows with their guns. Stanley was one of them; he could hear his voice.

"Goddamn stupid son-of-a-bitch Indian," Stanley said, and he fired his pistol real close so the oil splattered.

Smoke was clearheaded now. He lunged toward the wall and one of the cowboys fired a shot, and so he stood there in the middle and tried to devise a plan, unmoving because he knew if he moved they would shoot. And so that's how it was. He was shaking; he couldn't help it because it was so damn cold. And it was dark. The moon had gone into hiding. He stood—he didn't know for how long, but Stanley was getting bored. He picked up a handful of rocks and tossed them at Smoke, and a couple hit him in the head. And then the other men were tossing rocks, and Smoke sank low into the oil and backed up. He was lucky, he told himself, because they were drunk and their aims were off.

"What's going on there?" There was some talk behind Stanley, and then more men looked down on him. They laughed and someone else took a shot and someone threw a rock and this one made his head ring when it hit him. Then they were pelting him from all sides and he sank below the surface for as long as he could, then came up gasping for breath.

"Ah, come on. Let him go. He's had enough."

"He's had enough when I've said he's had enough," Stanley

said.

"Jesus Christ let him go." Smoke thought he recognized Clem's voice in the gathering crowd, and then he sank below the surface again and oily water lapped at his ears. A rock pelted him on the head. When he rose, Clem was still talking.

"Why don't you take me for a ride in your automobile?" He was creating a distraction, Smoke thought, feeling grateful.

"It's Jake's automobile," someone—not Stanley—replied.

"Hell it is," Stanley said.

"Give me a ride."

Smoke waited as the attention drifted away from him to the automobile parked down the street. When the voices had receded, he lunged up the cement ramp of the vat and ran as fast as he could though he was cold and stiff and sticky as hell and his head ached as much from the smell as the rocks.

"Jesus Christ," Wendell said when he made it to the barn. "What the hell happened to you?"

Smoke didn't answer, and so Wendell found him some rags and a bar of soap and carried a bucket of clean water in from the pump.

"G. Rover Cripes," Wendell said as he watched Smoke scrub himself. He went into the tack room and found a pint he had hidden on a shelf behind some saddle blankets.

"You're going to need this," he said, handing it to Smoke. "Holy tarnation . . . Someone's got it out for you . . . Hell . . . it ain't right . . . It just ain't right. Some son of a bitch has hell to pay . . ."

Smoke handed Wendell the bottle and he took a swig; it helped him think, and he needed to think, so he took another swig.

"Who the hell did this to you?"

When Smoke didn't answer, Wendell took another swig and handed the bottle back to Smoke.

"Who the hell did this?"

Smoke took several long swallows of whiskey.

"Son of a bitch," Wendell said, because he knew. "He's a goddamn shit-ass son of a bitch," he said, and the two sat for a long time drinking and thinking about the truth of Wendell's statement, and they thought they would get him back, they just had to wait for the chance.

CHAPTER 19

ADAM

A jab in the ribs woke Adam from his stupor. He opened his eyes and felt another sharp kick in the ribs and lurched into sitting.

"What the hell are you doing here?"

Glen, the stable hand, was staring down at him, a middle-aged reedy man with a couple of weeks of beard.

Adam was unable to speak; he had what felt like a wad of sandpaper in his mouth and his head was like a lead ball.

"You better get yourself home and cleaned up."

Adam took a moment to gather his wits. Slabs of light shone through the cracks in the roof of the barn, and there was a small stack of hay and another of straw. Jake had better start stocking up, he thought to himself, then glanced down. He'd thrown up in the night—the straw beside him was full of vomit, and he had some on his shirt.

"I don't feel so well." He sounded sheepish. He felt sheepish.

"I bet you don't."

Glen's face had softened into something more sympathetic. He was a decent fellow, a little soft in the head maybe—he'd been kicked a time or two by a horse—and he and Adam, while not exactly friends, were on friendly terms. Glen wasn't much for talking. He showed up to feed and muck out the stalls of what few horses Jake kept around, and sometimes he'd rub down Jake's car to make it shine. And he'd dilly dally in the tack room cleaning gear. But mostly he hung out at the barn because he didn't seem to have any place else to be. And Adam was often passing through on his way to one job or another off-site, so they rarely did more than nod.

Adam stood up slowly, then waited for the loft to stop spinning.

"You had yourself quite a night, by the looks of it."

"I guess."

"I'm not going to say anything to Jake."

Adam hadn't expected he would.

"I appreciate that."

"Hair of the dog?" Glen shoved a bottle at Adam and Adam pushed it away.

"Nah."

He found the top of the ladder and twisted around so he could manage the climb down.

"You be back later?" Glen called down as Adam's foot hit the barn floor.

"I don't know. Maybe."

The walk home seemed eternal. The sun was low in the east already sizzling up the town, though there was still that morning fresh smell to the air.

When he pushed open the front door, the house was quiet. Adam cleaned himself off and threw his dirty clothes in a pile in the corner of his room, then lay in his bed. Eventually, he reached beneath the bed and pulled out the diary.

The Diary

January 3

I was no more drunk last night than a preacher giving a Sunday morning sermon.

What do you expect? The filthy punters have never heard of a bath. Alice said I should lay off, that Josephine has her eye on me. To hell with Josephine. She's running this place like a convent.

January 14

Kentucky T. was drunk with a knife acting foolish and belligerent and Stanley hauled him out by his collar. I thought for a minute he was going to shoot a hole in him right then and there.

January 16

Well, old Snake (Daisy, rest in peace, gave him that name because of his beady eyes) froze to death in the privy. Went out to relieve himself and never came back. We thought he wandered off home. Sheriff said they'd have to thaw him out before they could bury him.

Adam sat up and adjusted himself until he could find a comfortable position, then flipped through the book until he found a section about the women crying. Why were they crying? He turned the pages until he got to what seemed like the beginning of this particular episode.

November 27

Daisy came crying to my room in the middle of the night. Said she is in the family way. Stupid girl! I had to get her drunk so she could sleep. Josephine's going to kick her out, no doubt about it. Babies are bad for business.

November 28

I was right about Daisy, but it doesn't make me feel much like working. Daisy said she'd get rid of the problem, and Josephine said she'd call the woman she knows. Last time Daisy bled a lot, so now she's panicked. I don't blame her. My second time I got an infection. It's a hell of a price to pay to keep working in this racket, which is why I'm going to find me a husband and get out of it for good. Or maybe I'll take over Josephine's job one day. That's not such a hard life . . .

December 14

Today is a dark day. We buried Daisy down by the river because they wouldn't let us put her in the cemetery. She died on Saturday. Doc said it was an infection. We took turns bathing her to cool her down and sitting up with her, and then the girls told her we were planning a party. They weren't planning a party, but they thought it might give her something to look forward to.

December 15

Josephine shut down the house for the night because everyone's crying and no one feels like working. They've been banging on the door, but Josephine tells them to come back tomorrow. Jake brought his partner. He's a nice young man with plenty of ambition. People say he has a wife, but I haven't seen her.

CHAPTER 20

ALTA

The night after the dance, Alta lay in bed listening to the revelry that went on late into the night. She must have eventually drifted off, because she was startled from her sleep by a crash in the front room. He must be really drunk, she thought as she listened to Stanley bump around the house. He flung open the bedroom door and ricocheted from one wall to another. She made herself small in the bed.

"Stanley?"

He mumbled something, and his voice was sludge.

"Stanley? Are you all right?" She sat up.

She didn't recognize the tumbleweed of hair that appeared in the moonlight flickering through the window.

"Who's there!" he shouted, a stranger's voice.

"Stanley?" She pulled the covers up like armor.

"Hey lady!" The man raised up his hands. "Christ Almighty."

"Get out! Get out!"

"Christ Almighty! What are you doing here?"

"This is my house! Get out!"

"Goddamn." He stood startled and confused. "I didn't mean!" He turned and crashed against the bureau, then out of the room, cussing as he went. She could hear him crash into the kitchen table before he banged out the front door, which was swinging when Alta rushed after him. She pulled the door shut and locked it. She leaned against the door trembling and trying to catch her breath, eventually moving to the sofa where she wrapped herself in a blanket and watched the door, waiting for Stanley to come home, with the broom at her side, which was hardly a security system, but it was something.

The next morning, Beverly stopped by early to check on her.

"You and Stanley left the dance in such a hurry, I was worried."

She hovered over Alta, clutching a tin covered with a towel in her hands, and cluck-clucked her tongue. Alta was still in her nightgown in a nest of blankets on the couch, her eyes both sleepy and wild. "Dear girl, you look terrible."

"Is that pie?" Alta straightened her posture and patted her hair, self-conscious.

"Chokecherry. I'll just set it in the kitchen."

Beverly took care of the pie then sat next to Alta and took her hand. "Now tell me. What's going on? Are you sick? Do you have a fever?" She brushed her hand across Alta's forehead.

Alta told her about the intruder.

"Oh, my goodness. Did he hurt you?" Beverly patted Alta's hand.

Alta shook her head and wiped her eyes with a handkerchief—talking about it resurrected the incident.

"A reveler who lost his way. That must have been terrifying. And Stanley? Where was he?" Beverly asked, though she was pretty sure she knew. The red-light district was a bad habit for too many men around town. When Alta's silence confirmed her suspicions, she clucked her tongue some more and shook her head.

"I don't know. I just don't know," she said, more to the

room than to Alta, then gave Alta's hand some more pats, as if agitating the appendage would somehow invite an answer. *What was wrong with that man, anyway?* was what she wanted to say. And what's to be done? He was going to do what he was going to do. Lew, thank heavens, didn't wander to that part of town.

"Sometimes, I don't know if this town was a good idea." She gave Alta's hand a squeeze, then cupped it in both her hands and gave it a small shake. Alta pulled her hand away and clasped it in her lap.

"You sit. I'll make some tea."

Beverly banged around in the kitchen. "It's going to be a hot one. Already you could cook an egg on a rock. Even Lew has had a hard time sleeping in this heat wave, and he could sleep next to a train."

Alta nodded, though of course Beverly couldn't see her.

"We could use some rain. That's what they're saying . . ." Beverly continued on about something, and Alta stared at the armchair opposite her, a cheap likeness of one from her father's house.

Beverly came to stand in the kitchen doorway to better talk while the water boiled. "Too many out-of-towners. They come in and blow all their money in the bars and make a mess of everything. It's good for business, mind you. I'm not complaining. But if they break a window, they ought to pay for it."

"Of course," Alta flashed her a smile. "I would hope that would be the case." Beverly dipped back into the kitchen and Alta wondered if they weren't all out-of-towners, considering the town was but a dream two years ago. Was the stranger from last night an out-of-towner, she wondered, and did it matter where he came from if he'd done what he'd done?

"Oh, dear, you are a mess," Beverly had come into the room carrying two cups of tea and saw the tears leaking down Alta's cheek.

"I'm sorry. It's just nerves, I'm sure." Alta dabbed her face with a handkerchief.

Beverly sat next to her again and did some more hand patting, but this did nothing to plug the fissure.

"Listen, dear. I have something that might help. It will calm your nerves."

"Oh, I'll be quite all right."

"You go get yourself dressed, and I'll be back in no time." Beverly stood up and wiped her hands on her skirt. The front door teetered back and forth after she had gone.

In Beverly's absence, Alta recalled the stranger from the previous evening. She had so narrowly escaped what danger, she thought, imagining all sorts of scenarios, each one equally terrifying, so that by the time Beverly returned, she was even more worked up.

"You need to rest." Beverly gave her a bottle of laudanum and explained the dosage.

"Everything looks better when you're rested." There was more hand patting.

When Beverly had gone, the anxiety condensed into something heavy and dark and spidered along her spine. Blood crashed in her skull with each beat of her heart, and she struggled for breath. Finally, she stood up, as if in water, and waded into the kitchen where she managed to give herself the prescribed dosage of laudanum. It had an almost immediate, transformative effect, like a warm light filling her.

When she awoke, a sliver of light sliced through the curtains and lay on the floor near the interior wall. She sat up, disoriented. Was it morning or evening? She couldn't tell. How long had she slept? What day was it? She searched the shadows, but they didn't provide an answer, and when she looked outside, there was plenty of activity. The bars were busy, so it was probably late afternoon. As she watched, the memory came creeping back, swarming her skin. She rubbed her arms as if to brush it away. Where was Stanley? Had he returned? He'd not been to bed, but then again, he wouldn't come to bed in the day—had she simply slept through the day? What if he didn't come back? . . . Had he left for good?

Alta decided to get her act together. It's Wednesday, she thought, and felt certain, though she had no way of knowing. She should do something useful. Get to work—it would calm her nerves. Wednesday was ironing day. Alta dressed and made her way to the kitchen where she turned on the stove to heat the irons. What would she do if Stanley were to truly leave? she wondered, still a bit off-kilter. She had no money, or at least not enough to keep her for long . . . That thought set off her nerves. She noted the laudanum on the table and thought just a little bit would help. She took some, then folded and spread a blanket across the kitchen table, then retrieved a clean shirt. She shook water from the tiny broom bristles over the shirt to moisten it. She would go home if he didn't return. She would plead her case with her father and apologize, and say that she'd seen the error of her ways. She wondered if her father would take her back. He could be a hard man. But she was his only immediate family. Was their rift so expansive that he would turn her away? She set the iron on the stove and detached the handle.

The light outside was fading. Alta was tired—she justified the indulgence. She turned on the lamp and went to the front door to check the lock and considered moving a chair to lean against it, but then, what if Stanley came home? His delinquency was maddening.

She prepared some tea and sat down, determined to get a hold of herself. She could go back to Minnesota now. Not tonight of course, but soon. She didn't have to stay. The thought gave her strength, lightened her mood. She would swallow her pride, plead her case to Cadwallader. He was not a cruel man. Of course he'd take her back.

She took another dose of laudanum so she could get through the night. She couldn't possibly sleep otherwise . . . There were so many clothes. Were the ones she was ironing even clean? The piles were looming, blooming, lifting like a giant wave threatening to break over her . . .

She went to the window and the sun slid down the gullet of the sky, and up and down the street men were coming and going from the saloons. Across the street, someone saw her in the window and waved, and she let the curtain drop and peeked out the other window, through the smallest slit in the curtain. She was trapped in this house like an animal, like a sacrifice. And then she saw Smoke in a shadow near the Tumbleweed, and she wanted to call out to him, and she did, in a quiet way, but her voice was trapped in the glass of the window, and when she looked again, he was gone. Had she dreamed him? A brawl began in the street. Inside, the walls arched and stretched as if they might lay upon her, as if she were the bed.

She took another dose of Beverly's tincture for courage and to calm her nerves, and then she set out to find Smoke. She needed to find him and tell him something. She couldn't recall what. And he would help her. She felt a glow of pleasure—he was a friend. As she made her way over the hard dirt road, the stars descended and danced along the edge of her forearm and the back of her neck before tumbling off and across the pale hide of prairie. Each star had its own delicate chime so that as she drifted, her feet moved on clouds and she was bathed in the song of a bell choir, and the air parted before her as if she were a prophet and rushed behind her to fill her wake. She placed her hand on her head to keep it from lifting off, but still, she suspected, it was hovering.

She made it to the barn and almost laughed at the silliness of the dark red structure, which could never withstand the collapse of the sky. Inside, the smell of hay was sweet and sharp and it washed over her like a wave and she couldn't breathe. She slid in the side door and a loyal dog of moonlight followed her the first few feet.

"Smoke," she said, her voice a raspy note *g*, a tiny sliver that couldn't break the surface of the hay-sea. "Smoke," she said again, and the sound dropped like a tear.

She pushed open the door to the tack room and he grabbed her wrist.

"What do you want?" His voice was a brick. She stared at the knife blade of his chin and his hair, a clutch of raven's feathers. She reached out to touch it.

"It's so soft," she said, and then she giggled because, of course, it was hair! His hair. And the giggle bubbled toward the rafters and popped, and that made her laugh louder. But then she grew silent in the heat of him. He hadn't moved yet was pulling on her. She floated closer and placed her hand beneath his sternum and his heart thundered. His breath was a fishing line reeling her in.

"I was looking for you." Her hands fluttered over the rough growth on his face.

"Why?"

She answered by brushing her lips on his.

"You can kiss me . . ."

He hesitated, because she was an insurrection, but then her hand burned a trail across the flat of his stomach and up behind his ribs, beneath his shirt, and her skin was warm, and when he bent toward her, she parted her lips and she tasted of lye and sweat. He led her to the hayloft and they somehow climbed up, and then she sank with him into the straw, and she felt as if the sky itself were resting upon her.

XXX

Sometime later, she was cold and itchy. She untangled herself from a blanket and then startled into wakefulness. The hay scratched her arms and the back of her thighs as she pushed herself to sitting. She wrapped the blanket around her waist and couldn't think where it came from. And she couldn't think how she'd come to wake in the barn. She listened for another, but there was only the occasional sound of horses swishing their tails and stomping their feet. And then she remembered her mission and the dream of the night—it most certainly had been a dream. Yet her breath caught in her throat and she felt herself blush, recalling his rough hands on her skin. She placed her hand on her heart and imagined it was his hand warm on her breast, and then she felt ashamed. For a moment, she couldn't move. Couldn't breathe. She adjusted her clothing in the dark barn, listening, like prey. As her head cleared, it became urgent that she get home. She used the blanket as a shawl and placed it over her head and slid from the barn and wondered about the time and if Stanley had returned—she hoped not, dear Lord, she hoped not. Not now. She would tell him she had been looking for him, for Wendell. She'd tell him about the drunk in her bedroom . . . What had she done? . . . Her heart raced as she realized the enormity of her offense. And there was another thought knocking on the door of her conscience: the desire, which had not been present in intimate relations with her husband. Desire was the domain of the prostitutes and painted ladies, wasn't it? Was she a whore?

The sky was lighting, and she moved in and out of shadows trying to catch her breath. She picked up her pace until she was practically running. She would redeem herself, be a better wife. She would learn to cook exquisite roasts. She would host parties for local dignitaries—a relative term, she had to admit—and she would host the most amazing salons and educate the local women about literature and art, teach them etiquette, how to be socialites. She thrilled at this thought. Of course, she didn't mean *socialite* in its more contemporary incarnation of high fashion, parties, and other self-indulgent entertainments. And she didn't mean anything having to do with the Social Register—even she lacked the necessary breeding to be so anointed! She meant it in the more old-fashioned way, when the socialites were essential keepers of the culture—the culture of ideas and manners and art.

Alta felt buoyed with determination and purpose, like a Susan B. Anthony (if Susan B. had limited her influence to a single, remote town and didn't bother with issues like slavery and suffrage). She walked the last bit to the house imagining she had a place in history—forgetting, for a moment, her mortification, until she arrived at her own door, and she could feel he was in there. He was home.

Inside, his coat was tossed across the back of the kitchen chair, and when she crept into the bedroom, he was sprawled across the bed, fully dressed and snoring loudly. She changed into her nightclothes and slid in beside him.

She must have fallen asleep because the room was light and had gone from cool to sweltering, and Stanley was clattering in the kitchen making coffee—she'd not felt him rise. Alta found her wrap and took her time putting it on, steeling herself for whatever was to come. When she entered the kitchen, he eyed her warily and poured her a cup of coffee. Alta looked for signs—clenched muscles, tightened jaw—but there were no signs. He'd come home too drunk to notice, she guessed, so she went on the offensive.

"Where have you been?" She sat down with her cup.

"Working. I had to work."

"You couldn't come home, just to sleep?"

"I do what the boss tells me to do."

"And he told you that you couldn't come home."

"What is this, the Inquisition?"

"I was just worried about you, that's all. I thought something happened. Or maybe you left."

"What? Skipped town? Why would I skip town?"

"I didn't know where you were."

"Well, I'm here now."

Alta stood up and retrieved some eggs from the icebox and cracked them into a bowl.

"How would you like your eggs?" she asked.

CHAPTER 21

WENDELL AND SMOKE

Wendell and Smoke were sitting in the Tumbleweed not talking, but rather watching the sodbusters through the window. There was a mess of them sprawling across every available space in front of the Mondak Townsite Company with their chests and crates and kids and mules, all looking worn and tired. The men were smoking or seeing to the livestock, and the women were talking or sorting through belongings. When Stanley eventually sputtered up in the automobile, a small swaybacked horse looking half dead burst to life, tearing its lead from a young man's hand and dashing down the street. Several boys gave chase to the horse, while Stanley made a production of lifting himself out of the car. He planted his feet on the road and paused, dusting off his hat, then strode through the crowd like the president of something and marched into the office building.

"His father, my brother, was a mean son of a bitch," Wendell said. He scratched at a rut on the table.

"Was he?" Smoke said, watching to see if Stanley reappeared. He was feeling sanguine after his encounter with Alta, as if he'd achieved a coup in war—some noble deed that would become a story retold in perpetuity, entitling him to name a child or to an invitation to the guest lodge.

"Meanest son of a bitch you ever laid eyes on," Wendell said. Outside the boys were leading the horse back—too decrepit to go far. "That's a sad excuse for a horse. A man could hang a coat off those withers."

Smoke grunted in agreement, and they watched a man take the lead from the boys and wrap it around a fencepost. Wendell thought the horse was hardly worth the hay it would take to get him through the winter. Smoke thought it was better off dead.

"The apple doesn't fall far from the tree," Smoke said, after pondering a good long time. He pulled his smoking tobacco from his shirt pocket and rolled himself a cigarette. Wendell signaled that he would like a smoke as well.

"Killed a man in a bar fight," Wendell said, accepting the cigarette and watching Smoke roll a second cigarette for himself. "Sliced his neck with the broken edge of a bottle."

"Sounds like a mean son of a bitch."

"Got himself hung," Wendell said.

"An eye for an eye."

"Not really an eye. More like a neck."

"A neck," Smoke nodded.

"Took my girl," Wendell blew out a ring of smoke and watched it climb toward the dusty ceiling. He motioned to Clem for another round of drinks. "Prettiest thing you ever laid eyes on. That was his mother," he nodded toward Stanley, who'd come back outside and was in discussions with a small group of men.

"His mother was your girl?"

"Sure as eggs."

"Damn. Your own brother."

"My own brother."

"Maybe that's why I felt I had to watch out for him . . . Not because of his dad."

Smoke released a ring of smoke, and the two watched it

dissipate. Eventually, Jake came out of the townsite building across the street and made a speech, which Smoke and Wendell were unable to hear. A small group of people followed him into the building, and several other folks drifted away, some with maps in their hands. Stanley got in the car with one other man. A wagon came by loaded with barrels from the Hamm's storage house.

"Sure was a hot one today," Wendell said. Smoke ordered another round. Outside, a number of kids dashed up and down the street screaming and carrying on.

XXX

Later that evening, the families had tucked themselves in and the streets were livening up with the evening crowd, and Smoke and Wendell were walking up from the riverbank where they'd caught and cooked up some fish. Stanley sputtered by in the car with his hat tilted forward and a fat cigar poking out of his mouth.

"Dad-blasted dandy," Wendell spat .

Stanley pulled into the field behind his house and swung out of the Winton. He tripped as he bolted up the steps.

"He could have been your son," Smoke said.

Wendell didn't reply, but he was thinking the same thing. And that got him thinking about that girl with the brown hair who would sometimes wait for him by the river so he could carry up the water for her washing. Her memory was like the taste in his mouth after the cake was eaten, something gone that had been delicious. Her face billowed, and he could not remember the shape of her nose or the line of her chin, but he knew her eyes had been big and brown and lovely like a doe because he could remember the words he had assigned to them so long ago. But that time was gone, she was gone, and the car was there on the side of the road with the moonlight spilling all over it, and he had to admit it was a pretty thing.

Smoke walked up to the car and kicked the tire.

"Damn car," he said. And then Wendell realized it was a damn car. And he and Smoke circled it, and each wondered what it was like to drive it. Wendell thought the car had caused them a shitload of problems. Smoke spat on it, and Wendell did too, but then he crawled up into the seat and leaned back against the leather. He wrapped his hand around the steering wheel, which floated nicely up from the floor, and he turned it but the wheel didn't move. He thought he could see why a man could get the hang of a car, and maybe he'd get himself one someday.

"How the hell do you start this thing?" he wondered to Smoke, who walked around to the front and studied it; then Wendell answered his own question.

"You crank it."

Smoke found the crank and turned it.

"Faster. Jesus Christ."

The engine revved and Smoke cranked, and then it sputtered and roared and Wendell roared.

"Goddamn," he said. "Get in. I think you and I are going for a ride!"

Smoke jumped in beside Wendell, and Wendell jammed the gears this way and that and pushed on the pedals and the engine roared. He shifted something and the car lurched. The two let out a couple of whoops and bounced forward across the field. Wendell pushed on the gas, and the car jerked. They laughed as they picked up speed, bouncing through the buffalo grass. Wendell cranked the wheel to one side and liked how easily the wheel moved when the car was speeding through the night. He swerved around a wagon and pulled the wheel the other way to avoid a shed. And then they were on a road that was more like a path, and he guided the beast beneath him on the worn dirt.

"It's not so hard!" shouted Wendell as they bounced and shook.

"You sure know how to drive this thing!" Smoke roared above the sputtering engine.

"I'm a natural!" Wendell yelled back, and they bounced on the path over the railroad tracks and headed toward the river. Wendell took his foot off the pedal and missed the turn in the road, and the car continued picking up speed.

"You're going to hit the river!" Smoke yelled as they approached the embankment.

"Dad-blast it! I know that!" Wendell cursed. He tried to turn, but it was too late. The car flew over the embankment, and for a moment, they were flying. They both shouted. Then the car slammed into the water.

"Goddamn!" Wendell cursed as the frigid water gurgled over his legs and over the top of the car. His neck hurt like hell from the whiplash. "Dad-blast it!" He stood up and stepped over the back of the car and into the swirling water.

"I can't swim!" he screamed as the river licked at his thighs.

Smoke grabbed hold of his arm and steadied him against the current.

"You can walk, can't you?" He held Wendell, so the older man could get his footing.

"Goddamn!" Wendell spat .

They made it up the bank and sat down to rest and dry off a bit—the night was warm—and watch the automobile settle into the river like a big dog bedding down in the weeds. There was the circling of water and the back and forth as the current pushed and pulled and the wheels sank into the muck, and pretty soon only the windshield was visible. But still the car lurched, getting just a bit more comfortable.

"Christ Almighty," Wendell said. "Did you see that?"

"That was something," Smoke replied.

"Now I know how it feels to be a sailor on a sinking ship."

"I think I'll stick to horses."

They were silent, both contemplating the miracle of the drowned machine.

"Well, that's that," Wendell said. "Stanley's going to be mad as hell."

"Jake too."

"Yeah. There's going to be hell to pay." They were silent again, thinking about how Jake could make their lives miserable.

"Sure is," Smoke finally said. He had a sinking feeling, like he was that car.

"Anyone could have taken it. He shouldn't have left it sitting alongside the road like that. It's an invitation."

"Yeah," Smoke agreed.

"A sodbuster might have stole it."

"Stinking thief," Smoke agreed.

"Or some drunken cowboy."

"Yeah," Smoke agreed. "I think I might head back to my brother's for a while."

"Might be a good idea."

Smoke stood up and grabbed Wendell by the upper arm.

"I better go make myself seem useful." Wendell brushed the dirt off his pants.

"Damn car."

"Yeah. Damn car," Smoke replied.

CHAPTER 22

STANLEY

"Do you know what it would do to this town?"

The question came from a short, skinny cowboy with a furrowed face. It was something to see, that face, plowed and planted it looked like, with deep lines running the length of it. Stanley could hardly pull his eyes away.

"What the hell are you talking about?"

He'd been sitting at the bar in the Tumbleweed minding his own business, and he didn't like his reveries being interrupted.

"They all want Prohibition. They get together and organize and raise Cain. It's happening all over the country. They want to shut down every saloon in the country. It'll kill this town. That's what they want. They want to kill this town."

"Are you trying to talk to me about my wife? Is that what you're doing?"

Stanley was leaning toward the cowboy in a way that made the cowboy think he might have pushed things a little too far. Stanley was a large, fierce-looking man.

"I'm just telling you what everyone is saying." The cowboy was dangling a lasso in his right hand, and now he switched to his left.

"You're saying that everyone's saying this? Sounds like

you're the only one saying anything."

"People are talking."

"What are you going to do with that rope, lasso me? Get the hell out of my sight."

The cowboy did just that, because he knew who Stanley was, and he knew Stanley had the power of the government backing him, the government being Jake and his connections and his resources, and so it was prudent not to get him worked up. But before he left, the cowboy had to get in his last word.

"You might as well burn the town down. It's the same thing."

"Jesus Christ," Stanley said to Clem, who was standing behind the bar drying glasses.

"Can you believe that? . . . You don't think that's what they're doing, do you? Organizing for temperance?" It was a difficult question to ask, implying he didn't know what his own wife was up to, but the cowboy had hit a nerve; and the truth was, Stanley didn't know what his wife was up to. She'd been preoccupied with planning a salon for several weeks. She said it was to bring culture to the women in Mondak. But what did that mean? Culture could be temperance for all he knew.

"It's harmless. Phyllis wouldn't take part in a temperance rally of any sort. This salon is just a fancy name for trading recipes. The women do it all the time."

That made Stanley even more nervous.

"Alta doesn't have any recipes to trade."

It would be just like her to organize and sabotage the town. He felt a flash of shame toward his wife, who didn't seem to know how to behave like a wife.

"Is that what people are saying?" he asked Clem. "Do people think Alta is a women's temperance organizer?" Stanley toyed with his bottle. In truth, the cowboy wasn't the first one to complain. Mondak was alight with rumors about what was no doubt a seditious event. Concerned ranch hands, businessmen, and farmers came to him citing the rise of the Anti-Saloon League while contemplating their doomed future if women pushed through their temperance agenda. Others imagined a more Dionysian-type gathering and lamented the impeding corruption of good Christian women. The concerned citizens berated husbands and fathers and sons for not better managing their wives and daughters and mothers, and many felt it was ultimately Stanley's responsibility to rein in his wife and put a stop to the coming catastrophe.

She had too much time on her hands, was the problem. What did she do with all that time? She barely managed to keep the house and get food on the table. And frankly, the food she served was mediocre at best. Maybe she needed a baby . . . Stanley considered this for a bit. He would have to work on that a little more. But then he wondered if there was something wrong with her. He took a drink and savored the burn of whiskey. Marriage was much more challenging than he had expected.

"Some, maybe. But they're fools. I wouldn't worry about what fools think."

"It's a goddamn riddle."

"What's that?" Clem was only half listening while wiping down glasses.

"Women," Stanley said, raising his drink and setting it down with great emphasis, like an exclamation mark. "Do you think I should put a stop to it?"

"Only if you want to be miserable in your home for the next six months. And then there'll be a backlash. Imagine every woman this side of the Missouri out for your blood."

"It's just not right, all those ladies getting together and talking. That's nothing but trouble. Who knows what they have brewing."

Stanley ordered another drink and lit up a cigarette so he could ponder his predicament. It was during this second drink that he had his epiphany. He finished it and shoved his money across the bar.

XXX

Josephine let him into the house and left him in the parlor to pace while she retrieved Lola, who arrived swishing into the room in a cloud of skirts. Stanley's grin stretched across the room when he saw her—he had a foolproof plan and she was the key.

"Hey!" he said, and imagined Lola face-to-face with his wife, which made him almost laugh out loud.

"Well, this is a surprise. Don't you look like the cat that got the mouse."

She led him through the door and up the narrow stairway to her room, which was small and sparsely furnished, with the bed taking up most of the space. The flickering lamp and velvet wallpaper made the room look fancy, but Stanley had seen it in daylight and knew the wallpaper was cheap and the furnishings unexpectedly scrappy after the grandeur of the parlor downstairs.

"Well," he said, and took her by the shoulders.

"To what do I owe this? I hardly ever see you on a Monday."

He sat on her bed as she unbuttoned her shirtwaist, a simple design that she expertly shed, and in a matter of seconds she stood in her chemise, and then she bent just so and one of her breasts fell out, swollen and heavy, and he caught his breath. His wife kept her breasts caged in layers of materials he couldn't name, and to see breasts swinging free, well it was a pleasure he never tired of. He watched Lola's swing as she moved across the room to pick up her drink, then something about the lack of symmetry, one still bound—he wanted to tuck the exposed breast back into her clothing or pull the other out.

That she was oblivious to this crux was irritating.

Stanley stood up and grabbed the majestic flesh of her and pulled her close.

"I had some time. I wanted to spend it with you."

"Well, aren't I lucky," she said, and there was something in her tone. Stanley felt the need to soften her up.

"I'm the lucky one . . ."

"Yes, you are." She pressed against him.

"I have something I need you to do for me."

"You do." She unbuckled his belt.

"Alta's having a party."

"Well, that's wonderful." Her sarcasm was palpable.

"I want you to go." His lips brushed her face.

"Why would you want that?" She pulled away to study his face.

"I want you to humiliate her," he whispered.

"You do? . . . How do you expect me to do that?" There was doubt in her tone.

"You just show up!" Stanley's grin was enormous. The simplicity of the plan was brilliant! It didn't occur to him that Lola might not be pleased with the subtext—that her mere presence was a humiliation, that the stain of her could ruin an otherwise elegant occasion—because she was a whore and Alta was high class. And it wasn't that Lola had any delusion about who and what she was. She couldn't say if it was the actual plan or the pleasure Stanley was experiencing at the thought of it all that struck her the wrong way, but it did just the same.

"All you need to do is show up," he repeated, thinking she should commiserate in the debacle of her own humiliation, and she paused in her stripping. Stanley was horny as hell at this point and pulled on her chemise to rush her along, but when she didn't respond and didn't take his cock in her hand but pushed him away, he sensed he had miscalculated, though for the life of him, he didn't know how.

"You know how I feel about you," he said, pushing her back onto the bed, and still, she was stiff. But it didn't matter really. She didn't have to like it, and he didn't have to feel anything; he was paying her, after all. But he liked it better when she was receptive, when she pressed her hips against his; and so he whispered into her throat as he reached between her legs and slide his fingers into the warm cocoon of her, because talking feelings always got a response. Even with the whores it got a response. And with Lola, well, everything was better when she was an enthusiastic participant.

"I could fuck you all day," he said, flipping her over so her ass rose in front of him like baked custard. "All day," he said as he pressed against her. "One day I will. I'll be rich as hell and we'll spend our days fucking." He slid inside her, his hands buried in her custard ass. "We'll be like husband and wife."

"You'll divorce your wife?" She spoke mostly to her quilt.

"Sure . . . Something like that. 'To everything, there is a season . . . A time to be born, a time to die' . . . a time to fuck . . ." He loved this ass. He pulled out and came all over her backside, then rolled over on the bed.

"She's useful, right now. One day she won't be so useful. Everything has a purpose."

"Would you really marry someone like me? If your wife wasn't in the picture." Lola poured them each a tumbler of whiskey.

"Hell, why not? . . . If she weren't in the picture." Stanley swirled his glass, smiling to himself, appreciating his own genius.

"So we'll be married." She stepped close to him and kissed him. "When your wife is done . . . serving her purpose."

"Sure," Stanley said. "Why not?" He took a big swig of whiskey. You can say anything to a woman when you're paying her, he thought.

CHAPTER 23

LOLA AND ALTA

Lola agreed to go, but didn't play the harlot at the salon, as Stanley would have liked. The following Saturday, she showed up at the schoolhouse in a conservative tea dress with her hair tied up and her face washed of its usual paint—she could have been anybody's mother or sister or wife. She had decided to placate Stanley but also use the opportunity to practice for the day when they would marry and she would need to perform the duties of a wife.

Alta didn't recognize her in the cluster of women with her basket of cookies. Of course, the two women had met only once, and Lola had been in her working costume, so Alta knew her more by reputation than sight.

"Come in. Come in." Alta stood in the doorway fresh and fashionable while the other women lingered in the hot sun waiting for direction: What was the etiquette for entering a salon? Did you walk in or did you need to be invited? Was this a salon or a social—they'd heard it called both; what was the difference? They were every one of them in a tug-of-war with the wind, which was yanking like a hungry teenager at the towels that covered their baskets and plates and bowls of fare. The wind grabbed the door from Alta's hand and slammed it into the side of the school as if in a fit of bad temper.

"Goodness." Alta stepped outside to grab it. "Please. Come in."

A towel broke ranks and flew across the buffalo grass. Doris dashed after it but quickly gave up and instead, covered her mashed turnips with her hand, as if a hand could block out the dust. "It's a breezy one," someone noted.

Several women introduced themselves to Lola as they filed into the school room, believing her to be a new arrival to the community, and she called herself by her given name, Martha. The women set their wares on the stretch of tables along the far wall in the room that was unrecognizable. Alta, with the help of Phyllis and Beverly, had pushed the desks aside and set up tables. Beverly had brought linen clothes for each of the tables, and they had placed flowers in jars for centerpieces. And all the women were nearly unrecognizable, dressed in their best clothes. Several paused to straighten their skirts, an unconscious gesture to fill the moment while they acclimated to their unusual context. Doris picked lint off Myrtle's shoulder while June flipped through the pages of the books on the front table, not reading a word. The others milled around the tables in the middle of the room. A few women seated themselves, and several helped themselves to the punch Phyllis was pushing enthusiastically. She didn't mention to any of them that it was spiked.

"None of these women know how to relax," Phyllis had explained when Alta tried to stop her as they were setting up for the day. "I'm helping them have a good time."

Beverly was the first to recognize Lola. She'd often seen her in the store. She weighed whether to say anything to Alta, but decided against it—better to let things lie rather than cause a scene, and it seemed Lola was going to behave appropriately. Katy Anderson asked Beverly about the agenda. Was it true Alta was going to read to them?

"It's what they do in the city," Beverly explained.

"Story time? Like with children?"

"Yes. Here. Drink. It'll be fun." Phyllis, overhearing, shoved a cup in her hand.

June, Constance, and Myrtle gathered around the banquet table discussing Myrtle's recipe for meat pie. Others discussed children, husbands, the influx of homesteaders, and whether Pastor Thomson was going to accept the offer of a permanent position. Having nothing to contribute to the conversations, Lola made her way to the book table. She'd fancied herself a reader in her younger days, before her parents had passed and she'd been left to her own devices.

"Is there one you like? Would you like to read an excerpt?" Alta asked, and Lola was pleased to see she had no idea who she was.

"I always loved *Little Women*. That Jo was really something."

"Please, ladies. Eat. Before it gets cold," Beverly motioned toward the food.

Doris would have known Lola if she were walking around with her face wrapped in scarves. "It takes a lot of nerve," she hissed as she passed the whore with a plate of meat pie, and everyone turned to see what the fuss was about.

"Oh, dear." Beverly saw the clash about to happen and clapped her hands to get everyone's attention. "Ladies. Ladies. We're going to begin. Fill your cups and plates." The next time Alta approached, Beverly whispered in her ear, and Alta's eyebrows arched, but she did her best to hide her anger. Why and what, she wondered, about the prostitute attending the event. Of course she'd heard rumors about Lola and Stanley, but she had made the choice not to believe them.

The others had heard endless stories about the red-light district and the women corrupting their men, so when they realized Lola was one of them, they pelted her with looks of disgust and disdain—how dare she, really? The hostility put

Lola on the defensive, and she no longer felt bound by manners and norms, but rather like a cat surrounded by dogs. She'd taken a seat in the back of the room and was picking at a piece of cake on the plate on her lap when she unsheathed her claws.

"A salon," she said, taking a bite. "What a lovely idea, sitting around so the lace curtain can flaunt her education. It's an insult, isn't it? She thinks she's smarter than you."

"Oh, on the contrary. A salon is a safe place for everyone to express their ideas. To be inspired," Alta defended herself, remaining calm.

"You hear that, ladies? She's going to inspire you."

"Come now. Sit. Sit." Beverly clapped.

"Maybe you should go," Alta said. She was furious. "This is a private event, and I'm sure you'll find the discussion tedious."

"No doubt the company is tedious." Lola gestured to the room. "A bunch of fops and go-alongers. I don't think I can bear any more of this dull affair." She left then, in a grand way, dropping her plate on a table and swinging her hips and her basket and flicking her head.

When she had gone, it was as if the party had sailed into the doldrums or time had stopped; there wasn't a sound.

"Good riddance," Doris shouted into the canyon. And then someone laughed a drunken laugh and the tension unfurled. Phyllis pushed drinks and food.

"Eat ladies. Eat. Look at all this food!"

There was more mingling, but then Alta—still agitated and off-balance from the encounter with Lola—thought they should get to the meat of the matter. She'd lost her sense of purpose and wanted to get the reading part over.

"Well, how about we get started?" she said, and no one seemed to hear. The wind rattled the building and a gust blew through a crack in the wall and fluttered the pages of the books. She took her place at the front of the room, and then Phyllis clapped her hands and ordered the women to sit, and they did, though Ethyl and June found sitting hilarious and broke into giggles. Alta gave a brief introduction explaining the purpose of the salon, then asked the group about Tennyson, which no one had read. (She had meant to talk about Louisa May Alcott, funny thing, but because Lola had argued for *Little Women*, Alta had to choose an alternative, though she was probably one of the more accessible writers for this particular crowd.)

She held up the book, then read "The Lady of Shalott," and when she finished, there was silence. Phyllis opened a bottle of bourbon. "Why not?" she mouthed, and walked around the room offering "tastes."

"It's very sad," Rose finally said, about the poem.

Eunice said she didn't understand, and June wanted to know how barley was bearded, which made Rose laugh, and then the other women laughed at them laughing. Constance wondered to Doris how her husband Kermit was doing, holding down the fort. She imagined her own husband Fred would starve since she wasn't home to cook for him—but fortunately she'd left him a bit of ham, and then they all laughed at how incompetent their husbands were in the kitchen, and they agreed their husbands would starve if left to their own devices.

Even with her audience distracted and at least partially drunk, Alta was determined to impose literature on them—otherwise it would be as if Lola had ruined the event. She read several poems over increasingly loud chatter and asked questions about the work. Several women offered their opinions, and others gazed at the floor. Most of the group outright ignored the guided conversation. Rose swayed like a tree, tilting from side to side in her chair, and then her face broke in a gush of laughter. June and Frances had spines of rope and nearly collapsed on one another as they talked. The entire event felt like a catastrophe.

"That was lovely, darling." Beverly sidled next to Alta—she could see the other woman was distraught. "It does make one's soul soar . . . What a wonderful life you must have had back in the city."

"Yes. It was wonderful . . . Of course, I had responsibilities." Alta was furious at Phyllis, feeling she had ruined the event by getting the women drunk. She wanted to scream or cry, but instead gathered her books and put them in a basket.

"Now what?" Phyllis seemed to sense her anger. She came to stand next to Alta. "They're having a grand time."

"Yes," Alta agreed, and flashed Phyllis a tight smile. Phyllis squeezed her hand. "Look at them. All day they cook and clean and haul water and chop wood . . ."

"It's true," Beverly agreed.

Then Alta did look at the women. They were talking and laughing, their hands wandering in a disembodied way, smoothing their skirts and touching their hair. Several picked up abandoned cups and wiped up food, but even this was funny, the way the punch spilled onto the floor or the watermelon splattered.

"These ladies will go home and remember a good time, and next thing you know, they'll be planning their own salons. They'll be telling their kids how much they love literature . . ."

Alta nodded. She had to agree that they did seem to be having a very good time. "Tomorrow might not be such a good day for them . . ."

Phyllis laughed, and then they were all laughing. And then the laughter became something like a small earthquake. They couldn't stand and they couldn't breathe and they couldn't see because they were crying from laughing. And then they had to sit down because they couldn't stand. The other women took a pause from their own malarky and watched the three of them. Eventually, Alta caught her breath and stood up to say something respectable to close out the event, and then she looked at Beverly, and they both broke into another round of laughter.

XXX

When she returned home, Stanley was at the table reading the paper and drinking a beer.

"How'd it go?" he asked, and she said it was fine and went about the kitchen picking up stray dishes.

Stanley pressed for details.

"I think everyone had a good time," Alta responded. She wasn't used to him having a keen interest in her affairs, so his questions were curious. She wondered if he had anything to do with Lola's appearance, and she wondered why he would be bothered to sabotage the event.

"They probably didn't have much interest in the books . . ." Stanley attempted to keep the conversation going. "Did everyone show up?"

Alta had her back to him and now she turned. She wanted to see his face.

"Mostly women from the church," she said.

"Mostly?" He took a long drink of his beer and set it on the table.

"Sure. Mostly." She went into the bedroom and shut the door.

CHAPTER 24

ALTA

Alta was preparing clothes for soaking when Clarence knocked on her door. She finished filling a large pot with water to heat on the stove, then rushed to the front door. When she opened it, he was there, the rickety manager from her father's mill. Clarence was wearing a smart but rumpled suit and leaning on a cane.

"Clarence! Goodness! What a surprise!"

"Good afternoon ma'am." He removed his hat and bowed ever so slightly. Clarence had always had the best manners. He was quiet and gentle and more like family than an employee.

"Come in. Come in." Alta held the door, and he stepped inside. She was immediately self-conscious and embarrassed about her situation—how far he must think she had fallen.

"Aren't you a sight for sore eyes," he said, though he could see she was drawn. "I'm here at your father's request."

"Of course. How is Father?" Alta motioned to Clarence to sit. "Tea?" she asked.

"Sure. I'll take some tea." He was studying the room, and she wanted to explain this tiny home was temporary, until Stanley's business took off. Then it occurred to her as she set the water on the stove in the kitchen that this was Stanley's catchphrase—"until his business took off." Stanley had made no moves to start a business or even advance in Jake's. He was an entrepreneur only in his fantasies, it seemed—an unsettling thought.

"He sent me to deliver a message," Clarence began when Alta returned from the kitchen. "Your father spoke with Mrs. Hill. She told him where you were. He had no idea."

Alta sat on the edge of her chair with her hands clasped on her lap waiting for the tea water to boil.

"He was out of sorts about the marriage. He thought you should know that." Clarence pulled a handkerchief from his pocket and wiped his brow, then folded the handkerchief into an increasingly small square, a tedious process made even more so by the tremor in his hands.

Alta waited until he was done folding to respond. "Of course," she finally said, then jumped up from her chair to return to the kitchen so she could organize her thoughts.

"It's quite a town." Clarence was making conversation from the other room.

"Isn't it?" Alta spoke from the other room. "It's growing quickly. Every day the train drops off a new batch of settlers."

"Truly something . . ." Clarence spoke softly, almost to himself. He continued as Alta returned to the room carrying a tray with the tea setup. She passed him a cup, and he perched it on his lap. The saucer slid sideways as he lifted the cup.

"He'd like you to come home."

These were words Alta had been longing to hear, but she held back her enthusiasm. "Is that so?" She managed to sound noncommittal.

"He wanted me to relay this message. You come home, make amends. He's willing to forgive you, but there are conditions."

"What are the conditions?" Of course there were conditions. She glanced at the blue curtains she'd made for the windows in this room. They could use another go with the iron, she thought to herself, but otherwise, she had to admit, they looked pretty good. A horse and rider passed outside the window, so close that the rider could reach out and touch the glass.

"There will be a divorce," Clarence said. He studied his tea like he was reading the leaves. He didn't like what he had to say, she could tell. She knew he had great respect for her father and was one of Cadwallader's most loyal employees, but there were times she imagined his loyalty challenged his own moral and ethical inclinations.

"Of course," she said, helping him along. She would expect no less. After all, Cadwallader had demanded a divorce from the moment of her marriage.

"He says he has a more suitable husband in mind."

"A more suitable husband?" Alta set her cup on the tray on the side table.

"Yes ma'am. After a respectable amount of time has passed, of course." Clarence bowed his head, falling back on formality.

"He can't be serious." Alta was enraged. This was the twentieth century, for goodness' sake.

"I promise you, he is very serious." Clarence had a pleading look—he didn't like conflict. She should obey and everything would be fine was the unspoken message. Fighting was pointless. At least, that's what it looked like to Alta.

"Why would I trade one husband for another?"

"He's an old man, Alta. He's not going to be around forever. He wants to know you'll be taken care of. And probably, he wants grandchildren."

"You came all this way." Alta concentrated on her tea. "What if I was already . . . in the family way?"

"Are you?" Clarence looked relieved. "Well then, we wouldn't have to worry about the marriage part . . . I'm sure we could come to an arrangement with your husband. Your father is worried about you. The Hills told him about your situation. These people . . ." Clarence shook his head.

"No," Alta said, in a tone that surprised even herself. She looked back at the window and took a breath. The thought occurred that she was late. But she couldn't be pregnant. She didn't feel pregnant.

"No?"

"You know I can't accept his terms, Clarence." How dare he? She would not be bartered like a horse, and that's how her father was treating her. Like a horse to be traded.

"I was afraid you'd say that . . ."

"How absolutely ludicrous."

"This . . ." Clarence gestured with his head at the room, but he meant to include everything that led up to this little house, the totality of Alta's new life. "He was very upset about this. Your marriage."

"Yes. You've made that clear . . . I'm sorry, Clarence. I know you mean well." Alta picked at a thread on her skirt.

"He's a good man. Charles Fisher. A successful businessman. Dashing, my wife tells me . . . I'm not a judge of such things . . . He didn't know what else to do . . ."

"Father didn't know what else to do?"

"I have a photo. Do you want to see a photo?" Clarence pulled a picture out of his pocket and offered it up to Alta, but she shook her head and stood up. Clarence looked hot in his coat. She hadn't offered to take it and hang it up, she realized. That's how distracting she'd found his appearance. But now it was too late. She wanted him to go.

"Tell Father I love him very much, but I have a new home now."

"Why don't you think about it? I'm going to get myself a room at the hotel down the street for a couple of days. Until Wednesday, if you change your mind." Clarence stood up slowly, leaning into his cane, and Alta took hold of his arm to help him balance.

"Thank you, Clarence, but I won't be changing my mind."

Clarence took his leave and Alta carried the tea set back to the kitchen and dumped out the remains, then filled a tub in the sink with water. Washing dishes increased her fury—the water, the bubbles, the teacup. She paused in rinsing off a saucer, then flung it into the wall. The shattering felt good.

XXX

Alta avoided the public as much as possible while Clarence was in town. She was afraid if she ran into him, she wouldn't have the strength to stand up for herself, and that's what she was doing, standing up for herself—she would not be forced into marriage like some impoverished backwoods country girl. But after the train left on Wednesday with Clarence presumably on it, there was a finality, and she felt she'd been stranded anew. She could see her homeland slide off the horizon and disappear from the maps. Before, she'd felt there was a remote chance that she could return to Minnesota and make amends with her father, but now that possibility felt nearly impossible—how could she jump from her marriage to Stanley to a marriage with a stranger?

She spent the next days focused on her chores. Now especially, she had no choice but to make her life here, which included her marriage, work. She thought of the success of the salon as she prepared her ironing—it had been a success, hadn't it? She lit the stove and set her irons close to the fire to heat them up. Of course it had been a success. Everyone said it had been a success. It hadn't gone as she expected, of course; she had to account for that. But it had worked in its way. And now, it simply needed adjusting. She tossed a blanket over the kitchen table and covered it with a sheet, then spent some time smoothing out the wrinkles before sprinkling the sheet with water so it had the perfect dampness. Next, Alta wrapped a towel around the handle of an iron and pressed it into the sheet. There would be no creases, she promised herself.

She worked the iron over the sheet and thought of the small changes she could make to the salon to make it more appealing to the women. More accessible books, for certain. Jane Austen. Why hadn't she presented her in the first place? Could it be she was keeping Elizabeth Bennet to herself? Well, no more of that. *Pride and Prejudice* would make an appearance at the next one. Of course they would do a reading. She got goosebumps just thinking the thought. And then Jules Verne. Of course. Jules Verne! The ladies would love him. And they could bring their pies and exchange recipes. Alta set her iron on its stand and folded the sheet just so and carried it outside to hang it on the clothesline.

She would be the patroness of culture in Mondak, she decided. Who better to take the reins of educating the local population about theater and art and music than herself? And really, it would be a waste of her upbringing and education if she didn't make use of it, and how else was she to make use of it?

She considered this new role for several days, and the more she did, the more she imagined she had found a calling, one that had to be more meaningful than becoming the wife of one of her father's business associates.

She was chopping carrots for a pot roast, imagining Mondak as a booming cultural center, with people coming from miles around to listen to music and visit the theater—coming soon, she'd make it happen—when she noted the ache in her breasts. She paused and realized it had been there for days. She pressed on them irritably with the heel of her hand. Her breasts were swelling. She set down her knife . . . And she had indeed missed her cycle. She placed her hands on the counter as if for balance. She was late by two weeks, and she'd never been late. And she was feeling off in other ways. A bit nauseous. She felt a rush of panic. She was pregnant. Of course she was. She walked to the table and took a seat and folded her hands on her lap. She wanted a baby, of course . . . but . . . she did the math. It might not be Stanley's . . . In fact, as she pondered it, she thought it was unlikely Stanley's. And if it wasn't Stanley's . . . Dear Lord, she'd tried to pluck the memory of that night from her head. But the numbers added up.

She stood up and circled the kitchen, then pushed open the door and walked outside. A heaviness hit her, and she sat down on the step and stared at the laundry flapping in the breeze. There were rusty stains on the side of one of Stanley's shirts that she'd been unable to vanquish. Like blood, she thought, then reprimanded herself for her own morbidity. Where did that come from? But dark thoughts came tumbling: Stanley choking her in the kitchen—she'd been sure then she would die—and his enthusiasm for the lynching. How he'd tossed Smoke into the dipping vat. She understood from these lessons that she was in danger if he learned of her indiscretion. And he would know, she suspected. Of course he would know. And he would hurt her and the baby . . . Well, this changed the situation with her father. He wanted a grandchild, and he wouldn't push her into marrying a stranger if she gave him one. She would go home, back to Minnesota. Once the decision was made, she was relieved. She thought of the big house and all the help—someone to do the laundry and cooking—and it was like a weight being lifted. She felt a rush of homesickness. She touched her stomach and imagined the person growing inside her.

She went inside and filled a bucket of water from the pump and carried it out to the tomatoes, splashing water onto her dress so it clung to her calves as she worked through her plan.

She couldn't tell anyone, even Beverly—though she trusted her implicitly—because she couldn't take a chance of her telling Lew and it somehow leaking back to Stanley. Stanley could absolutely not know . . . She'd take only the essentials—there was nothing here that she couldn't replace once she was home. She felt a certain thrill anticipating her escape.

She finished watering the garden and went inside to fix dinner. When Stanley came home, she distracted him with trivial conversation, worried he could read her mind and discover her plan. But he was preoccupied and hardly glanced at her when she slid a plate on the table in front of him. When he finished his meal and excused himself to go to the bar, she was relieved.

XXX

The next day after Stanley left for work, she dressed and packed a few things into a basket, and set off for the station a few minutes before the train was scheduled to arrive at noon. She purchased her ticket, took a seat in the station waiting room, and paged through a magazine.

The train was late. Alta eyed the clock that seemed to have slowed, or maybe stopped. A few people came and went, looking for passengers, and passengers got bored and walked out onto the platform to stretch their legs and watch for the train's approach. A young man, drunk, it appeared—he was slurring his words—and argued with the clerk, which distracted her for several minutes. Seats were sold out, the clerk argued, and the man kept insisting on a seat until several other men jumped up and, after a quick scuttle, pulled him outside.

There was another lull and then Jake came in and had a conversation with the clerk. Alta lifted her magazine up to cover her face and pulled down her hat, wondering what possible business he could have. And then he was standing over her.

"Good afternoon," his voice boomed. "Off somewhere?"

"Oh, goodness, how are you!" Alta smiled. "Just to Williston. To do some shopping."

"You don't say? Stanley was there just this morning. He should be back soon. You could have gone with him, then you wouldn't have to wait." Jake seemed distracted by the crowd. His eyes kept glancing up as if he were looking for someone. "I'm sure he told you we got a new car—runs like a charm. This was the maiden voyage." He winked knowingly, then nodded toward the clock on the wall. "Probably ran into some cattle on the tracks."

It took Alta a moment to realize he was referring to the train. She watched as he took out a handkerchief and blew his nose as if to punctuate his point. His eyes darted toward the door and he rocked back and forth on his feet.

"I had some business to take care of this morning," Alta responded. "And I really don't mind the train. It's quite pleasant . . . it's almost like part of the family business," she said, reminding Jake that she had her own powerful connections.

"No doubt . . . Well, then. Have a pleasant trip." Jake tipped his hat.

When he was gone, Alta stood up and stared at the clock, willing it to move more quickly. The clerk announced another forty-five-minute delay.

There was nothing to be done. Alta took off her hat to fan herself and thought of her bedroom back in her father's house. She thought of the cooks and maids. She thought of the baby she was carrying, and when she did, she thought of Smoke, which made her blush. She clenched her magazine and wished she had water. It was terribly hot, and the heat made her light-headed, and she felt sick to her stomach to boot.

When the whistle finally announced the arrival of the train, she gathered her belongings and stepped onto the platform. The engine trembled into the station, and she hurried to her coach. Only when she was settled into her seat was she able to relax. In no time, she'd be home. She laid her head back against the seat and imagined her father's surprise when she appeared at the door. He'd be delighted—until he remembered he was angry, she supposed. She'd have to talk him down, but she was up to the task. She smiled thinking how she could, eventually, when he was in the right mood. She missed him—she never thought she would. And she couldn't wait to see Greta. Was she still employed at the house? she worried. Would her father have let her go? The questions made her catch her breath. Oh, dear, he may have. She would have to make him hire her back. Greta could help with the baby. She placed her hand on her belly. She was having a baby!

Alta glanced outside just as Stanley burst onto the nearly empty platform, dodging the few porters still moving baggage.

The whistle blew a warning while he chatted with a porter. The porter shouted, and he was swarmed by other porters and they were talking. Alta shrank into her seat and lifted the magazine to hide her face and wondered where she could flee to. But then a porter was standing over her.

"Ma'am, I'm afraid there's been some mistake," he said. Stanley stood beside her seat, staring down at her.

"Alta dear." He smiled a sinister smile.

"Hi, Stanley."

"Where are you off to? You never told me you were going away."

"I'm going to visit my father."

"Your father?"

"My father. In Minneapolis."

"She's confused," he said to the porter. "Her father's been dead for nearly three years, but she thinks he's living in Minneapolis. A flour baron." He whispered this last part. "The doctor said it happens from time to time with the high-strung ones. Hysteria, he called it."

"He is a flour baron. Cadwallader Woburn! What are you doing, Stanley?"

The porter gave Stanley a sympathetic look, and Stanley took her by the arm. "Come on, dear, we're going home."

"I'm not going with you!" She ripped her arm away, and the porter turned so as not to invade this private moment.

"Come along." Stanley smiled again, and his fingers clenched her arm. "You don't want to cause a scene, dear." And then he addressed the porter. "She'll be fine. She just needs to rest."

Alta had no choice but to follow Stanley off the train. The other passengers turned away as she passed, as if embarrassed by her and her affliction. Stanley was silent until they were through the depot, and then he didn't feign politeness.

"What the hell do you think you're doing?"

"I'm leaving, Stanley. One way or another, I'm leaving."

"The hell you are. You're my wife and you're going to act like it," he hissed into her ear. "People think I can't handle my wife." He pulled her over the rough ground, and she stumbled trying to keep up.

"When my father hears about this!"

He tugged her arm, throwing her off balance, but his grip was so tight she didn't fall.

"Your father . . . as far as he's concerned, you're dead. You're dead to him. You ran away, remember? Your father's not the forgiving type."

"He'll make you pay for this!"

Stanley stopped and turned to face her.

"I'll make him pay . . . You're my wife. That gives me certain rights and authority under the law. Your father can stomp and shout, but he can't help you unless he pulls out his wallet." He tapped her on the sternum.

"I'm sure he would make arrangements with you."

Stanley laughed. "Why take the golden egg when I can wait

for the goose?"

Alta was aghast. "What is that supposed to mean?"

"He's an old man and his health is not so good, and you're his only next of kin. He'll come to his senses. Even if it's on his death bed."

"That's a horrible thing to say."

"Who else could he leave his money to?" He pushed her along the rutted road toward the house.

"Make yourself useful," he said when they arrived. "Make me dinner."

CHAPTER 25

ADAM

Adam and Cecil drove the wagon toward the Todd ranch on a warm day in late summer. It was a bumpy ride. The grass was so tall it caught in the cracks between the dash and the floor of the wagon, and the cut tops bounced along the floorboards under the seat, shimmying toward the back of the wagon and popping up like popcorn. Adam glanced behind the bench to make sure his rifle was still there, lodged between some boards nailed to thefloor. Cecil was saying something, and he grunted in response. "War," he said. And something about joining up. Adam had heard that story too many times to pay much heed. He slapped at a grasshopper that had landed on his arm. An especially aggressive cloud of them parted like a bubbly Red Sea as the horses trotted along, and the click of grasshopper bodies hitting the sideboards reminded Adam of a lot of hail.

"Jesus Christ, where the hell is the road?" Cecil rumbled.

"There's not much of a road. Just some wagon tracks."

"Goddamnit!" Cecil brushed a grasshopper off his arm. "I don't know why Jake won't let us take the truck."

"It's broke down."

"That's what he says."

"It might really be." Adam felt a jolt of loyalty toward Jake.

Cecil pulled off his straw hat and waved it in front of his face to quicken the air. Just then, they came over a rise and saw the house. It was a small sod block, barely distinguishable from the surrounding country, with a corral and a lean-to nearby for the stock.

"They were murdered," Cecil whispered, putting his hat back on his head. Adam had heard the rumor—the parents and three kids had died a mysterious death, and when the neighbor found them, the bodies were decaying and smelling like hell. Some folks said the death was from sickness, but just as many folks thought foul play. Seeing the house now, Adam had a bad feeling.

"I bet the murderer is still around. Probably watching us right now." Adam slugged Cecil in the shoulder to shut him up.

They parked the wagon and let the horses graze—the team was old and the boys didn'tworry about them spooking.

"I'll go check over here," Cecil said, motioning toward the lean-to. Adam thought Cecilwas afraid and didn't want to go into the house, but he didn't say anything.

Adam stepped into the house and let his eyes adjust. Already the roof was beginning to collapse. Clumps of it were strewn across the hard dirt floor. He stepped in and kicked a mattress, and several mice charged out, aiming for the wall and then turning at right angles. There was a fair amount of furniture—a table and chairs, bedding, and a rocking chair near the one glass window on the opposite side of the room. Adam had taken to calling such windows the "proving up" window because so many homesteaders included a small, blurred square of glass in their elementary homes to make them legal. He set about removing it, because even in these hard times Jake could sell it at an inflated price.

"What a shithole." Cecil had snuck in beside him. He spat on the floor.

"Let's get this done." Cecil picked up the mattress and carried it, straw-filled and lumpy, out the door. A gust grabbed it and lifted it into the air. Adam set the window down and rushed to assist Cecil with the mattress.

"Bring the mattresses back, Jake said. They died, for Christ's sake. It's probably full of disease."

"Not if they were murdered," Cecil corrected.

"Would you want a mattress someone had been murdered on?"

"Hell no . . . But he wants everything. 'Don't leave a scrap of paper, or I'll know,' he said."

They dropped the mattress in the back of the wagon.

"What's he do with all this anyway?" Adam asked. It was a redundant conversation, one they'd had many times before at many house cleanings, but they repeated it over and over again like a bad vaudeville bit.

"Lord knows . . . Maybe he sells it."

"Who buys this shit?"

"Hell if I know." Cecil kicked a wheel on the wagon.

"You're an ass," Adam said.

"Better than being a no-account pile of horseshit."

"At least I'm not a no-account son-of-a-bitch scalawag."

"Scalawag?"

"Yep." Adam nodded.

"You hear that from your uncle?"

"Probably," Adam laughed.

Cecil spat, and Adam went back into the house.

He took his time excavating, feeling a bit like a detective digging through the lives of the departed inhabitants. As was the case at most of the homesteads, he learned the Todds' lives had been unbearably simple in the way of material things. There were two mattresses total, and a rocking chair backed into a corner. The blackened remains of some meal remained in tin bowls on a primitive table. The blankets were filthy and probably full of fleas or lice, but Jake liked to look such things over before declaring them trash, so Adam carried these out to the wagon. In a box in the corner of the house, he found three faded photographs, a bruised doll, stained ribbons, and letters hidden in the cover of the family Bible. The sum of five lives, he thought, as he carried the box to the back of the wagon

It didn't take long to empty out the house. Everything, no matter how meager, the boysgathered up.

"People buy this shit," Cecil said. It occurred to Adam that he liked to hear his own voice.

"Sign of the times," Adam said.

Cecil stalked off to the yard, grasshoppers lifting off around his feet as he walked, and Adam returned to the house. Each time he entered or exited, he had to pause so his eyes could make the adjustment from bright sunlight to the shadowy interior. This time, as he circled the interior, his foot caught on something, a lump, and he bent down to feel it. It felt soft like a pelt. He grabbed it by the edge and pulled. The ripping sound was like uprooting a plant, and it came up in a tattered clump. When he held it to the dim light, the shades were familiar, but it took his brain a moment to process. He brought it close to the window hole. There was no evidence it had once been magnificent. Adam ran his hand across the filthy fur. The lines of fire had cooled into something like dead ash.

He stood in the middle of the single room thinking about the tragedy of the Todd family, now joined with the chorus of the dead, and this house fodder for rodents and the wind. And then he thought, Cecil is right, the Todds probably had been killed, and among the transient population of Mondak, a killer wandered unnoticed.

Adam was feeling a general unease thinking these thoughts when the hand gripped his shoulder. He assumed it was Cecil's, though of course Cecil was outside, and he shrugged.

Thebony fingers wrapped more tightly around his clavicle, and Adam was annoyed as much as surprised—the pinching hurt.

"Hey," he said, glancing over his shoulder at no one.

He spun around, and he was alone in the house. He slapped at a twitch in his arm, and the right side of his torso avalanched in a series of spasms. He collapsed, and his body ground into the hard dirt while his thoughts raced. He'd dropped the pelt, and it lay in a loose clump in front of him. He sat up and pulled rolling paper from the pocket of his shirt.

He took a deep breath and thought he must be coming down with something. He leaned against the wall, not caring about the twigs and brambles poking into his back. His heart came back to normal, and ghosts rushed into the vacuum left by the departed, proof of a something after, a gauzy bindle to hold the rotting relics of lives extinguished. Adam imagined apparitions rising like the odorous tang from a bush left by a passing dog, and the requiem of piss was a bulwark against oblivion.

He inhaled the cigarette and watched the universe of dust floating in the slant of light from the open door—the world broken into infinitesimal pieces suspended between what was and what was to be. Adam imagined the particles were small planets or stars with entire populations mucking barns or hunting prairie dogs or riding rafts on rivers that moved backward, up to the peaks of the mountains. And then, why backward, he wondered, and he pondered that thought, and the smoke curled in the air above him.

I'm breathing them in, he thought. Then sucked in on his cigarette.

I imagined it, he said about the hand. But it felt so real . . . He lingered over his cigarette, ashing onto the hardened dirt.

"What are you doing?" Cecil blocked out the sun and then kicked Adam in the thigh, not hard, just enough to lurch him out of his reverie, and then he noticed the pelt.

"Goddamn," he said. "Fuck! That the tiger?"

Adam nodded.

"Jesus Christ. That's right. Old Myrtle shot it." When he noticed Adam's confused look, he continued.

"Didn't you hear? Everyone was talking about it. Big old cat walked right into the yard and sat down. Myrtle, who was practically blind, went in the house and got a rifle and shot it. Just like that. Right between the eyes, folks said. She even collected the reward. Fuck. That was about a month ago. How the hell did you not hear?"

Adam didn't respond but walked out and tossed the pelt in the tall grass to feed the hoppers.

"That's why Jake wants all this crap," Cecil said climbing into the wagon. "Thinks there's a reward hidden in it someplace and he's too goddamn fat to come looking himself."

Adam climbed into the seat beside him. "Let's get out of here. This place gives me the creeps."

CHAPTER 26

SMOKE

They came for him during the harvest. He was husking corn with Duck, his brother, who was much more experienced and therefore a faster husker. Duck was much older than Smoke, with gray streaking the hair he kept long, in the traditional way. Duck wore a western-style shirt and wide-brimmed hat to keep the sun from his eyes, and he moved through stalks that were taller than men, tearing off ears with his husking peg and tossing them into the rig—he was used to this kind of work. Smoke was worn out from trying to keep up. He paused to wipe the sweat and dirt that had turned to mud from his brow, and that's when he saw them through the stalks, two riders and a wagon approaching off a rise, pushing aside the veil of heat. Smoke glanced over and saw Duck was watching too. His back was turned, but he was seeing with the hair on his neck and by the skin on his cheek, which had paused in its chewing. He was seeing how far to the shed where their rifles were leaning. He was seeing how the peg in his hand could work like a blade. Duck slid over to the horse and took hold of the bridle and walked the horse and rig toward the shed, and Smoke followed. They walked slowly, not appearing to notice the approaching party, like they were heading back for lunch. At the shed, they unhitched the horse and moved inside, and

Duck glanced out the window to watch the riders break away from the wagon and lope into the yard, a two-man cavalry. They were bringing trouble. The white men always brought trouble. He had no doubt he was watching a funeral march; it was just a matter of identifying the dead.

Smoke and Duck came into the yard with their rifles to meet the riders—one, Duck recognized, was the BIA agent, a man with a vast ranch who called himself a friend of the Indians. His name, Duck recalled, was Carson. He was a trickster with many faces, and so Duck had no use for pleasantries.

"Afternoon," Carson said, fingering the rifle that lay across the pommel of his saddle.

"What do you want?"

Carson nodded toward Smoke. "I need to take him in."

"What do you need him for?"

"It's my orders."

By now, the wagon was pulling up. Carson motioned to the other rider—a man Duck named Toothless because he had no front teeth—and to the man driving the wagon. They dismounted from their respective rides. Smoke and Duck raised their rifles and the two men stopped.

"No one's taking anyone."

The two men stood facing off in a casual way. The outcome was predetermined, so there was no urgency. Both knew how the story would end, the way it always ended. But still, Duck pointed his rifle, because there were so many ways to arrive at the ending, so many plot points and arcs, and there were characters that overcame and some that had to be sacrificed, and it was always better to arrive at the end after a fight.

"You kill us and they'll send in the army. You know that," Carson said.

"Yeah, I know that," Duck said, and fired. But the man driving the wagon was fast. He pulled a Colt from his hip and shot back. Then there was a flurry of shots. Duck twisted as the driver caught him in the shoulder. And then Toothless hit Smoke, it looked like in the side, because he was bent over and blood was running through his fingers. At that moment, Toothless and Carson leapt forward and caught Smoke and wrestled him to the dirt. The wagoner kept his gun on Duck while they dragged Smoke like a roped steer to the wagon. They lifted him as he twisted and kicked, and they rolled him into the back of the wagon, then jumped in and cuffed him.

"Where you taking him?"

"There's something wrong with your brother." The driver grinned.

"Where you taking him?"

Carson was down from the wagon. He swung up onto his horse.

"Hiawatha," he said.

The driver clicked and lifted the reins, and the horse circled with the wagon slowly out of the yard. The riders with their guns across their laps followed behind. Smoke was slumped over in the back of the wagon, bleeding, Duck knew. He wondered if he'd even make it where he was going. Duck could see he was afraid, but there was nothing Duck could do for him. He watched until the wagon disappeared, and still, he stood. He stood until the sun set and the sky went black. In a way, he never stopped standing.

Later Duck learned the men had driven Smoke to Poplar, where Carson shoved him and Toothless on a train, and those two rode to Canton, South Dakota. He wept, because he knew he'd never see his brother again.

CHAPTER 27

WENDELL

Wendell pushed himself up and pulled his legs one at a time over the side of the cot, grabbing one calf to swing it over the edge and then the other, and then he sat with his feet dangling and stared at his legs all papery white covered in a web of blue veins, and he wondered how the hell he'd grown so old, and if he'd ever been anything but. He listened to the snores coming from the next room and was envious of the boy's deep sleep, because even sleep came hard these days. He wondered if going on was worth it, but then, what's a man to do but take it a day at a time?

He had a memory of a boy, a skinny thing with golden hair. Maybe it was himself, but it could have been another kid. I must be close to the end, he told himself. Truth was, he'd been telling himself the end was near for years, but now it felt true. Recently, the climb to the attic had become impossible, so he'd set the cot up in the front room. And now he stared at the door and thought there was something he should do to prepare for his passing. The boy wouldn't have anyone after he was gone. But then, he thought, I haven't been much of a father. It won't be much different without me. This thought made him sad. The kid had lost everyone.

Wendell sifted through a blur of faces—some he couldn't

name. He caught a flash of Alta in magenta and blue, and then he remembered she had a father, an important man, and he was Adam's grandfather, but then the memory was gone, and his head was pounding, thundering like a running horse. He stumbled to the kitchen in spite of it.

When the boy eventually came in, Wendell gave him coffee. Residue of his earlier recollections must have lingered because he was feeling unusually benevolent toward the boy. He set down the coffee pot, and then, because moving across the room and even standing took too much effort, he sat at the table across from Adam. The boy was holding something.

"Why the long face?"

Adam shrugged. He let go of what he was fingering and it rolled across the table. Wendell picked it up and saw it was a carved tiger.

"Did you know Myrtle Todd killed the tiger?"

"The tiger?"

"The circus tiger. That everyone's been hunting."

"You don't say?"

"You didn't hear? It walked into her yard and she shot it."

"No fear," Wendell said knowingly. He held up the totem. "Where'd you get this?"

"Mom . . . It was in her stuff."

"Smoke used to make carvings like this." Wendell studied it more before rolling it back to Adam. His fingers, left empty, tapped on the table. Adam didn't reply because there was nothing to say, but then Wendell blurted. "Your ma sure had a fondness for him. The way she looked at him. It made Stanley half mad. And he had eyes for her too."

"You're an ass."

"A truer thing could not be said."

Adam glanced around for a bottle.

"She didn't know what she was in for, coming out here. A real fish out of water. They both were. Two peas in a pod, really, if you think of it that way . . . I don't know . . ."

Wendell's fingers sped up so they were fleeing ponies trot-trot-trotting across the table, and he bounced his leg. His fingers were bounding, all four on his right hand hurdled, as if small logs were rolling across the table and under his hand, and the fingers were leaping over them. Adam watched and was irritated. He wanted to slap Wendell's hand.

"I should have done something," Wendell said, and the fingers slowed their pace, tap-tap-tapping to cool down after a race.

"Smoke was a good man."

"What could you have done?"

"Hell if I know. Tell Jake the truth of it. He may not have been so hard on Smoke . . . He couldn't have had me put away, like him." The realization sucked the breath out of him. He closed in his eyes and slowly filled his lungs, which set him coughing. Adam glanced at the stove, noting there was nothing cooking, and he was quite hungry.

"Why don't you tell him now?"

"Wouldn't do no good. Jake had it in for him."

"Would it have done any good back then?"

"I don't know. Maybe. I can't say."

"Do you think he's alive?"

"I don't know. Cripes Almighty."

Wendell waved his hand and sat still now. There were too many thoughts, and he was too old.

"Listen," he said, because he needed to say something. He needed to give Adam something. "You have your whole life ahead of you. None of that matters. You're a good kid."

"I killed that tiger."

"Jesus Christ. Myrtle killed the tiger. You let it go. Maybe that didn't turn out to be such a good idea. But a tiger shouldn't be in a cage either. You gave it a chance. So that's something. Probably spent its whole life in a cage. It didn't know how to be a tiger . . . Some things you just can't save."

His words felt good. Adam felt a smile working on his face, but the fact that Wendell had turned all sentimental was uncomfortable. Next thing he was going to be crying and Adam couldn't bear that, so he changed the subject.

"Did I kill my mom?"

"Jesus . . . you been drinking, boy?" Wendell stared at Adam. Any early morning sunshine he'd been feeling was gone.

"By being born."

"No. Christ Almighty."

"If Stanley didn't, and I wasn't born, she'd be here."

Wendell lifted his head toward the door as if expecting someone. When he spoke, he spoke slowly. "That's crazy talk . . . Listen, kid. It doesn't do any good. Wrestling with the dead. They're all gone now. You can't bring 'em back."

They sat quietly, dust lifting in the blade of sunlight coming through the torn curtain. Adam shook his head. It mattered. Of course it mattered. Weren't the living walking the path cleared by the dead? If his mom wasn't dead, if his father were here, he sure as hell wouldn't be living in a house eviscerated by a drunk old man.

"The grasshoppers are sure bad this year."

"Yeah . . ."

"You know, in '75 we had locusts. They came in a cloud as wide as you could see. They ate everything. They ate a man. He fell asleep in the hay. They don't come like that anymore."

"Is that true?"

"Yes."

"Where'd they come from?"

"The devil."

Adam nodded. He scanned the small kitchen with its rusted-out stove, the empty cupboards. The pump in the sink had a constant, slow drip.

“This place is a mess,” Adam said, but Wendell didn’t hear him.

CHAPTER 28

ALTA

Alta sent letters to her father explaining her change of mind and her situation. Send Clarence back, she told him; she was ready to come home. Once a week, she walked to the post office and the clerk took her letter. She waited for a reply, but none ever came. Clarence didn't return—no one was coming for her. She felt abandoned, and she panicked. The reality of her predicament settled over her like a storm cloud. She wasn't safe. And if she wasn't safe, of course, a baby wasn't safe. The episode in the kitchen with Stanley's hands at her throat replayed in her mind over and over again. She couldn't bring a child into such a dangerous world, and the window in which she could do something was closing. Of course Stanley would know the child wasn't his; of this she was certain. She laid her hands on her stomach and felt sick with the thought of it, and she made up her mind.

She sent for Lola through a cowboy who'd been passing by the house, an out-of-towner visiting to blow his paycheck. While she and Lola weren't on friendly terms, she had no choice in the matter. A moment such as this required a stalemate in which women supported each other. If the reverse was true, and Lola was in such a predicament, she told herself, she would lend a hand—begrudging of course, but a hand just the same. Women stick together. It's a fundamental truth, like the sun rising every morning. Besides, Lola was the only one who could help, and so she must.

Alta ran a rag across the counter and then the table to keep moving while she waited for Lola to stop by—not certain she'd even received the message. She considered that Lola might not like her, especially after their encounter at the salon. Alta admitted she hadn't been the most Christian in her reaction, but what did Lola expect coming uninvited to an event for the good wives and mothers and daughters of the community? And Alta had an obligation to protect the reputation of her events and her guests. Besides, the woman had meant to disrupt; this knowledge increased the distaste Alta had for what she was doing. But liking wasn't a prerequisite for helping or sticking together.

The clock on the shelf ticked past the hour with no sign of Lola. Alta tried needlework but quickly gave up. She stepped out on the porch to watch wagons rattle down the street to the depot to dump their loads. The dust rose like smoke and scattered in the gathering wind. It was well past dinnertime, but this time of year, the light lingered. Boys wandering in front of the depot jumped into the piles of wheat and sank so the wheat avalanched over their arms, and the farmers and ranchers and the men working nearby driving cattle through the vats or waiting on the train yelled at them to get out—they could suffocate, for goodness' sake. Occasionally, one of the men slapped a boy alongside the head or chased the lot of them out of the pile, but eventually, the boys always returned. The elevators Jake was building in the spring would keep them out of the grain.

Alta went back inside and shut the curtains. She hoped Lola had the good sense to come to the back door. She didn't want anyone to see that they were meeting. But the knock, when it came, was at the front door. Alta smoothed her skirt and touched her hair as she rushed to open it.

Lola stood on the doorstep with a scarf wrapped around her head. She stepped inside, unwrapping the scarf, and her hair cascaded down her shoulders.

"Thank you for coming," Alta said.

"Of course I came. I wouldn't miss this for the world. I couldn't imagine why you wanted to see me." Lola's voice dripped sarcasm, which Alta ignored, though she understood in that moment the degree of Lola's animosity. Alta directed her guest to have a seat and disappeared into the kitchen where she set water to boiling—she needed something to focus on to calm her nerves.

"Would you like some tea?" She peered into the front room. Lola had made herself comfortable and seemed to be studying the wall opposite, where Alta had hung a landscape painting—a poorly executed one at that. Even in what felt like a dire moment, she felt a blush of shame.

"I'd prefer something stronger."

Alta dumped the tea into water to steep.

"Sugar?" she called from the kitchen, choosing to ignore Lola's comment. She took a deep breath to steady her hands as she arranged the cups on a tray, then carried the tray to the front room and set it on the table next to Lola. She passed the other woman a cup, looking her over for the first time since her arrival. Lola wore a plain dress and her face was unblemished with paint. Though no longer young, she was still a beautiful woman. Their eyes met briefly, then Alta glanced away.

"This is fine," Lola said, not hiding her irritation. She ignored the bowl of sugar Alta offered.

Alta took a cup and sat down across from her.

"Well, then, how are you?"

Lola didn't say, but gazed at Alta over her teacup.

"Is this why I'm here? For pleasant conversation?"

"No. Of course not. I'll get to the point." Alta set her cup on the side table without taking a drink. "I asked you here for your advice. On behalf of a friend."

"Advice. For a friend."

"Yes. A friend."

"I see," said Lola. She wondered if Alta really thought she would fall for the friend ruse. She sipped her tea and waited for Alta to continue.

"I believe I can trust you to keep a confidence . . ."

"What makes you think so?"

"In your line of work . . ." Alta paused. Just what did she know about Lola's line of work?

"I can be very discreet," Lola smiled, enjoying Alta's discomfort.

"Sometimes women need to stick together."

"What does your friend need?" It turned out Lola wasn't interested in the philosophy of women sticking together.

Alta took her time. She wasn't sure how to form the words. She stared at her hands, and she felt herself grow hot.

"Would you like some more tea?" She stood up and took the tray back into the kitchen—though Lola hadn't yet touched her drink—and refilled the kettle, then set it back on the stove, wondering as she worked how to say what she needed to say.

"My friend is pregnant," she spoke to the stove, making sure her voice was loud enough to carry.

"I'm sorry. Can you repeat that?" Lola asked when Alta reappeared. "I couldn't hear. Did you say you were pregnant?" She knew exactly what Alta had said, but wasn't about to make the conversation easy.

"Of course." Alta was flustered. "My friend is pregnant . . . and circumstances . . ."

"I see." Lola set her cup down and let the silence hang over the room. She had to concentrate to keep from laughing. It was an obvious lie from an inexperienced liar. She surveyed the room waiting to see if Alta would continue, wondering how she herself could put this information to work. The house was modest for someone as high and mighty as Alta, she noted with a sort of glee. The household furnishings were rather lowly. Josephine's place was much nicer. It occurred to Lola that Stanley wasn't such a great provider—they wouldn't be living in a mansion when everything eventually played out, but then, one can't have everything. At least he would make her respectable.

"She can't have a baby." Alta stood up and picked up her cup and walked back into the kitchen, still trying to calm her nerves.

"Why is that?" Lola called after her, imagining Stanley's outrage if he knew of this conversation. When. Because of course she'd tell him . . .

"I assume your friend is someone like you," Lola encouraged, sweetening her voice. "By that, I mean she has a husband and a house. I would imagine a baby would be a welcome addition."

Alta stood out of sight wondering what it would be like, an abortion—the mechanics of it. She'd heard some stories that sometimes women died. She wondered if she was committing a sin so great that she'd be consigned to hell.

"Unless the baby is someone other than the husband's," Lola said, careful to keep her voice even. The thought of Alta having an affair was truly funny, but of course that was the reason. That was the only possible reason. She watched Alta return to the room with a line of perspiration on her brow. She was concentrating on her teacup and looked like she was close to tears. Lola almost felt sorry for her. She tried to think of who the father might be. She'd heard the gossip here and there but hadn't paid it much mind. Back then, it didn't really matter.

"Oh, honey. That is an old story. Old as the hills." Lola

wondered, as she spoke, if she would just move into this house when Stanley divorced Alta. Abortion was certainly grounds for divorce. No one would dispute that. She'd never thought much of God, but it seemed He might be looking out for her. "No husband is going to know the difference. When a daddy sees he's got a son, or a daughter, he's going to be the happiest man on earth. It really doesn't matter who plants the seed. The man who harvests the crop is the father. That's the way it is. That's the way it's always been. Men never know the difference. As for the other thing, I wouldn't recommend it. If that's what your friend wants, of course I can make arrangements. I know people. But it's dangerous."

Lola reached out her hand and covered Alta's in an unusually maternal gesture—she was feeling generous.

"A man is going to see what he wants to see. Tell that to your friend."

Alta nodded, because Lola was right. Of course she was right. Stanley wouldn't know he wasn't the father. How could he? The realization filled her with relief. She'd been worried for nothing.

"Well, then." Lola stood up. "I should be getting back before someone notices I'm missing." She glanced around the house, looking for something, she didn't know what, and so she swung the end of her scarf around her neck.

"Talk about it with your friend. Let me know if she changes her mind."

"How can I thank you?" Alta said, getting ahold of herself.

"Well . . ." Lola said, and then let the unfinished sentence speak for itself.

"Of course," Alta said. "One moment."

Alta disappeared into the bedroom and returned with a handful of bills. Stanley had searched through her things but had not found the money she'd been skimming from her household allowance.

"Will this do?"

Lola took the money and threw her scarf over her head. Alta was relieved when she closed the door. Lola was right. Women had been raising illegitimate children as their own since the beginning of time; there was no need to worry. She'd been foolish to think differently.

CHAPTER 29

ADAM

It was there in black ink. "The thing is not his." Adam paused and felt the blood drain from his face. There was no misunderstanding. He clutched the book like he was squeezing the words out of it, then released it like something burnt. He leaned back against the bed frame to catch his breath, then leaned forward and pressed the book into the floor as he read it again, slowly, moving his fingers beneath the words to make sure he didn't jump a line.

> *September 5*
>
> *Stanley's wife came to me in the family way, and the thing is not his. He ought to know it's not. Of course, he'll know. All high and mighty and she's nothing but a whore. She thinks she's better than all of us, but she's just like us. Lying with an Indian, of all things. Even old Hazel wouldn't have sunk that low, or maybe she did. Maybe that's how she ended up with her neck choked . . . And them folks who said God don't watch over the whores, well he just handed me a free ticket on the gravy train.*

The story didn't get any better, but Adam couldn't stop reading. The entire past, every question he'd asked about himself and his family came into focus in those three miserable entries.

March 27

He kilt her. I know he did. He didn't say, but I could see it. It was in his eyes and he smelt of it. I felt sorry when I knew, but he's my ticket. I'm not scared because I know him. I never wanted a child, but it'll be OK. He'll be mine.

May 22

He's a Judas! All lies. I'm not his pigeon, the sap. And a wet nurse, of all things, after what he did to his wife. I know what you did. You're finished! You'll get your just desserts!

He set the book down and stared at the rotting walls. "The thing is not his." He repeated the lines in his head over and over again. "He kilt her." Two thoughts, each one stunning in its own way. Bastard, he thought about Stanley. He'd held off the rumors, like a dam holding back water. But now the truth burst in his brain and he felt a surge of rage. God damn son-of-a-bitch murderer. And then there was the relief—and confusion. "That thing is not his." Stanley was a murderer, but the murderer was not his father . . . But then, lying with an Indian? It couldn't be. His mother wouldn't do that, would she? It was too much really. He found his rifle—fortunately Wendell hadn't sold it yet—and set out walking, grabbing a couple of beers off the railing of the Tumbleweed from two cowboys too busy arguing over which one of them was a better roper to notice. He stuffed one in each of his back pockets and set off toward the whirl of the river, then drank the first as he followed the river east along the bank. His feet tangled on the dead brush and brambles, snapping twigs and catching on branches, and he yanked them out, pulling up roots as he pulled on his knees. After a time, he came up on the rotting remains of the Fort Union Trading Post, once the commercial center of the Great Plains. He tossed the first bottle into the brush and finished off the second while walking through the abandoned fort. He stopped and stood swaying ever so slightly, liking that the world seemed muffled as he studied the grounds, which had been disassembled and gutted so mounds and scraps of wood and rusting nails marked the foundations of the long bunkhouse and storage sheds and the house of the officers of the American Fur Company, which had built the post. He continued on for two more miles, pausing to shoot at prairie dogs, not flinching at their squeals—damn varmints—then stumbled on to the abandoned military outpost, Fort Buford, near the confluence of the Missouri and Yellowstone rivers. By now the sun was hot and beating down on him, and he was too depleted to continue. He wandered listlessly through the barracks, his brain a tumbleweed of prickly thoughts. Most of the barracks had been transported to Mondak to be transformed into bars and other businesses, but a line of them remained, standing in an orderly line like old soldiers, gray and bent. These he gave a mock salute.

He walked through the cemetery beyond the buildings along the southwest boundary with headstones sticking up like rotted teeth from the dried grass, the buried men known by their afflictions rather than their names—Disease, Suicide, Killed by Indians, Died of Inebriation. So much dying, Adam thought. So many ghosts.

He thought of his parents. All he had of his parents were the stories that had been handed to him. His mother. She'd been beautiful and good—this knowledge was skin. But maybe not so good. And his father. Who was his father? Not Stanley—the man who had kilt his mother. He could shatter that golem. Was it the Indian? And so he was born of what? Sin? Violence? What did that make him? He kicked a headstone once, then twice, then again, 'til he wondered if he'd broken some toes. Who was he? *Half breed?* The thought sent him into a rage, and he kicked another headstone.

"Fuck!" He jumped up and down holding his leg. It's all a bunch of crap anyway. He was tired of the weight of them. They're all dead. The whole lot of them. They're all ghosts. They had nothing to do with him. They were all just stories. He let those thoughts circulate and took a seat, leaning against Died by Suicide (there were quite a number of these). What if the ghosts of all ages crossed time and gathered together, and so his mom, the Indian, and maybe that goddamn Stanley might be huddled with the soldiers? He felt clever thinking the thought. What would they talk about? He brushed off a swarm of mosquitos, leaving a trail of blood across his arm. It's the land that killed the soldiers, he thought. All dry and desolate in the summer. Frigid winters with ferocious winds. And the oppressive immensity. He imagined the soldiers with their vague twisted forms and growling voices telling swaggering stories, and his heart throbbed in the boney cage of his ribs from thinking. And then the soldiers were circling him, wearing sackcloth shadows, and of course they were jealous of his flesh, but they were amicable, slapping one another on the back, smoking, and bragging about battles. Their thoughts were his thoughts. But then he saw in the shadow of Chief Sitting Bull dressed for battle in this very place he had surrendered, and the soldiers realized Adam was not of their tribe but of the enemy, and their camaraderie turned to fury. Adam broke into a sweat and tried to tell them differently, but they scattered like clouds. Then he saw the chief's eyes were vast lakes, and men were drowning in their depths. Adam could hear the screams and he froze, and then the chief became a pile of rotting timber. And he felt his mother's breath across his face whispering, "It's all right."

Adam startled awake and lay catching his breath. He sat up and wiped the ground dirt from his elbows and wasn't sure if he'd been visited or he'd been dreaming. He dug his hand into the dirt where he sat and thought that all the dead were dirt. And he thought here in his hand could be the dust from a hundred men from opposing armies.

He stood up and shook his head, then picked up his rifle and began the long walk home. He was too tired to care about any of it, although his mind kept returning to the images from the cemetery.

He slept fitfully that night, in fits and starts under a mountain of blankets, and he had the feeling of being weighed and measured and prodded by frozen fingers that may have been the night air seeping through the cracks in the wall and along the window or may have been something else. Sometime in the night he awoke gasping for breath. It took a moment for him to realize the hands at his throat were his own. His pulse beat against his palms and at first, his hands were too heavy to lift. And then he did lift them and lay groggy in his nest of blankets.

He gazed at the shadowy walls of his room and thought the house was like a dying thing—small and empty, collapsing in on itself. A flower folding. The house and town and everyone here, Adam thought. It's all peeling away, conceding the prairie to the rabbits, quail, deer, and hawks.

He glanced in the mirror on his way out of the room and saw his face was covered in a rash like tiny bites. He lifted his shirt and the rash covered his torso and his arms, and it itched, so he had to scratch. He made his way into the kitchen and started water boiling for coffee.

XXX

Adam didn't say anything to Wendell about what he'd learned from the diary. What was there to say? And what did it change? He hired himself out to a farmer for the harvest and still attended to Jake's business. Keeping busy was key to keeping all his crazy thoughts at bay. And school was starting soon. He had that to think about. Beyond school, he didn't think about his future or the past. He thought about the harvest and driving horses, pulling a binder, or tossing bundles of wheat into the threshing machine. The physical work was a relief. In the evenings, Jake had him running errands in his Model T, which he'd taught him to drive. Any time he wasn't working, he was off hunting for pheasant or grouse, and so he was too tired to even go fishing with Cecil.

All that came to an end when Wendell got sick. One morning at breakfast, the old man stood up and walked toward the stove with his coffee cup, then dropped to the floor like a burlap bag of horse feed. The cup shattered, leaving a minefield of ceramic shrapnel.

Adam's first thought was that Wendell was drunk, so he was more irritated than concerned. It was ridiculous being drunk so early in the day. He watched Wendell's hand twitch. Then it hit him that something wasn't right.

"Hey," he said, and Wendell didn't respond.

"Christ!" Adam jumped up. He rolled the old man onto his back. "You OK?"

Wendell's eyes were wide and frightened; spittle leaked from the side of his mouth.

"Can you get up?"

When Wendell didn't respond, Adam patted him on the chest. "You're going to be OK. I'm going to get the doctor."

Adam rushed out of the house and came back a few minutes later with the doctor hobbling after him.

"Stroke, it looks like," the doctor said, waving his fingers in front of Wendell's unresponsive eyes. They carried him to

Adam's bed because it was the most comfortable, and the doctor moved around him, poking until he repeated his conclusion.

"It looks like a stroke. You'll have to take care of him. Do you think you can do that?" The doctor explained the signs to look for and how to make sure Wendell was hydrated and how to monitor his breathing. After the doctor left, Adam sat in a chair next to the bed and stared at the old man with sloughing skin.

"What the hell are you doing, you bastard," Adam whispered, feigning anger rather than let Wendell see he was worried. After a while, the boy stood and paced, then brought in a cup of water and sat by the bed. He tipped the cup into Wendell's mouth, and the water poured out the side, so he went to the kitchen to fetch a spoon. Slowly, he pressed the water between the old man's lips.

Over the next few days, Wendell occasionally gained consciousness and blubbered nonsense. "Hiawatha," he said several times, pointing his bony finger at the ceiling.

"What? Who's that?"

Wendell shook his head, defeated by the effort.

Several days later, he lurched up and grasped Adam's hand, squeezing painfully hard, but Adam didn't pull away.

"Go see Duck," he mumbled. "Smoke's brother. In Poplar . . ." He chewed his lip and seemed to be focusing extremely hard to get his words out. A drop of blood slid from the side of his mouth. Adam wiped it carefully and helped Wendell to lie down. "Sm . . . brother . . ." Wendell mumbled before falling asleep.

XXX

Wendell passed away several days later. Adam came into the bedroom to look at him early one morning, and he was gone.

Adam stood next to Clem at the funeral, and no one said it out loud, but each wondered if it weren't for the best. Still, the death was an untethering for Adam. For all his drunken foolery, Wendell had been a constant for the boy, a leaky boat on a rough sea, but a boat just the same.

Adam sat in the house for days. It was like an abandoned place with its chipped paint and scarred floor. What furniture remained was worn and tattered. Adam paced and opened and closed cupboards and moved cups around. He sat at the kitchen table and stared at the walls, waiting, he realized, for Wendell. But of course Wendell was gone.

At some point, it occurred to Adam that there was probably something that needed to be done, things to take care of. It's what people did with the dead. Probably there were items to be seen to or a person to be notified, a wrapping up of the loose ends of a person's life. Adam climbed the ladder with a lantern banging against his leg, the rungs worn soft, and pulled himself into the dusty attic. It took a moment for his eyes to adjust to the dim lighting of what was barely a room—just a triangular space under the slanted roof with exposed beams. He could stand straight in the two feet that ran down the middle, but as he moved away from the center of the room, it was necessary to lean over. He gazed around, trying to remember when he'd last been in the attic—it had been a long time. It was a place where Wendell used to retreat, like a rabbit hole in the roof. It seemed the old man had never cleaned the place. The dust was thick along walls and corners, and the two small windows looking east were so filthy they barely took in any light. The only furniture was a straw mattress, worn and stained with a blanket twisted on top and a wooden chair. Clothes were strewn in piles on the floor. There were several crates along one wall.

Adam bent to get to the crates under the sloping roof. He pulled one out and lifted out piles of filthy clothes, which made him reconsider—it was all probably trash. But Adam persevered and kept digging. In the next crate, under torn gloves and holey socks, he found a faded and worn box. Inside were several faded photos, some old coins, and a button. Adam picked up one of the pictures, a young woman—pretty, he supposed. The other pictures looked like they could be family, but there was no way to identify them. Wendell had never talked much about his family or where he came from, and there was no identifying information. Another box had a stack of letters, newspaper clippings, and ties and bow ties, and several more photos. Adam picked through the photos. Among them was one of Alta and Stanley's wedding. He knew it was them because he'd seen pictures before. She sat in a chair in a pretty dress with a veil holding flowers and he stood over her shoulders in a fancy suit. They looked happy, he supposed. He set the photo aside and fingered the ties. To the best of his knowledge, Wendell had never owned a tie. It was strange indeed to find him with several. Adam picked up the stack of letters and his heart stopped. The return address was Alta Olson, and the address was to Cadwallader Woburn in St. Paul, Minnesota. He opened a letter.

Dear Father,

I am writing to you with a heavy heart. I understand now that I made a mistake disobeying your orders and coming out to Mondak. I was an impetuous child, and I hope you can forgive me. You see, I am expecting your grandchild, and I wish to come home and raise him (or her) under your guidance. If you can not forgive me for my own sake, I hope you can for the sake of this baby.

If you have it in your heart, send Clarence here to accompany me. I am afraid it is not safe for me to travel on my own for reasons I can not explain in this letter.

I am waiting, forever hopeful and with all my love,

Alta

Adam stuffed the letter in his pocket and glanced through the others; they were more of the same. Why on earth did Wendell have these? he wondered, but then it occurred to him that this was a box of Stanley's possessions. Probably Wendell had stuck it in the attic and never bothered going through it. Stanley had had a reputation as a dapper dresser, and he often, if not always, wore a tie. The letters, it appeared, had never been mailed. He wondered why as he set them aside.

He continued through the other crates and boxes looking through a batch of newspaper clippings, obituaries mostly, of people Adam didn't know—Wendell—or Stanley, whoever's belongings he was sifting through now—had been a sort of chronicler of the local history, it seemed. Adam found an obituary for Phyllis—passed in her sleep, it said. And there was an article about Lew and Beverly leaving town to return to Billings so they could care for Lew's sick mother.

Adam leaned back against the wall and wiped his forehead with the back of his hand. He pocketed the letters from his mother, then carried the contents of the crates down the ladder. In the backyard, he gathered together kindling and lit a fire, and then he shoved the photos and clippings and buttons and ties into the flames. He pulled up a log and sat watching the flames until they slowly faded and the red glow of the wood turned to black. Then he found a shovel and buried the ashes before he made his way to the livery to see if Jake had some work.

CHAPTER 30

STANLEY

Stanley was in the parlor at Josephine's on the night Lola visited Alta. He was sitting on the couch with several of the girls flirting with him while he drank a glass of whiskey when she returned, but she was in an exuberant mood, and so it didn't bother her at all. On this day, she recognized the futility of fighting nature—he often spent evenings making sure the clients paid and didn't harm the women, and it was in a whore's nature to flirt. Her mission, she'd already decided, was to weaponize Stanley's nature and use it to her advantage. Besides, there had been an unusually ruckusy crowd the last few nights, and Jake was worried that some men who had been forcibly removed previously would return.

Stanley needed to know Alta's child was a bastard, Lola thought as she made her way to the stairs, feeling like she'd won the lottery. She had to convince him without him knowing she was convincing him. And more importantly, she had to convince him that he could not benefit financially from his marriage to Alta through this child because then, if he thought it was necessary to eventually claim Cadwallader's wealth, he might overlook the paternity. No, she had to appeal to his pride, and Stanley was nothing if not prideful. She had to let him know his wife had betrayed him without appearing to knowingly reveal the news. He would become enraged; the rest would work itself out.

He followed her from the room and nuzzled her neck, but she pushed him away. She needed to go to her room and think and plan. Later that night, he came upstairs quite drunk from a party downstairs and lay back on her bed chatting enthusiastically about the goings-on. She let him ramble without really listening and offered him a drink. He sat up and took the glass from her. Music and laughter from the party downstairs shook the floor.

"I hear congratulations are in order," she said, getting straight to the point.

Stanley mumbled.

"The news is all about town. I overheard a couple of those church ladies talking when I was at Lew's the other day."

"Oh, yeah?" He rocked on the end of the bed, not interested.

"I'm sure you're very happy."

"Yeah. Why's that?" He gazed at his glass. He wasn't making this easy.

"You're going to be a father."

He didn't seem to hear, so she leaned over and whispered in his ear. "Congratulations! You're going to be a father!"

"You're pregnant?" he asked. He pulled his tobacco out of his shirt pocket.

"No. Your wife is."

"Who? Alta?"

"Do you have a different wife?"

"How's she pregnant?" He stopped rolling and stared at her.

"Well, I think you know how that works." She pulled the tobacco from his hand and set it on the table and straddled him, her hand reaching for his crotch.

"Alta's going to have a baby?"

"That's the gossip. You didn't know?"

He pulled her hand away and pushed her off him, and looked dazed. She moved to her dressing table and brushed her hair, measuring his reaction in the mirror. He picked his tobacco back up and rolled a cigarette.

"I'm going to be a father."

"Well, that's what I heard. That's what the women were saying."

He smoked now, flicking his cigarette, and she could see his face working into a smile.

"A father."

"Jake has children, doesn't he?"

Stanley nodded and watched the smoke from his cigarette curl.

"The family is in Minot?"

"That's what I heard."

Lola stood up and poured him a tumbler of whiskey.

"Rumor is he moved her there after she cheated on him with a wealthy rancher from Butte."

"That true? I would have beat the living shit out of her." He ashed his cigarette and picked up the whiskey.

"It's not as uncommon as you might think for women."

Stanley finished his whiskey and stood up to pour another. Normally she didn't mind his drifting away. Most punters figured their five dollars paid her for listening, so giving a rat's ass was good customer service. But now she wanted his attention without appearing to work for it.

"Do you think Alta would ever cheat on you?"

"Hell no. She's too much of a prude."

"Yeah, she is that . . . Of course, some women just play like prudes."

Lola held out her own glass so he could fill it.

"Whatever happened to that Indian? Smoke, that was his name, wasn't it? Didn't he do some work for you around the house?" She turned into the mirror to sip her drink.

"Yeah . . ." He let his voice trail off, as if he was thinking. "I took care of him."

"Did you?" She let a note of doubt creep into her voice. It took him a moment to catch it.

"What the fuck are you saying?"

"Goodness, Stanley . . . You're in a mood. We're just making conversation." Lola rolled a cigarette for herself.

"You heard about our Daisy here? She got herself in the family way. It's not good for business, as you can imagine." Lola could see Stanley's mind working, making connections. He toyed nervously with this cigarette.

"I was here for that. I remember."

"It's just that some father lost his child. He didn't even know it. He didn't know he was a father. It happens a lot in this business."

She stood up and planted a kiss on his mouth, then turned away to light her cigarette.

"I heard Minni Johnson had a baby that didn't belong to Mr. Johnson. He never knew the difference."

When Stanley finally lunged for her, Lola knew he understood the message. She knocked over her chair to escape his hands.

"Jesus Christ!" He jammed his shin on a leg of the bed as he caught her by the throat. He lifted her and pushed her against the wall.

"Goodness, Stanley. I'm just making conversation."

He could choke her right here, she knew. He was cutting off her air, but she didn't let the fear leak into her eyes, which were steady on his face. He squeezed harder, and she imagined he was seeing a new and different picture of his wife. It was coming in clear.

"Everything OK?" There was a loud knock on the door.

Stanley held on just a little longer to show her he could,

and then released her throat but still pressed her, now by the shoulders.

"Everything's fine, Josephine," Lola said, catching her breath. "Just knocked over a chair."

"Well, you've been up here a long time. Why don't you come on down? I've got someone I want you to meet."

Stanley was breathing heavily, and he brought his face close and still she was looking, and then he pressed against her, his whole body, and that's how it was, and he took her against the wall, and that way he worked out his rage so it was OK.

After he left, Lola examined her neck and there were red marks from his hands. She would have a bruise, which was never for the best, but downstairs the lights were dim and people had been drinking for hours, so it was doubtful anyone would notice. She cleaned herself in the basin, straightened her dress, patted her cheeks, and made her way to the party.

XXX

Stanley came home in the wee hours of the morning, and he was too tired and drunk to recall his conversation with Lola. He didn't remember until he was drinking coffee much later and Alta was at the counter making bread or pie or something, and it came back to him.

"I heard something," he said, and she glanced at him and continued pressing her hands into the dough.

"What's that?"

"I heard you're going to have a baby."

Alta stopped and felt her face drain, because obviously Lola had said something. And so Alta's thoughts were scrambling to recall exactly what she'd said to the other woman. She didn't think she'd confessed that the pregnant party was herself, and so she responded to Stanley from that point of view.

"Well, it's possible, Stanley. I just don't know. It's too early to be sure."

"Well, why were women gossiping about it?"

"I don't know. People gossip. What women? Where?"

"Down at Lew's . . ." Stanley trailed off because he couldn't name the women and he felt like he'd been trapped. He tried to recall the rest of his conversation with Lola, and it seemed there'd been talk of infidelity, and he recalled she'd suggested Alta had been cheating, but then he wasn't sure at all if that's what had been said. The facts seemed to be jumbled.

"Do you think you might be?"

"It's possible. Maybe. I'm late . . . But I wanted to be sure before I said anything. Many times, early on, the baby is lost."

Stanley squinted his eyes and stared at her all dusty with flour and her hair drifting down from the stack on her head into her eyes. That last thing she said seemed awfully suspicious.

"Lost? How?"

"Miscarriage. The baby doesn't take."

"Well, you'd sure as hell better not miscarry." He growled, because he knew miscarry was code for calling some midwife with a hanger.

"Well, I don't think anyone intentionally miscarries."

Stanley slammed his fist into the table and Alta startled, knocking a bowl to the floor so it shattered. He stood up and shook his hand at her.

"If I find out you miscarried, you'll be sorry . . . And don't try running off again with my child. I'll be watching you."

XXX

She'll say anything, Stanley thought, later. It was one of the qualities he liked most about Lola—even if in this case her jealous ramblings were full of shit. He knew Alta hadn't had an affair because that would involve fooling him, and he was not a fool. Just the same, he was attentive in the months preceding the birth. The suggestion that his wife could betray him fascinated him, in a morbid kind of way, and made him a wee bit wary. She became an enigma—what was she capable of? He studied her like a puzzle or some kind of prey. She was sly, he knew that. She'd tried to leave him, and he couldn't have that with the impending birth of his fortune. So, he tried a new approach to husbandry. He became attentive. Doting. He helped her carry washtubs and haul firewood and advised her on how to avoid the chill as winter descended, and she let down her guard and didn't divert her eyes from his quite so much—though if he was honest, she did seem to avoid his touch. But he figured that was the way of pregnant women. Besides, he had outlets. He didn't need to worry about bedding his wife. As the days shortened and grew cold, he huddled with Alta in the kitchen and played cards and talked by lantern light while she stitched clothes for the baby, and sometimes he would touch her growing tummy and feel his son kick, because of course she was carrying his boy. And he had to admit that if one put store in domestic things, the days were quite pleasant. When he wasn't around, he had a farmer here and a cowboy there and an agent at the depot—a small army of men who he paid each a buck or two to let him know if Alta approached the station or attempted to hire a man to take her out of town, and the postal clerk always kept her mail—though of course she wasn't a prisoner. When he stopped by Josephine's to collect "rent" for Jake, he avoided Lola. Sometimes she'd happen by the parlor where he'd be joking with the other girls, and he'd tug at her skirt and flirt a bit, and then he'd follow Kittie or Alice or Madeline up to their room. In this way, the whore knew he was punishing her for insinuating he had married a tramp.

CHAPTER 31

ADAM

The Erickson job is a big job, Jake told him. "Do you think you can handle it?"

Of course he could handle it. He spat into the dirt to illustrate his point. He was done with these tests. He was ready for anything Jake could send his way.

The family had forty acres about five miles north of town. And they had two big boys and at least two guns, Jake explained. This was a two-man job.

It had rained recently, so the roads were bad. For this reason, Jake said they'd take the horses. There was Lady, of course, and another sorry buckskin, probably nineteen years old with withers as high as a mountain—a sign of its ramshackleness more than poor diet because it also managed to be fat. The backstrap on the saddle barely fit around its belly. Adam felt the insult of mounting such a sad beast, but he patted its neck as they left the barn—it wasn't the horse's fault, after all.

They kept at a steady trot, Jake spilling over the saddle and jiggling in a way that made Adam's outrage worse. And his breathing was heavy like he was doing the work rather than the horse. Adam had never mistaken Jake for a horseman, and today the big boss compensated for his lack of skill by using a particularly sharp bit and tugging on the reins, even though Lady was an easy, responsive ride. Adam found himself having to concentrate on the horizon to keep from commenting on Jake's lack of riding skill, a surefire way to get into trouble.

They slowed to a walk as they neared the homestead—relatively prosperous compared to many Adam had seen. The house was little more than a small box, but it had wood slabs for siding rather than the oft-seen tarpaper, and it had a brick chimney. There was a lean-to in a relatively large corral for the stock. Several chickens roamed the yard, and two milk cows and a donkey stood lazily flicking flies in the corral. A buckboard was parked not too far from the house, alongside a plow and some other equipment.

The family, it seemed, was expecting them—they all came out to meet them as they approached. The father was a lanky man with a gray beard and crumpled hat. He cradled a rifle like it was something dear. Two boys—young men really—lined up behind him, tall and sturdy, one with a tumbleweed of red hair, the other blond. Adam figured them to be just a few years older than himself. The mother had a thin, lined face, and the daughter was doe-eyed with silky brown hair. Very pretty, Adam thought, then shook his head to dismiss the thought. He needed to focus on the task at hand.

"Howdy, Tom," Jake said, lifting his hat. Adam wrapped his hand around the rifle stock; his eyes were on the boys, but his mind was on the girl.

"Good afternoon," Mr. Erickson said. He had both hands on his gun, though the barrel was pointed to the dirt.

"What can I do for you?"

"You're past due on your note." Jake held out a piece of paper, but none of the Ericksons made a move to take it.

"It's been a lean year."

"That is has," Jake said. "But according to our terms—which you agreed to"—he shook the paper to illustrate his point, or perhaps to get Tom to take it—"you no longer own the property. I'm going to have to ask you to vacate."

"No," the mom whispered. The daughter covered her mouth and let out a yelp.

The blond boy lurched forward, pointing a pistol. "Nah. I don't think so."

The mother pushed the daughter back into the house and disappeared behind her.

Jake raised his rifle at the boy, and Tom raised his pistol and pointed it at Jake. Jake glanced at Adam to make sure he had backup, and Adam had a whole mess of thoughts. He was pointing his rifle at the blond, but that didn't feel right. And then Jake's saddle squeaked as he adjusted his position in a particularly irritating way. Adam stared at him. He was a grotesque human, he realized. A blustery, insatiable, greedy man. Why would he ever want to be like Jake? The Ericksons—Adam glanced their way—he had no gripe with them. But Jake. He thought of all the stories Wendell had told him over the years. Of Jake and Stanley. And he thought of Smoke, who Jake had had dragged and hidden away—to what end, he couldn't possibly know. And he thought of Mrs. Lund, who was really a harmless old lady when he put his mind to thinking of it.

Lady shook her head to rid her face of flies, and she stomped her feet. Jake jerked on the reins.

"What the fuck do you think you're doing, son?"

Jake was staring at him, and Adam realized he had his rifle pointed at the big man's chest.

"I don't think we're going to settle this today," Adam said. "You don't need this place. You have plenty of land, more than you can use . . . And these folks, maybe they had a couple of bad years, but they're going to make it."

"What are you, a fortune-teller? Lower that gun."

When Adam didn't respond, he added, "Lower your rifle, son." And then, "There will be a price to pay."

“That may be,” Adam said. “Get off that horse.” He cocked the rifle. At the sound, the blond boy stepped forward still pointing his rifle, so there were three guns on Jake. He lowered his.

“Get off that horse,” Adam repeated. He nodded to the Ericksons and dismounted from the buckskin.

“That horse is too fine for you,” he told Jake, dropping the reins of his mount. Tom Erickson removed the gun from Jake’s hand.

“If you don’t mind, sir,” Adam said to Tom. “I’ll let you fellows work this out.” He picked up Lady’s reins and mounted her.

“You can’t hang on a horse’s mouth like you do,” Adam said to Jake. “You’ll make it hard.” He reached over and pulled the saddlebags off the buckskin and threw them over his lap. He’d tie them on later—best to get out while he could. He nodded to the Ericksons and turned the horse north, then squeezed his legs and put Lady into a cantor and left the others to work out their situation.

CHAPTER 32

ALTA

What all heroines have in common is some level of self-determination. This was the thought in Alta's head when she woke up in the middle of the night to what felt like a barn-raising in her uterus. She held her hands over her enormous belly and stared at the darkened ceiling and listened to the rattle of Stanley's snores. Her cheeks felt cold—almost no light had penetrated the slit in the curtain, but somehow the chill had clawed its way into the room. The wind howled outside. Her breath, she imagined since she couldn't see it, was like the exhaust from the smoke stack on a steam engine. But she was warm under her bundle of blankets.

The baby's foot pressed into her side and she pushed her hand against it and thought she could distinguish between the heel and the toes. He or she, they're coming, she thought to herself. The baby's real—this is not a story. Of course, it never had been. But now there was an urgency to that thought. Her eyes roamed the space—they'd adjusted a bit and the dark came in degrees. A solid black for the bureau and the wardrobe and all the knickknacks and baskets that lay about, a lighter shade everywhere else. There was something expansive about it, like space or possibility, and she felt a quickening. Life is much more complicated than a book, she told herself, but still, there are lessons to be learned, inspiration to be drawn from the stories. Elizabeth Bennet—she would not have let herself be a victim of circumstances. And isn't that what Alta had become? A victim of circumstances and poor choices? Well, no more. She had to do things differently. For the baby.

Alta inhaled and did the calculations in her mind, locating her essentials—what drawers she would open, what baskets she would pull from, the boards that squeaked on the floor that she would need to avoid. Once out of the bedroom, she retrieved her scarf and cloak and determined her allies—not just friends, but those beyond suspicion who couldn't be blackmailed or bribed. If she could catch a ride to Williston or beyond, to Minot, she'd be safe at that point. Jake's pull beyond this little conclave was small at best.

All this, she determined before she slid out of bed. She had a couple of weeks. That was enough, she thought as she moved quietly about the room.

She hadn't accounted for the weather. She pulled her coat tight around her luminous belly and clutched her bundle as she stood listening to the wind scream outside. I can do this, she said, before she pushed open the door. The wind yanked it and slammed it behind her, and she felt a rush of panic—Stanley must certainly have heard.

There was nothing to be done but to push ahead into the storm, one step at a time, lifting her feet before plunging them into the drifts that had piled up in the night, past her calves. The wind slashed at her face like tiny knives. Almost immediately, her cheeks were stiff and her nose was dripping and her eyes watered.

She moved toward the mercantile because Beverly would certainly help, and Lew had some immunity from Jake, at least enough to buy time. She leaned forward and a sharp pain cut across her abdomen. She stopped. A contraction. It couldn't be. It was too soon. She waited for it to pass, then took a breath and moved ahead, the snow spilling into her boots, which were thin-soled, with binding up the front that offered little protection.

The next contraction caught her mid-stride, and she stumbled. She reached for something to grab onto, but there was only air, and her enormous belly meant she was ungainly. She fell and lay a moment with the snow spilling down her collar and freezing her wrists, and then she shifted to her side to push herself up to sitting. But she couldn't pull herself to her feet because she had nothing to hold on to in order to lift her huge weight. She pressed her hands into the snow in an attempt to push herself up, but to no avail. She was as stuck as a turtle tipped over on its back. She pulled her coat tight and closed her eyes, trying to devise a plan.

She glanced up and at that moment, the wind, it seemed, took a deep breath, the snow slowed and a shot of moonlight illuminated the sky. She could see the Tumbleweed not too far in front of her, and in front of that, the thin lip of railing. She felt a wash of relief, then elation. She could pull herself up by the railing. She could do this. She was saved. She smiled to herself at the absurdity of her situation, moving forward on all fours with the snow up to her chest, seeping through every seam of her clothing. She thought of her father's house and the warm fires, and the image gave her strength. Soon she'd be wrapped in a blanket in a rocking chair in front of one, rocking her dear little baby.

She didn't hear Stanley approach her, but then he was there.

"Jesus Christ." He pulled her up by the collar on the back of her coat. "Where the hell do you think you're goin'?"

She didn't need to see him to know the look that was on his face.

"The baby," she whispered, as another contraction gripped her. "It's coming."

He spun her around to stare at her.

"Stanley, please."

She didn't remember much after that. The next thing she knew, she was in her own bed surrounded by what seemed a gaggle of clucking, scurrying women.

"Are you OK?" Beverly sat on the bed alongside her and took her hand, her brow creased in worry.

Alta nodded. "Is it time?"

Beverly shook her head. "Not quite. Sometimes this happens. False labor . . . But you should rest . . . What were you doing in the snow?"

What was she doing? How foolish, she thought, too exhausted to lift her head. She shook it back and forth on the pillow.

"The doctor was by. He said you should rest . . ."

Alta opened her mouth to respond, but Beverly shushed her. Phyllis came into the room with a stack of diapers and set them in a basket on the bureau.

"You need to listen to the doctor," Phyllis scolded gently. "You just relax and let us take care of everything."

"You are all too kind," Alta said, and Beverly shushed her again.

"Rest."

XXX

Alta went into labor two days later. Beverly and the midwife attended, and Phyllis stayed in the kitchen cooking food, along with a couple of other women from the church. There was nothing unusual about the birth. After several hours the baby presented, and the midwife guided him into the world. Then she and Beverly cleaned and wrapped him, and Phyllis assisted Alta. Someone stripped the bed and replaced the sheets and blankets, and the midwife passed the baby to the exhausted mother whom the women had propped up with pillows.

"Adam," she called him, touching the baby's delicate nose.

"That's a fine name," Beverly said, and the others agreed. In the background, the women were planning who would bring meals and when for the new family.

XXX

Stanley retreated to the Tumbleweed when Alta went into labor because birth was women's business. He bought a round of drinks for everyone. And then Jake joined him and bought another round. The two men sat at the bar waiting to hear that the baby had arrived.

"How many kids you got?" Stanley said, making conversation to pass the time. He was nervous about the birth and the baby. And he was disturbed by Alta's recent attempt to escape. He was beginning to think she was too much trouble. On top of that, the thing Lola had said kept popping into his head. Of course, he didn't believe her—she was up to no good. She'd become attached, which was a problem. Even whores, it turned out, got attached.

"Two girls . . . maybe I got another one out there somewhere."

"You think you might bring them here someday?"

"Nah. I see 'em on holidays and such. They're good with the wife . . . Now a son . . . It might be nice to have someone to take hunting and fishing. To teach the business to."

"I didn't think you cared for hunting and fishing."

Jake laughed. "No. I don't. You're right about that . . . You're a lucky man, Stanley. You got yourself quite a wife, and now a family." Jake raised his glass. They toasted, but Jake could see Stanley was still troubled.

"She'll be just fine," Jake patted him on the back. "Women are designed for having babies."

"Do you think women are loyal?"

Jake laughed and slapped Stanley on the back.

"Ah, hell. Some of 'em are, and some of aren't, I suppose."

Jake motioned to the bartender, and they drank another round, and Jake told Stanley a series of cheating stories, which got Stanley worked up. And then Jake said he wouldn't trust a woman as far as he could throw. But Alta, he assured Stanley, was a good woman. "Classy," he finished. "Now get home to your new baby."

XXX

Stanley didn't know what to expect when he opened the door, but it wasn't silence. Someone had taken down the clothes and stoked the oven and cleaned the kitchen and there was a stew warming on the stove and it was a peaceful scene, but there was no one around. And then Beverly rose from a rocking chair in the front room where she was knitting with a blanket strewn over her legs. Phyllis was sitting across the way on the couch. Stanley lifted his hat.

"Howdy," he said. He kicked off his boots and unbuttoned his coat.

"Congratulations! You've got a son!"

"A boy?"

Stanley let out a whoop and threw his fist into the wall, which started the crying in the other room.

"They're sleeping," Beverly said in a raised whisper.

"I should be going," Phyllis said, but she didn't move.

Stanley stumbled a bit then threw his hat onto the kitchen table and looked at Beverly expectantly. He wasn't sure of his role.

"You can go on in," Beverly nodded. She could see he was drunk.

"We didn't want to leave her alone, in case she needed something."

"Well, I'm sure she'll be fine. Why don't you go on home?"

"She's very tired."

Stanley had already disappeared into the bedroom. Beverly and Phyllis gathered their knitting and put it in a basket, listening for just a moment to the excited sounds as Stanley met the newest member of his family.

After a few minutes, Beverly popped her head into the bedroom. "You should let them rest," Beverly said. She turned to Phyllis, who had on her winter coat with a scarf wrapped around her head and a basket cradled on her arm.

"Do you think we should leave them? He's pretty drunk. What if they need something?" she whispered. They listened, and all they heard was the wind bellowing outside.

"She'll be fine. She just needs to rest. We'll stop by in the morning."

"You go. I'll just pop in one more time," Beverly waved Phyllis off. She opened the bedroom and Stanley was looming over the bed. He glanced her way and grinned. Alta was lying back in the pillows with the baby nestled in her arm.

"Do you need anything else? I was going to get going."

Alta looked at her, her eyes enormous and wild, a mix of exhaustion and all the feeling that went with giving birth, and something else—Beverly couldn't be sure.

"Are you doing all right, dear?" Beverly asked. Alta nodded slowly but didn't turn her gaze.

"I'll be back in the morning," Beverly said.

Strange, she thought to herself as she pulled the door closed. Something's off. Then she shook her head. It must be nerves. Sometimes she got anxious for no reason. Lew teased her when she got a case of the nerves and called her his "crazy cat." Beverly put on her coat and stood for a moment in the front room, listening, but no sounds came from the bedroom.

The next morning when she approached the house with sweetbread, the anxious feeling returned. She stopped a few feet from the door, pulled her coat tight and stepped up to the door. When she knocked, an unfamiliar voice bid her to come in. She walked inside and the doctor was there, along with the minister and his wife. The young woman from the church, Gracie, sat cradling the infant Adam.

"What's going on?" She stood frozen in the doorway, the chill inside matching the cold outside.

Her eyes turned to Stanley, who appeared in the kitchen doorway. He nodded to the minister, who stood up and took Beverly's arm.

"Why don't you have a seat." The minister guided her to the couch and waited until she'd positioned herself, then got to the point. "She's gone," he explained. "It happens sometimes." The minister's wife reached over and took her hand.

"But I was there. She was fine." Beverly looked at the doctor, disbelieving. He shook his head.

"It was too much . . . the exposure so close to giving birth."

Alta had seemed depleted the last couple of days, Beverly admitted to herself, but she also couldn't forget the look in Alta's eyes the last time she'd seen her. Fear. The realization felt like a freight train bursting through her. Alta had been afraid. Beverly looked over at Stanley, who was pacing back and forth, clasping and unclasping his fists, until the minister stood up and guided him to a chair. Beverly continued staring at Stanley, but he wouldn't meet her eyes. His hands gripped his knees as he studied the pool of water on the floor from someone's wet shoes.

"It was an easy birth. There were no complications. She was fine. I was there," Beverly pleaded. "Something must have happened." She kept her gaze on Stanley as if sending a message to the others in the room.

"It happens all the time," the doctor repeated, not clairvoyant. "One never knows about these things."

"But I was there."

The minister's wife gave her hand a reassuring squeeze.

"We need to discuss some matters," the minister interrupted. "There's a baby to think about. Logistics need to be attended to."

Beverly remained seated but couldn't contribute. She was in shock. Things had been going one way, and now they were going another. Her mind couldn't make sense of it.

"Him . . ." she said quietly. The minister's wife looked at her curiously, then Beverly jumped out of her seat. "Him!" she lunged at Stanley.

The doctor and minister both stood up, each taking an arm.

"You're in shock," the doctor said, guiding her back to her seat. Stanley glared at her. Gracie looked at her with a mix of fascination and fear. Like she was crazy.

"Maybe you should go home and rest," the minister's wife said. "I can walk you."

"Can I see her?" She glanced over the faces staring up at her.

"Of course," the doctor finally responded. The minister's wife accompanied her to the bedroom door while the others watched, as if afraid of what she might do. She closed the door softly behind her, as if afraid she might wake her friend.

CHAPTER 33

WENDELL

"Last one. You need to get yourself home." Clem slid a beer down the worn bar to Wendell, who was tea-kettling, aiming for a splashdown. It was against Clem's better judgment to serve Wendell another, but he was feeling the need for some company, even if it was sloppy-drunk company.

The Tumbleweed was quiet for this time of night. There was a relatively polite game of cards in the back of the room and several strays silently sipping whiskey, and there was Wendell. Clem wondered if there wasn't something going on somewhere in town that he didn't know about as he wiped down the bar.

"Home," Wendell thought, and it was the house rather than the livery. Stanley had taken pity on him after Alta's death and given him a room in the attic. It was a cramped, barely insulated space where Stanley seemed to dump useless things, such as old clothes and boxes with documents and letters. Nothing much of interest or value, though Wendell wasn't one to snoop. And it wasn't for free. Stanley charged him rent—a bit much by Wendell's reckoning—but Wendell wasn't looking for handouts. And he helped out. He chopped wood for Gracie, who Stanley married soon after Alta's death, and helped with the gardening and hauling water for laundry, and Gracie in turn fed him meals and washed his clothes. So Wendell found himself becoming acclimated to civilization in unexpected ways. He even spent a good deal of time entertaining the baby when he wasn't working in the livery, which meant significantly less time drinking. And with square meals and his new, healthy lifestyle, he felt more clearheaded and energetic than he had in years.

"We're on the same side," Stanley had winked, when offering him the room. "We're family. Family sticks together." It had been a funny sentiment coming from Stanley, but then after losing a wife, who wouldn't turn sentimental?

Wendell's new room might have been cold and dark, but it didn't smell of horse shit or car exhaust, and the house was alive with activity. However, Gracie, it turned out, wasn't the most pleasant of women. She was demanding and loud and constantly ordering him and Stanley around, so Wendell started to wonder if Stanley hadn't invited him to stay to give Gracie someone other than himself to boss. Occasionally, he thought he might be better off in the barn. But it had been a long time since he felt like a he was part of a family, so he stuck it out. That didn't mean he didn't occasionally go on drinking sprees, which was how he ended up at the Tumbleweed talking to Clem.

Wendell raised his glass in a toast.

"Thank you, sir!"

"That nephew of yours is sure getting big."

"Keeps growing," Wendell said. He drained his glass faster than he'd meant to and set it down.

"That's what they do." Clem removed the glass and wiped a rag across the bar again.

"The mercantile's not closing down," Clem said by way of conversation.

"Oh yeah. Why's that?" Wendell didn't care, but making conversation meant he didn't have to leave quite yet, and he wasn't ready to leave.

"Looks like someone finally bought it. When Lew and Beverly picked up and moved so quickly, seemed like it was finished. His father got sick. That's what people say."

"Yeah, I heard." Wendell looked longingly at the bottles behind the bar, while Clem moved things here and there. A cowboy came in and sat farther down the bar and ordered a drink. Wendell watched as Clem filled a glass, then continued with his cleaning.

"What was the name of that friend of yours?" Clem said after a long silence.

"What friend?" Wendell was trying to think if he had any friends.

"The Indian."

"Smoke?"

"Yeah. That was his name . . . Whatever happened to him?"

Wendell shrugged. It had been a long time since he had thought of Smoke. A year. Maybe two.

"Lot of rumors. Maybe there's something to 'em."

"Yeah. What's that?" Wendell concentrated on the bottles, thinking Clem might forget he'd cut him off.

"Some people say they took him away."

"Took him away? Where?" Wendell turned his gaze to Clem.

"Some hospital. Hiawatha. Said he wasn't right in the head."

"Right in the head? Who the hell is right in the head?" Wendell shot. Lord knows I'm not right in the head, he was thinking. Was he going to be taken away? Clem's words cut into the fog lingering in his brain and caused his spine to unfold like a blooming flower. He pictured Smoke lying in bed with his head wrapped and raised and felt a surge of remorse. He had something to do with it, he had a feeling, then he thought of Jake.

"Jake," he mumbled. Things were coming back. He remembered the horses and the car. Clem passed Wendell a glass of water, which Wendell gave a disappointed once-over. Then he lifted it, his hand shaking and the water darting side to side. Probably Smoke could use a drink, he thought.

"He sure had it out for Smoke."

Clem bobbed his head in something like agreement. "All I know is that those fellows from the bureau won't lift their asses if someone isn't riding them. They're lazy sons of bitches, that's for sure."

"Taken away," Wendell mumbled.

"That's what folks say . . ." It must be a slow night, Clem thought, regretting he'd brought it up. He'd probably had this conversation before—probably multiple times. In his line of work, words were pebbles in a pond—he tossed them out and maybe customers caught on or maybe the entire conversation sank and burrowed into the muck. He certainly didn't keep track of tossed stones.

"That's too bad." Wendell set his glass down and gave the bottles a hopeful glance, but Clem shook his head.

Eventually, Wendell abandoned hope. He slid from the stool and made his way to the door, pausing in the doorway to gather his balance before leaving the saloon. His head was feeling awful heavy, like it might roll off his neck, so he tilted his neck from side to side until he got his head balanced just right, like a fruit basket on a pedestal between his shoulders, and he stepped onto the boardwalk. He focused his eyes and walked, one foot in front of the other, and sometimes his feet seemed to land on air and then the basket wiggled, and a couple of times he stumbled. He focused his eyes like lamps on the front of the Winton and stepped. He got a good pace going, and he was walking down the moonlit road, and the thought drifted cloud-like by about Smoke in the hospital, but it wasn't a hospital, not really, because the bureau put him there, and he wasn't sick. Something about it wound Wendell into a fury, and his thought cloud was billowing all gray and ashy, but he kept walking, off the boardwalk and across the road, and then soon he stumbled through the brush and he heard voices. They were laughing. He directed his feet toward the voices and tilted his neck and the basket tipped and the weight of it carried him down. Sticks and pebbles poked his hands, and one stabbed him in the cheek, but he managed to pull himself back up to his feet by grabbing a tree branch. There was more laughter and the slamming of doors, and he was in the shrubbery but didn't know where. Then he saw Stanley in the moonlight, mouth pulsing like a wound, talking at someone, a woman most likely. She had yellow hair coiled like a snake on the top of her head. Wendell was seeing it through water or a foggy window, everything muffled and moving slow. Music thumped, and Stanley grabbed at the woman. His mouth split open and there were words spilling into the night, but Wendell couldn't make out a single one as he stood clutching the side of the tree. He tilted his head this way and that until it felt right. In front of him the two were moving back and forth in a violent dance, shaking the ground and shouting. Stanley seemed to leap or blow backward as an engine burst from the trees. It caught him and tossed him to the side, somewhere in the woods, and then the train moved past like a storm. Wendell lurched away from the thundering train, and his basket twisted once again, and then the whole mess of it spilled and he tumbled to the ground. Wendell kept thinking, as the curtains descended, that he'd have to ask Stanley about his dancing.

XXX

He didn't know how long he'd been sleeping when he awoke to the shouting. He tried to lift his head, but it was stuck to the ground like a stone, and he was cold and covered in dew. Through trial and error, feeling like a rusted-out tin man, Wendell pushed himself to sitting. There was a glimmering of eastern light, but it was mostly dark, as if the sun was about as anxious to get the day started as he was. Over by the tracks, lanterns wobbled and men shouted.

"Didn't see it coming!"

"In an instant, Jesus Christ!"

"Drunk! Fuckin' hell, what a mess! Never seen anything like it! Holy shit!"

"Is Arnie bringing a wagon?"

Wendell moved his hands and feet to check if they were attached. He concentrated on bending his fingers. Damn, he was cold! Damn near frozen. He rubbed his hands together and slowly worked his way to the edge of the light, crawling through the bramble until he was warmed up enough to stand, and then he pulled himself up by hanging on the arm of a tree. Through the branches, Wendell could see the men were bent like trolls over something, poking and prodding and lifting here and there. It was a body, Wendell saw in the bobbing lantern light. He leaned forward for a better look as someone held the swinging lantern over the corpse. It was badly mutilated and blackened with blood. He recognized the single-breasted vest, the bowtie, and the snakeskin boots.

"Stanley," he mouthed. He crept forward, his eyes roaming up the cocked neck and ravaged face all blanketed in shadows. In the distance, the wagon creaked, growing louder. Horses snorted and harnesses jangled, and the wagon stopped on the edge of the woods, if you could call it woods, a strip of trees that lined the tracks along the banks of the river. The ladies from the nearby cathouse had come out and were congregating at the edge of light; their whispering was loud and airy. Wendell heard Stanley's name spoken several times. The temporary sheriff—because the town hadn't yet hired a permanent sheriff—told them to get back, they shouldn't see.

"Really Sheriff, if you'd seen half the things we've seen," Josephine said. You had to hand it to Josephine.

Then the sheriff was looking at him. Wendell stared at his face, trying to make out his words, thinking of Stanley's wound. The sheriff came through the foliage to where Wendell was planted.

"Did you see anything?" The temporary sheriff was fierce.

"What the hell happened?" Wendell growled just as fiercely. The temporary sheriff was large and probably intimidating, but Wendell wasn't going to be crossed.

"He was drunk," one of the whores said; he couldn't tell who.

Wendell shook his head.

"What happened?" he repeated, though he knew.

"Got run over by the train."

"He wandered onto the track, it looks like."

"He was drunk as hell when he left us," Josephine said.

"You didn't see a thing?" the sheriff asked. "You were sleeping right here and didn't hear a train come by?"

"Must have come after the train," Wendell said. Something was crawling up inside him, snakelike, winding through his stomach and into his throat, and he turned and heaved into the bushes, bending down with the force of it. He straightened up shakily and gazed at the scene.

"Jesus Christ," the temporary sheriff said from behind him. Wendell could make out disgust in his voice. And now the world had become clear as ice.

"Stanley," he said, turning back and wiping his mouth. The circle of people had widened to give him distance, and all sorts of eye barbs were firing at him. The snake was constricting his heart, and he had a feeling, a thought—he remembered the train and Stanley and his clown mouth wide and foaming, and all that fancy dancing . . . the snake was squeezing and then he remembered Stanley jumping backward all crazy-like. Had he done it? Had he pushed Stanley? His heart lurched like it had been chomped . . . It was suspicious that he was here and Stanley was dead. And he probably hadn't meant to, but it would be just like him. All those people looking at him, like they could blame him. He could see it in the way they were closing in, but hell if he was going to say. Right then and there he thought he'd have to give up drinking.

He put his hand to his throat to stop any words, and Josephine put a hand on his shoulder.

"Are you OK?" she said, and Wendell nodded, thinking she was an angel with that halo of sun-colored hair.

"Oh, dear, he was your nephew, wasn't he?"

Wendell nodded.

"I'm so very sorry. You shouldn't see this. Can someone help him home?"

Lola volunteered and bent down to assist Wendell in standing, which he found irritating. He didn't want her assistance.

"It was a terrible accident," Lola said, taking his arm.

Yes. That was it. It was an accident.

"He's dead," Wendell said.

"I'm very sorry."

"What are you sorry for?"

"Your loss. I'm sorry for your loss." She gave his arm a bit of a squeeze.

"Thank you."

"He was drinking a lot when he left the house."

"Makes a man stupid," Wendell replied, thinking he ought to know. He was king of drunk and stupid.

"Sometimes you do things when you're drunk." They'd moved away from the river bottom and were on the hard dirt road that led into town.

"What things?" Did she know? . . . He glanced her way and

she had that stack of hair. She'd been there too. She and Stanley had been fighting. Had she seen?

"I'm just saying . . . he wasn't the first man to get drunk and step in front of a train."

That's what had happened, he told himself. Stanley had stepped in front of a train.

"You knew him real well?"

"Well enough . . . He was a good man."

"He was no saint."

"Not all men can be saints."

"Don't be making him a saint."

"I have no intention of making him something he was not." Her teeth snapped in a growl.

"He did plenty of things. Maybe things you don't know of . . ."

"You shouldn't speak ill of the dead."

"I didn't speak ill of him," Wendell wondered who made that rule, about the dead. The dead were sinners just like the living.

"I loved him. We were going to get married."

The jaundiced eye of the sun cast the town in a yellow light, and already wagons and cars were filling Main Street. Wendell and Lola moved to the side of the road to avoid two cowhands trotting their horses into town, then Wendell stopped and turned to face Lola.

"Why the hell would he marry you? . . . He was married. He was married to Alta. Then he married Gracie. He wasn't marrying you. That's some pipe dream you're having . . . No offense," he added. He looked Lola up and down and saw a not-young woman with a pretty face. She wore a light-colored dress—he couldn't name the color—beneath which he could see she had a figure any man could appreciate. But still—she was who she was. "I see . . ." He turned and kept walking. Home seemed a long way away.

"What? I'm not good enough? He was sleeping with

prostitutes. What do you think that makes him?"

Wendell kept marching and she rushed after him.

"Did you see it?"

"What are you talking about?"

"Last night, you were there, weren't you?"

"I didn't see anything. I was sleeping." He stopped again to look at her. She looked worried. Tired. She hadn't seen, it seemed, or she wouldn't be asking.

"Only a dead man could sleep through a train that close."

"Well, I sure as hell ain't dead. Not yet."

Wendell glanced at the shadows beside them, hanging on like a posse or a lynch mob. He felt impatient with all this talking. His head hurt, and he wanted to get home.

"It's none of my business," Lola said. "What's done is done . . . But it's a terrible thing. First the mother and now Stanley . . . Now that baby is an orphan."

"Fuck." Wendell hadn't thought about the child, but now he did, and his heart went out to the fat, smiling, dumpling boy. Of all the things! He'd left the boy fatherless . . . He felt his mind churning. He'd make it right. He'd take care of the boy. He was blood. He was nearly his grandfather.

"He's going to need a mother . . . Being's we were pretty near married. I was as good as his mother. I'm going to adopt the boy." The thought occurred to Lola as she was saying it, but she knew it was perfect. The baby was its own sort of retirement fund, after all.

Wendell guffawed and nearly toppled over from the force of it. Lola grabbed his arm and patted his back.

"Jesus," Wendell said, coming up for air. "You weren't married. The boy has Gracie now. And I'll take care of him."

Lola's laugh was genuine. "You! . . . And Gracie . . . she's nearly a child herself. She's not going to stick around. She's going to find some other fellow, not raise someone else's bastard."

"What did you say? What the hell are you talking about?"

Lola turned to face him. Her mouth pursed in defiance. "The kid wasn't even his. He knew it, and that's why he killed her."

Wendell reached out and grabbed Lola by the collar. The snake that had been winding around inside him coiled in his throat, and the memory came back cleaned, cooked, and plated.

"You were fighting with him, weren't you?"

"People fight. There's no law against that."

"You pushed him. You were jealous, and you pushed him." That was it, he told himself. That had to be right, but he wasn't sure. His mind was like that. It was him or her, but if anyone came asking, then he'd say it was her.

"You really are crazy."

"I saw you. You were arguing and you pushed him."

"You're still drunk . . . He killed her. Did you hear me?"

"You're crazy. You're a goddamn nutcase, and if you come anywhere near that boy, I'll tell the sheriff you pushed him."

"The sheriff knows the truth. Stanley was drunk and stepped in front of the train. Anything else is drunk ramblings."

He wasn't a reliable witness, that was true. No one was going to believe him, given his reputation. But she was no more credible. She was lying to protect her own crimes, of that he was sure. A feeling of fury rose inside Wendell, a fury on behalf of Alta and Adam, and even a wee bit for Stanley. He'd held no affection for his nephew, but he wasn't a murderer. Was he?

"It's best you leave town. Before the sheriff finds out what you've done."

"Your threats don't mean nothing to me," she said, but she was thinking, weighing her options. She probably should go. She wondered where. Where could she fade away, because maybe they'd come looking for her? Maybe she'd go to Butte. It was far enough away . . .

"I think you can make it from here." She left Wendell a block from his house and rushed back to Josephine's, where she packed quickly—a westbound would be coming into town in less than an hour. The other ladies had gone back to bed and would sleep most of the day, so they didn't see her leave, but it wouldn't have mattered if they did. They'd called her departure grief and an itch and reassign her room. It wasn't until she found a room in another house hundreds of miles away that she remembered her diary tucked in the floor below her mattress.

XXX

Her words settled in as Wendell watched her dash away. Stanley had killed Alta. The baby was a bastard? None of it made sense. He let the thoughts roll around in his head for a moment, trying to find a place where they would fit. But it was like finishing a puzzle with drizzles of water. There was no way to work them into what he knew of the world.

A few moments later, when he stumbled into Stanley's house, it was swirling with women, three or four of them at least. One of the church ladies was rocking Adam, and they were all weeping.

"Poor little fellow," they kept saying. "Already an orphan."

Phyllis clutched the child and kissed its forehead. Gracie stood in a corner looking like an abandoned dog.

"What the devil!" Wendell said.

"Good Lord," someone said, and then they all said, "Good Lord."

"You haven't heard?" Phyllis looked at Wendell, all accusing.

"Of course I heard!" he bellowed.

Phyllis touched his arm and guided him to a chair.

"It's just terrible. And what he was doing over there, drinking and having his way, when he had a motherless child needing him at home, is beyond me, I tell you. It's a shame," a woman named Donna said.

"He's not motherless." Phyllis glanced toward Gracie, and then they all turned their eyes toward Gracie, who then crumbled into a chair. They seemed to have forgotten she had been married to Stanley. She had that way—when she wasn't demanding or complaining—of disappearing.

"Oh, dear me. Just barely married and already a widow," she cried. Donna walked over and stroked her arm.

"I'm so sorry, dear."

Wendell felt a little like what he'd left on the riverbank was a fire of sorts and now he was standing in the eye of a cyclone, and his brain couldn't process the transition. He stared dumbly at Phyllis.

"These two are going to need some looking after," Phyllis was saying, like he didn't know.

"Don't you think I know that!"

Wendell pulled up from the chair and escaped into the kitchen, bee-lining to the dishes on the table, which he moved to the sink. He pumped water into the sink and watched it disappear down the drain, right behind his courage, which was slipping away after the sight of the cluster of women. He could hear them now, jabbering in the other room about the child or Stanley's death, or maybe they were talking about him—he felt a dread. He opened and closed the cupboards as if relief from their conspiring was lying inside on a shelf. Alone, each could be talked to and even intimidated by a loud voice or a threatening fist. But together they were an indomitable army of moral righteousness, and they could see into him as if he were made of glass, and he was made of glass. He was a weak man. He thought maybe he'd head over to the Tumbleweed, but it was too early to open. And then Phyllis walked in with the child. Adam cried and gurgled and mumbled "dada" and was reaching for him, Wendell.

"Hey there, fellow," he said, and Adam practically leapt into his arms. Wendell felt a burst of something. Love, some might call it. And the fierceness returned. He could do this. He would do this. He had it in him. He knew he did. He'd see to this boy's upbringing.

"I'm going to take care of 'em."

"That's noble of you. But he has Gracie now."

"Gracie's no more than a child herself."

"She's quite capable. And she'll have plenty of help."

"I'll take care of the both of them."

"Listen, Wendell. Don't take this the wrong way."

"Then don't say it," Wendell said.

Phyllis stared at him a long moment, then left him and returned to the front room where he heard a lot of mumblings.

Adam clawed at his face and drooled. Wendell thought of what Lola had said, that the boy wasn't his nephew. He cursed and pushed that thought aside. Lola was a liar. She was jealous and wanted the child but couldn't have it, so she had lashed out. That was the story he settled on.

When he walked into the front room, the women sat in a silent circle, and he felt like he was on trial. "Baby's need . . . a certain type of living . . . Clem and I would be happy to take him. We don't have children of our own . . ." Phyllis said.

"Goodness," one of the women replied. Wendell had seen her around but didn't know her by name. "He's got Gracie."

As if on command, Gracie came and took the child from Wendell. Adam clawed her face, and she placed him on the ground, and they all watched as the baby crawled to the davenport and pulled himself to his feet.

"We'll be just fine," Gracie said, though she looked

terrified. And Wendell thought they would be. He had this new determination. He was going to be a better man. He knew he could be. He owed it to Adam.

CHAPTER 34

ADAM

He couldn't go back to town, so Adam pointed his horse west, toward the reservation. Wendell had said go to Poplar, so he figured he'd go to Poplar. The journey took two days. He stopped to camp alongside the Missouri River when it was too dark to continue, eating a rabbit he shot along the way. When he arrived late the following afternoon, he was stiff and bowlegged.

Popular was much bigger than Mondak. It was the tribal seat of the Assiniboine and Sioux tribes, well developed and bustling. It had grown up as a trade center for government-contracted fur traders and trappers, and the success of these trades was evident everywhere. The graded main street was filled with cars and horses and wagons and trucks, and both whites and Native Americans filled the sidewalks, darting into the banks, restaurants, shops, bars, and liveries. Adam was surprised to see an establishment devoted singly to pool.

He tied his horse up in front of Mrs. Bain's Farmers Restaurant and enjoyed a steak before asking around for Duck's place. The only information he had to go on was from stories he'd heard over the years, but it was enough. Adam found a cleric in the tribal office who directed him several miles north.

Adam figured he'd wait until morning to get his start. He put his horse up in one of the liveries and spent the night in the Poplar Hotel. In the morning, he rode for a couple hours to a small farm with a house made of tarpaper and tin and a teepee in the side yard. A dilapidated shed sat in the foreground. The crops were anemic in the field. Adam approached slowly, looking for the brother or any other inhabitant, but with the exception of two slope-backed horses lazing in the corral, the place looked abandoned.

He knocked several times at the house, and no one answered, so he walked around the property. Farm equipment was scattered around the shed, and behind it a beat-up wagon was planted in the weeds. As he came around the back of the house, Adam heard chanting coming from the teepee. He stood and listened near the entrance flap, not sure how to proceed.

"Come on in," said a gruff voice. Adam fiddled with the flap. Inside was hot and stuffy, and smelt of dust and sweat. As if he'd been cued, Adam began to sweat profusely. It was hard to breathe.

A man sat on the ground leaning against a backrest of hide and willow, rolling a cigarette. A tobacco pouch lay on the dirt in front of him. His eyes, clouded with cataracts, were directed at Adam. Adam pulled at the collar of his shirt.

"What do you want?" the man said, but his tone didn't indicate he was interested in an answer. Adam wasn't sure if he should sit or stand or approach the man.

"I'm looking for someone."

"You must have no luck, asking a blind man to find someone." The man chuckled at his own joke and leaned back against the backrest. He pulled a slip of paper from his pocket and set it on his pant leg, then pulled a plug of tobacco from his pouch.

"Smoke. I'm looking for Smoke."

"You want a cigarette?"

"No. I'm looking for Smoke."

Adam watched the man's agile fingers roll a cigarette in a quick motion, then roll another, and then he reached into the pocket of his shirt and pulled out a book of matches. Adam at this point felt uncomfortable looming and sat on the hard dirt. He watched as the man lit a cigarette and inhale slowly, seeming to relish the smoke.

"I was told you would know where to find him."

The man passed Adam the second cigarette and the matches, and once again, set his cloudy eyes on the boy. Adam thought he must see.

"Who told you that?"

"The guy at the tribal office. And someone I know back in Mondak. Are you Duck?" Adam lit his cigarette. The smoke burned his throat, and he coughed it back up.

"At your service." Duck again reclined against the backrest. "Smoke." He let the name linger, then when he spoke, he spoke slowly, deliberately. "My aunt named him Hungry Coyote when he was a wee thing . . . A warrior from our tribe named him Napayshni. John Jones is his white name—the name the white men gave him at the mission school. Our father called him Trouble. Some called him Big Dog when they saw he had a way with horses. I called him Ugly Bastard." Duck held up his cigarette and chuckled. "Sometimes I called him Asshole." He paused for a moment, inhaled his cigarette, then lifted it up. "Smoke fit. He was drifty."

The ash hung like a stubby worm from his cigarette. "And who are you?"

Adam said his name.

"The first man." Duck held out his hand. "Nice to meet you . . . Adam. What do you want with my brother?"

"I'm just looking for him." Adam wriggled, uncomfortable.

"Looking for him. And how old are you, Adam?" Duck

motioned to his eyes. “I can’t get a good look at you, though I’m going to say you’re hardly out of your baby moccasins.”

Adam said his age, and Duck thought for a while, maybe doing math. His brother had spent a great deal of time rambling and a great deal of time in Mondak, so the thought of paternity occurred to him as a possible justification for the boy’s visit. The only justification, when he gave it a thought. Adam was the right age . . . But then, having a young man pay a visit, for whatever the reason, felt a bit like a blessing.

“Help me, will you?” Duck reached out his hand to Adam, and Adam helped him climb to his feet.

“I’m not as young as I used to be.” Duck felt his way to the tent flap and motioned for Adam to follow him.

“Sometimes I just like to get out here and think,” he said. “It gets crowded in the house.”

Adam followed Duck to the house and paused to let his eyes adjust.

The house was nearly as hot as the teepee, and it had seen better days. It was two rooms—the kitchen, with a scarred table and some wobbly shelves, and a tiny room in the back.

“Well, what do we have here?”

Adam turned toward the voice. A small Native American woman sat in a chair in the corner, sewing.

Adam said hi and stood awkwardly.

“Mrs. Duck,” Duck said by way of introduction

The woman didn’t say anything but watched Adam in a way that made him nervous.

“Adam’s looking to find Smoke,” Duck said.

“Is that so.” Mrs. Duck looked down at her sewing. “He’s not here.”

Duck waved his hand dismissively.

“We know that. I may be blind, but I can see,” Duck said, chuckling. He motioned to a chair, and Adam sat. Duck sat next to him, and the three sat in silence. Mrs. Duck sewed and glanced and sewed and glanced, and so the sitting felt like an interview of some sort, though he couldn't tell how.

Finally, Mrs. Duck spoke. "Are you hungry?"

She didn't wait for an answer but stood and went to a shelf, coming back with a thick slice of bread on a tin plate. It was crusty, and when Adam took a bite, it was dry. Mrs. Duck watched as he ate.

"He looks like him," she said.

"Well, does he now?" Duck asked. "I thought he might. Does he have his eyes?"

"Yes," Mrs. Duck said. "But prettier."

"Good." Duck laughed.

"Is he your father?"

Adam blushed at her directness. "I don't know," he said. "Some think so."

Mrs. Duck nodded. Duck stood up and walked out of the room. Adam sat at the table staring at the breadcrumbs, wondering if Duck's departure meant he should leave. But then the old man returned carrying something in his hands. He set the bundle on the table, then unwound several layers of leather and picked up a small folding knife, which he handed to Adam.

"You should have this," he said.

Adam took it and pulled out the short metal blade, and ran his finger along the edge. The handle was yellowed, scratted bone.

"It was his. He left it when they took him away. Years ago. They said he was dangerous, and they loaded him in the back of the wagon and hauled him off in chains. He wasn't dangerous. He was a good man. We tried to visit him in the prison. They call it a hospital."

"Hiawatha."

"You know it?"

Adam shook his head. "I've heard the name is all."

"It's no hospital . . . if you get put in, you never come out.

Nobody leaves."

"Except in a coffin," Mrs. Duck added.

"Visitors interfere with his care, they said. What kind of hospital doesn't allow visitors? The guards—they call themselves doctors—said he was crazy. Maybe he's alive. I don't know. It was a bad place."

"We traveled a long way to see him," Mrs. Duck said.

"All because he displeased the fat man," Duck said. "The boss down in Mondak."

"Jake," Adam said.

"You know him?"

"Everyone knows him."

"He's the devil himself. That's why we call him the White Devil. A bad man." Duck shook his finger at Adam.

"You haven't seen him since they took him?"

Duck shook his head and Mrs. Duck stared at Adam. The boy looked down at the tin plate on the table. "Where is it?"

"South Dakota. A place called Canton."

They all sat in silence for a long time, then Adam stood up. "I should be going," he said.

"Next time you come, bring some tobacco," Duck said.

Mrs. Duck shoved some money in his hand.

"You'll need this," she said.

XXX

Adam had the money from Mrs. Duck and a little he'd saved. It was enough to pay for a ticket on the train for himself and Lady in the stock car. They took a train from Poplar to Fargo, then another to Sioux Falls. From there, it was a short ride to Canton. They arrived on a gorgeous fall day and entered town through a canopy of red and gold leaves, passing in front of the hospital. The Hiawatha Asylum for Insane Indians was a formidable building on a rise behind a rusting swing set surrounded by several barren acres. Adam rode along the edge of the property studying the brick facade, thinking about his father inside. What was he like? All kinds of conflicting images crossed his mind. He must be handsome and brave—after all, he'd attracted his mother, who by all accounts had been an intelligent and beautiful woman. And he was an adventurer and loads of fun from all the stories Wendell had told him. There was the bit he'd heard from Duck, who was much older—Smoke couldn't possibly be as decrepit as his brother, but of course he'd been locked up for so many years . . . Adam shook his head to rid himself of images of an old, blind Smoke. His father had a way with horses—Adam felt a surge of pride—he'd inherited that. He patted Lady on the neck and ran his free hand through her mane. He found himself getting excited, anticipating meeting with a legend. He settled on an image of a middle-aged Native American sitting on a chair in a hospital room with his feet propped up on the bed, hands clasped in his lap, waiting patiently for the charade to end. But Duck had said Hiawatha was a prison, so there were bars on the door. But this prison couldn't damage Smoke's spirit, of that Adam was certain. Adam turned the horse toward town thinking he'd find a place to board her.

Later that afternoon, after he got Lady settled and had a good meal, he approached the asylum on foot. Occasionally, bursts of hot wind rattled the chains of the swings and lifted the wooden seats in a display befitting mad-swinging ghosts. The windows of the buildings were dark, many shuttered and barred, and a drip of people spilled through the doors and down the steps of the wide front porch. A small cemetery stood off to the side with rows of white crosses, many of them chipped and faded.

Adam pushed open the heavy front door and stepped into a grand foyer, the largest and most ornate room he'd ever seen. It was three stories high with a chandelier hanging in front of a sweeping staircase winding into separate wings of the building on the second floor, before continuing to the third level in a much more restrained manner. There were two sets of doors on either side of the foyer on the main floor. Behind the doors was a drone of noise, including occasional shouts and bangs, though Adam couldn't identify any words. A large oak desk with carved winged-griffin legs sat empty beneath the chandelier.

As his eyes adjusted, Adam saw the elegance was illusory—the chandelier was derelict, casting just enough obscure light with missing or broken bulbs to illuminate the stained and peeling wallpaper and the threadbare rug. And the stagnant air had a sour smell that made his lips curl. Adam stood for a moment trying to identify the odor, then gave up and adjusted his breath to minimize the affront.

He waited, assuming someone would come to greet and assist him. He walked over to the folding chairs that lined one wall and considered sitting, then circled the room to study the paintings on the wall—peaceful prairie and garden scenes—elementary even to his untrained eye. A display of medical equipment was locked in a glass cupboard—a curved knife, forceps of various sizes and shapes, saws, and plugs. Next to the instruments were several leather-bound books with gold gilt fading from their spines.

Adam approached one of the side doors and listened, then pushed it open. A chorus of wails, cries, and singing tumbled out, so he let the door fall back. He turned around, expecting someone of authority to be watching him, but there was no one. He thought of leaving, but he'd come too far, and if Smoke was here—well, he just had to go in. He walked to the door opposite and listened, and then made up his mind. He put his hand on the banister and ascended into increasingly swampy air, his eyes darting back and forth between the room below and the second-floor landing. As he stepped into the hallway at the top of the staircase and pushed through the doors into the north wing of the building, he was overwhelmed by the smell of shit and piss. And then, too, the wailing. It seemed to be coming from the far end of the hall, a piercing sound that set the hair on the back of his neck to standing.

He set off down the hallway, past a gurney pushed against the stained wall, a bundle of something—a dog? on the floor beneath. He turned and owl-eyed the figure. It was watching him, a skeleton in rags with a chain attaching its ankle to the radiator. A child. Adam's heart thumped. A scar bubbled along the edge of the child's foot. The child held something, a crude doll, and mumbled words Adam couldn't understand. Adam turned away and glanced down the hallway. Most of the rooms were shut, but he could see into them through the tiny windows.

"Smoke!" Adam hissed, shaking a door handle. The door opened to reveal a man pissing into a bedpan. This person too was shackled along the ankle, in this case, to his bed.

"Smoke!" Adam said, opening the next door. The patient spat in his direction.

And this was how it was. In one room, a young man was chanting, rocking on his bed, and in another, a woman was lying, unmoving, in a bed soaked in piss. There seemed no end to it, patients identical in their misery: dirty, incoherent, skeletal figures strapped or chained to beds or bureaus or radiators on stained mattresses with buckets of human waste on the floor or under the bed, or sometimes the skeletons were sitting in their own filth, and their dark or graying hair was shaved roughly to various lengths of stubble, and they were crying or moaning or chanting. It was as if they were speaking in tongues, each a different language from a different tribe, so that not even the words of one could penetrate the prison of another. They were mostly boys and men, though there was an occasional woman or girl. A few of the rooms were locked.

Adam could only look through the windows at the hopeless inhabitants. He was reminded of the menagerie of half-starved animals in the circus pacing in their cages, their eyes blank or burning.

Hell was the only word he could think of to describe the place. It was neither a hospital nor a prison, but so much more horrifying, He couldn't imagine the crimes that justified such mortification. He felt desperate to find Smoke. He would save him.

"Smoke?" he called into room after room, and then he remembered Duck had told him the other names. "Napayshni!"

"Smoke, do you know Smoke?" He asked all the patients that seemed to be coherent enough to hear. A few patients glanced in his direction, and several even spoke to him, but he couldn't understand their words.

"Smoke," a young man repeated and motioned for Adam to approach.

"Smoke!"

"Do you know him?" Adam moved closer. The man, no, a boy, Adam saw as he got closer, was no older than himself. He sat cross-legged and rocking on his bed.

"Smoke!"

"Do you know Smoke? Napayshni?" Adam repeated. The boy shook his head wildly and mumbled, then made as if bringing a cigarette to his lips, and Adam understood he wanted one. He shook his head—he didn't have any—and the boy yelled angrily. Adam continued down the hall. An old man shuffled by, glancing blankly in his direction, and then a cart burst through the doorway at the end of the hall. Adam dove into an open room and pulled the door closed.

The cart rattled closer. Adam pressed himself against the wall out of view from the window in an elderly man's room. The man stared cross-legged from his bed, one leg bound by a long chain to the bedpost. He sang softly. And then he mumbled, a little louder. Adam held his finger to his lips to indicate silence, but that seemed to encourage the man, and his voice grew even louder. The cart slid past and Adam heard it enter a room down the hall.

"Smoke!" Adam whispered.

The figure didn't respond, so Adam walked over and tapped his knee.

"Napayshni!" Adam hissed. The figure lifted his head and the eyes were clouded.

"What the hell are you screaming for?" came a deep voice from the hallway. There was ascuffle and a yelp, and then more voices came through the hall speaking a hushed English, mumbling to themselves or each other. Adam thought they might be feeding or cleaning patients, then reconsidered. Neither of those things likely happened here. He rubbed his knee, which he'd banged when he'd landed, then glanced up to see the figure on the bed was staring at him. The voices in the hallway made their way closer, one room at a time. Adam glanced at the figure and crawled under the bed and almost put his hand in a shit-filled bedpan. The stench was suffocating, and he held his breath to keep it from penetrating his lungs. He backed as close as he could to the wall. The figure moved above him, causing the springs to squeak and caving in the cardboard-thin mattress. The door swooshed open, and footsteps came into the room wheeling some sort of cart. The figure on the bed chanted and sang in a low voice, rocking and squeaking the mattress.

"Howdy there, John," said the newcomer. "Got to dump your shit pail."

The man bent down and Adam saw his fingers, and then John screamed and there was a scuffle.

"Jesus Christ! You crazy son of a bitch. Keep your goddamn shit pan."

The attendant left with a squeak and a rattle, but the

rocking continued.

"Napayshni, Napayshni," the man on the mattress chanted. Adam scrambled from under the bed.

"Napayshni?" Adam said, gulping at the air that was only slightly fresher than that under the bed.

"John," the figure said. He scratched at the stubble on his chin. He was a scarecrow without stuffing.

"Are you . . . ?"

The scarecrow waved his hand. "On the other side."

"On the other side? Where?"

"Room 212. . . . What do you want with Smoke?"

"You speak English?"

The scarecrow laughed. "I speak English, I speak Ojibwa, I speak Dakota, I even speak Canadian."

"That's English," Adam said, after thinking for a moment.

"Is it?" the scarecrow asked, and then he laughed. He was not as old as Adam had previously thought. Middle-aged, most likely, judging by the mapwork around his eyes and the way the skin on his neck sagged. His chopped hair was mostly gray with a few islands of white.

"What do you want with old Smoke?" the man asked again.

"I want to see him. Take him home."

"Impossible!" The man blew, then chuckled. "No one leaves."

"Why not?"

"No one leaves," he repeated, and his voice was rising. "Can't you see they're fixing them? Look at all this fixing." He lifted his chained leg. "No one leaves, and no one comes in!" He was yelling now, and Adam panicked, thinking someone might hear, someone on staff, like the man who'd emptied the bedpans. He held his fingers to his lips to shush the man.

"Who are you?" The scarecrow-thin man bared what remained of his teeth, a gray scattering of rotting tombstones.

He stared at Adam and Adam stared back. The face was parched earth, but there was a force in those black eyes that made Adam avert his and stare at the filth on the floor, spreading, it seemed, like late-day shadows.

Adam said his name and the black-eyed man spat and rocked.

"I need to find him. He's my father," Adam said nervously. "He might be. Most likely."

The scarecrow spat angrily.

"Napayshni didn't have a son."

"Yes, he did." Adam stood taller and poured his eyes right back into the captive's. Scarecrow closed his and sat back on his haunches rocking and chanting, and Adam glanced around the room's cracked, yellowed walls. On a shelf stood a row of delicate wood carvings—a beaver, a buffalo, a wolf, a bird. Adam walked closer, and there was one that looked like a tiger, like his tiger. A crash in the hallway followed by scuffling and shouting caused him to jump. Adam pressed himself against the wall, waiting for he knew not what. A congregation of urgent voices approached, and then the scuffling died, and the urgency died, and the scraps and rustling and mumbling quieted into something methodical, followed by silence.

Scarecrow continued his chanting and didn't look again at Adam.

"You have no business with the dead," the man eventually said, and he waved and then opened his eyes.

"It's the living I'm interested in. I'm hoping he's alive."

The scarecrow nodded toward the totems.

"You choose . . . Maybe not the beaver."

Adam walked over and studied the carvings then picked up the tiger, realizing he'd left his behind. He held it up for the scarecrow to see. Scarecrow didn't respond. Adam put the tiger down and studied the animals. He picked up a wolf. A wolf, Adam thought, is strong. Fierce. He showed the wolf to

Scarecrow and the man held his gaze. Adam put the wolf back and studied the animals again. Finally, he picked the eagle. He felt the weight of it in his hand, and it felt good. It felt right. He held it out to the Scarecrow, and the man slowly nodded. Adam squeezed the totem in his hand, then slid it into his pocket.

"Napayshni," Scarecrow said. "Go to room 212." He gestured toward the opposite wing of the hospital and waved Adam out.

Adam stepped into the hall looking up and down, then moved quickly, returning the way he had come, past the gurney (the child was no longer there) and across the landing to the opposite wing of the sanitarium.

Conversations in English were coming from a room immediately off to his left, so he ducked into a closet. "Better talk to Helen," he heard as a door swung open. "She's the only one the cooks will listen to."

"Two-twenty is on his way out. Can't eat anything but air anymore, and that just barely."

They kept talking, but Adam could no longer hear. His eyes adjusted and he saw he was in a supply closet of some sort, with linens stacked on a wall of shelves from ceiling to floor and another shelf of soaps and detergents. He took the eagle from his pocket and examined it, running his fingers over the knife cuts.

When he could no longer hear conversations, he returned to the hall and walked past what he assumed was a cafeteria to the patient rooms. The stench was as terrible on this wing as on the other, as was the wailing and crying and mumbling. Adam glanced through the windows in the doors to see people circling their rooms in filthy gowns. Behind him, a door opened and before Adam could duck out of the way, a man in a white coat entered the hall. His pace was fierce and soon he was walking alongside Adam as if they were colleagues on their way to check on a patient. But the man didn't look at Adam or show any sign that he was aware of his presence, and then he cut away and disappeared into a room. Adam paused and took a breath—was he invisible? But of course, that was ridiculous. He caught his breath again and searched the numbers on the doors. They were rising—261, 262, 263. He turned around and walked back to the beginning of the corridor and found room number 250. He felt a rush of panic—where was 212? How had he missed it? He walked back to the wing he'd originally visited.

"Hey!" someone shouted, and he kept going; he was no longer careful. He was back in Scarecrow's corridor, and it was vast and empty except for the suffocating smells.

"Hey!" came the shout again, louder, angry. "Hey!"

The numbers went up—208, 210, 212, on the left side. Adam stopped.

Room 212 was Scarecrow's room. The door was ajar, and Adam pushed it open. It was empty.

A hand clamped his shoulder and spun him around. "What the hell do you think you're doing?"

"I'm looking for someone," Adam said, and the hand squeezed harder. Adam faced a tall man wearing a white coat—the asylum uniform, obviously. Adam figured the man was a doctor.

"How did you get in here? You can't just waltz around a hospital without accompaniment, without permission. There are sick people here, people in treatment. You're disrupting patients."

"Smoke," Adam said. "Napayshni." Adam swung his head toward the room behind them.

"I don't know who you're talking about. There's no one here by that name."

Adam pointed to the room behind him. "He was right there."

"That room belonged to John Jones . . . You need to be on

your way."

"Where is he?" Adam asked, craning his neck. "He was just here."

"That room's been empty for a while."

"I just talked to him. Where did he go?"

"I don't know who you talked to, but John Jones died a while back. The flu. It hit us pretty hard."

Adam tore away from the man's grip and rushed into the room. The bed was shoved against the wall, and the thin mattress was bare and empty, as were the several drawers of the bureau alongside the wall, which were slightly ajar. The shelf that had held the totems was covered in dust.

"He was here," Adam spun.

"Look, son." The voice was threatening. "You can't be back here. Either you leave the property right now or I'll take measures to make sure you leave."

Adam looked around the room for some sign but saw none, so he followed the doctor to the foyer where a young woman in a nurse's cap sat at the heavy desk. The doctor opened the heavy front door and held it for Adam, turning the lock once he was outside.

Adam stood on the porch looking out over the grounds, contemplating his next move.

XXX

Adam walked to the cemetery he'd spotted upon his arrival and found a relatively fresh mound of dirt with a white wooden cross and the name John Jones, 1879–1918, painted carelessly in black on the horizontal slab. Something about seeing it made Adam angry, and he kicked at the cross without even thinking. He kicked and kicked and then he stomped and shattered it until it was nothing but white splinters. When he looked up, a large man was charging across the field toward him.

Adam fled.

For the next several days, Adam wandered the tree-lined streets of Canton with his hands in his pockets jingling his change, his thoughts all a-jumble. Then, one afternoon not long after his visit to the asylum, he sat in a restaurant near a window and set the eagle totem on the table and stared at it as he scooped egg yolk onto his toast. The eagle was perfectly shaped, delicate knicks detailing the fine array of plumage. The beak was sharp, the eyes piercing, and the talons dangerous. It must be magic, he thought to himself, a gift from beyond. He felt something bloom in himself at the site of it, something wonderful and light. A smile crept to his face and settled there. He glanced outside and the colors were different—brighter and more golden; he swore it was so. He wondered at the figure he'd met on the bed at Hiawatha, the scarecrow—of course it was Smoke. Napayshni. His father. Adam felt a pang for the misery of Smoke's stay in the hospital. But he was here now, in the sunlight streaming through the window.

Adam had a fleeting thought of the cemetery back in Buford with the wooden markers and the swirl of soldiers beneath the dirt, and he had an idea. He paid for his food and, with directions from the waitress, sought out Heritage Memorial and commissioned a headstone. When it was completed two days later, Adam directed the shopkeeper to place the headstone in a small wagon he'd found to carry the load.

Adam rolled the wagon up to the cemetery with only the moon and starlight to guide him. Once there, he dug a shallow hole to root the slab and then packed the dirt around it. When he was finished, Adam picked the shards from the broken cross and tossed them into the wagon. He stood up to survey his work: The name was in large cursive letters across the top of the marker, "Napayshni," and beneath it, the engraving he couldn't quite make out in the dim light, a tiger striding fierce and free across the stone.

XXX

The next day, Adam and Lady boarded a train for the Twin Cities. He pulled a crumpled envelope from his pocket, a letter from Alta to her father, and studied the address, then lay back against the wall of the car and felt the prairie chug past. When the train stopped, he looked out the slats at the whirlwinds whipping the topsoil toward the heavens and thought of his mother and his father, all dust now and blowing, lifting into the air.

Later, he slept. And he picked a dream from a ditch filled with trash and broken farm implements and chicken bones and pieces of clothing, and he understood it was her dream, faded and worn, like a much-loved child's toy, but it had once been beautiful, in a delicate sort of way. He showed it to her and her hands trembled when she touched it.

"I don't even know where I got it," she said. "I just picked it up somewhere along the way. It didn't really belong to me. It never really fit." She took it from him and held it like a child close to her heart and when she released it, it was winged.

When the train stopped to move passengers on and off, Adam awoke, sweating beneath the coat he held like a blanket across his chest. It was dark, but he could feel Lady beside him. She nickered quietly and adjusted her position in the straw. Adam stood and glanced out the slats of the car and the sun was just peaking over the prairie.

EPILOGUE

It was an unusually warm day of an unusually warm season. The sun beat down on the prairie already bursting with color, but Adam didn't notice. His attention shifted between the young mare staring him down in the round pen and the house, a white four-square with a wraparound porch and a swing rocking quietly in the light breeze.

The gray roan was sniffing the saddle splayed in the dirt, which she'd tossed off in a bucking frenzy the moment Adam had tightened the cinch. But she was calm now that the object of her derision was off her back. She nibbled on the leather then lifted her head inquisitively and watched Adam approach, like maybe he would help solve the mystery of the annoying object.

"Maybe you should call it a day." Charlie, the help, was leaning on the fence smirking, enjoying the show.

"It's OK, girl." Adam spoke softly to the mare, ignoring Charlie. He sent darting glances to the house, looking for a sign. There's been screams—spine-tingling screams, but those had gone silent. It was too quiet. That's what had him worried. He wondered if he should check, but Martha would let him know if something was wrong. He swiped the back of his hand across his forehead and turned his attention to the horse, feeling too much tension to be breaking a horse. The mare was feeling his anxiety. As Adam moved toward her, she stomped and spun around and walked along the edge of the pen nibbling at grass, the lead dragging in the dirt beside her.

"Want me to take over?"

"Don't you have work to do?"

Adam didn't look at Charlie, and Charlie didn't respond. He was used to Adam cajoling. Adam played the disgruntled boss well, though he was hardly disgruntled. Just the opposite. He was good-natured and thoughtful and focused on the work. But of course, he was distracted.

"She going to be ready?"

"She'll be ready." Adam picked up the lead and wrapped it around a post, then patted the mare gently on the neck. Her shoulder twitched as he rubbed the blanket over her back. He'd promised a trained horse to the buyers, and he would have her ready. They were driving down from Canada to pick her up. It was like that now, people coming from all over for his horses. The ranch did all right on its own with its herd of Angus cattle on thousands of beautiful acreage in eastern Montana. He'd purchased the property with the inheritance from his grandfather, and by all accounts it was successful. But Adam's heart was with the horses, beautiful performance quarter horses—some of the best in the country for ranch work and rodeos. The bloodlines alone were enough to drive up the prices but people wanted the training, and no one was better than Adam.

"You just going to stand there all day?" he said to Charlie. It was something to say. He wasn't worried about Charlie.

"Just watching the show, boss." Charlie grinned.

Just then the door to the house flung open, and Martha came dashing out.

"It's a girl!" she shouted.

Adam dropped the lead and was over the fence in a flash,

out of breath by the time he stumbled into the kitchen.

Martha held the bedroom door and he paused in the doorway, uncertain. Martha's daughter was there too. She darted into the bedroom to scoop up a pile of linens then dashed back into the kitchen. Viviane was propped up with a bundle in her arms, and she smiled when she saw him, the light in her eyes reminding him of that first day when she looked at him all doe-eyed—though then she'd been standing frightened behind her bulky brothers in front of her sad little home, which Jake had, eventually confiscated, but not on that day. And Adam had eventually bought it back and returned it to the family.

Now, Adam approached slowly, reverently. Viviane pulled aside the blanket and Adam gazed on the face of his daughter, his beautiful daughter. He stood awkwardly until Martha told him to sit. So he did. On the edge of the mattress, afraid to get too close, afraid to touch.

"Would you like to hold her?" Viviane said, and held the baby out for him. He paused—how do you hold a baby?

"It's OK. She won't break."

Adam took her and pulled her close to his chest and gazed down at her tiny red face, so peaceful in sleep.

"She's beautiful," he finally said. "She looks just like you."

"I think we should call her Alta," Viviane said.

Adam gazed at his wife, his love, and he thought his heart might melt. He didn't speak, but nodded. Viviane moved over and patted the bed, and Adam followed her instruction. He scooted over and leaned back against the mountain of pillows. Viviane lay her head on his shoulder, and they stayed like that for a long time watching the life they had created.

ACKNOWLEDGMENTS

I am deeply grateful to friends and family for their love and support through all the iterations of this story. Dad, you pointed to the bones and lit the spark—you are the original teller of stories. Anna Forse, Kimberly Zerby, Erik Hammen, you've been oh so patient readers! Your enthusiasm made me believe. And to the others, if not for this, then for that—you rooted this writer. Kristin Woodward and Gretchen Morse, I am blessed to call you sisters. Jack Stadel, thank you for your support, your kindness. Kari Thorstensen, Sue Unkenholtz, Anne Gienapp, Tania Henderson—not all sisters share blood. And of course, Izzy and Viggo, you are forever my heart.

ABOUT ATMOSPHERE PRESS

Atmosphere Press is an independent, full-service publisher for excellent books in all genres and for all audiences. Learn more about what we do at atmospherepress.com.

We encourage you to check out some of Atmosphere's latest releases, which are available at Amazon.com and via order from your local bookstore:

Icarus Never Flew 'Round Here, by Matt Edwards

COMFREY, WYOMING: Maiden Voyage, by Daphne Birkmeyer

The Chimera Wolf, by P.A. Power

Umbilical, by Jane Kay

The Two-Blood Lion, by Nick Westfield

Shogun of the Heavens: The Fall of Immortals, by I.D.G. Curry

Hot Air Rising, by Matthew Taylor

30 Summers, by A.S. Randall

Delilah Recovered, by Amelia Estelle Dellos

A Prophecy in Ash, by Julie Zantopoulos

The Killer Half, by JB Blake

Ocean Lessons, by Karen Lethlean

Unrealized Fantasies, by Marilyn Whitehorse

The Mayari Chronicles: Initium, by Karen McClain

Squeeze Plays, by Jeffrey Marshall

JADA: Just Another Dead Animal, by James Morris

ABOUT THE AUTHOR

Karin Rathert grew up in North Dakota, close to where Mondak once flourished. When not writing, she loves yoga and photographing abandoned buildings. This is her first novel.